THE BEST AMERICAN
EROTICA
1996

EDITED BY SUSIE BRIGHT

A TOUCHSTONE BOOK

Published by Simon & Schuster

TOUCHSTONE
Rockefeller Center
1230 Avenue of the Americas
New York, NY 10020

TOUCHSTONE and colophon are registered trademarks of Simon & Schuster Inc.

Designed by Brian Mulligan

Manufactured in the United States of America

1   3   5   7   9   10   8   6   4   2

ISBN 0-684-81830-2

ACKNOWLEDGMENTS

I would like to thank Jon Bailiff, my reading assistant, for his superb discrimination and hard work, and my agents and managers Joanie Shoemaker and Jo-Lynne Worley. My deepest appreciation also goes to Shar Rednour, Bethany Clement, Alexandra Koelle, and Bill Bright for all their editorial and production assistance. Thank you to Michael Anderson for alerting me to the end of the century. This volume of *The Best American Erotica* is dedicated to Rebecca and Ross's child.

CONTENTS

8   Contents

Contents 9

INTRODUCTION

I HAVE an announcement to make. In fact, I thought of calling this chapter "The Announcement" instead of "The Introduction." It's something I never dreamed of saying this soon, this early in a "Best of . . ." series that's only three years old. But now that the facts are in, the news is here, well, I'm sort of relieved.

Erotica is dead. I've felt her cold little fingers tap-tap-tapping on my shoulder all year long, occasionally reaching over to pinch my tits and laugh at my irritation. Then just to show how really far gone she is, when Erotica got sick of all my denials and rationalizations, she'd take my head away from my computer screen, turn me toward a full moon shining outside my window, and begin to HOWL.

You see, when I say erotica is dead, I certainly don't mean lifeless, quiet, or finite. I don't mean that the literary lovers are all wearing black, that what once was a stroke book is now a vale of tears. It's just that certain tenets of the genre have finally kicked the bucket.

Chief among those dead mysteries is "What is the difference between erotica and pornography?" No one can stay awake for that one anymore. There's a new question about sex writing and it comes straight from the authors to the readers: "Did I move you?"

The E. vs. P. debate is the modern version of an ancient set of class distinctions that are also wisely bowing out of the picture. That old chestnut was whether REAL literature could be sexually explicit, or if REAL porn could be literary. A lot of writers have been in hiding for years over this taboo, their pseudonyms hovering like protective cover. But now the bell has tolled. Those pretensions and snobberies are yesterday's hangover and no one wants to hear them anymore. The questions readers put to writers today are: Were you honest? Was it real? The sex doesn't always have to get us off, each and every one, but we damn well better believe it had its author by the short and curlies.

Erotica's death is a rebirth, a bonfire of old values and a kick in the pants to the end of the century. The artists writing about sex today are writing more prolifically and competitively about sex than ever before. There is a spontaneous consensus gathering that contemporary erotic writing is not about a warm, trusting glow or "expert" lovemaking, but about the hair-raising, erection-bolting, clit-tingling chills coming at you from behind. Erotica is dead, not like a doornail, but like a grip that you can't shake.

Some of the new school of erotic writing does flat-out embrace horror and the supernatural. In past editions of *The Best American Erotica*, we've seen Anne Rice's notorious vampires, Nick Baker's anti-hero possessed by a horny succubus, a werewolf making his match, and assorted other blood-loving Casanovas. Their adventures were a pure gothic delight—and so romantic we couldn't help but fall in love with them too.

But now, naturally, the ante has been raised. Many characters in this volume of *The Best American Erotica* are non-gothics, as alive as you and me, but like their supernatural predecessors they are not afforded redemption. The flame is never extinguished. Neither the protagonist nor the reader ever makes it off the hot seat.

When I first read Lucy Taylor (her story "Choke Hold" represents her work here), she had me so bug-eyed I didn't know whether to call a cop, a priest, or just turn the vibrator up a notch. Taylor's work represents a new genre—erotic horror—that takes every precious notion of the intact body and punches right through it. Another example this year is Aaron Travis's story "The Hit," which mixes a grisly crime thriller with hungry sadomasochism. Travis told me his story was rejected by the gay leather mags that he routinely publishes in—not because of the sex, but because of the "crime"—the moral outrage *out* of the bed rather than *in* it. Travis was ahead of his time, a predictor to the pop cult sensations of films like *Pulp Fiction*. Another prime example is this past year's most talked-about erotic crossover novel, *in the cut*, by Susanna Moore. Moore is just as relentless as Travis in her deliberate—and heterosexual, this time—mixture of suspense, fatal attractions, and the erotic persuasion of submission and domination.

The power of sexual desire to take us out of ourselves, our normal behavior, is legendary. The very nonsense of "normalcy" is really what the erotic funeral is all about here, because authors of the new school are spitting on the grave of conventionality, of moribund expectations. Sometimes I think this volume is one angry answer to that chart-topping bestseller, *The Book of Virtues*, by William Bennett. Bennett, a politician, offers a list of character traits that make a man great, the qualities that make for a stand-up sort of life. He's got the WASP work ethic down to a "T," but his list is a list for a toy soldier, not a person. It completely omits the fire that makes us creative: our sexuality, our erotic thumbprint, our desires so fierce they defy what is expected of us.

If William Bennett, or one of his followers, were to critique the turn in erotic fiction today, I think they would say that the reason there is so much PERVERSION, VIOLENCE, and CYNICISM in today's fiction is that this whole country has gone to hell in a handbasket of MORAL DECAY. If everyone would just take a good hot BATH and refresh themselves in the ten commandments, GET A JOB AND STOP BELLYACHING, then we would see stories about good old-fashioned romance and marriages that last.

It's a snap to give the status quo explanation of what's happening to arts and entertainment today rather than to contemplate the contradictions of real life. For starters, there are no jobs, not the way Americans ever understood a "job" to be, a place of security and opportunity. The very notion of "job" sounds like a retro item, something to pitied and escaped from, as writer Doug Tierney's protagonist does in "The Portable Girlfriend." As for bellies aching—well, they are. We have the ache of need and betrayal among the have-nots, and the ache of fear and loathing among the haves. Bellies are churning, period.

"Perversion" is the right-wing code word for gender chaos, the alarm that boys and girls are not keeping their pink and blue uniforms on at all times. Ken and Barbie don't live here anymore, and there's no putting that fragile little relationship back together again. Women have had it with the madonna/whore game, and authors in this volume like Amelia Copeland, Camille Roy, Linda Smukler, and Shar Rednour prove it. Over on the boy side, there's a similar antipathy for the double standard. Men know that the only thing more terrifying than being swept away is to never have been lifted off their feet. See this year's authors Estabrook, Robert Gluck, and David Shields for more persuasion. Word is out; to succumb is bliss.

Next up on the conservative's naughty list is violence. Liberals are similarly alarmed. Sex-and-violence is that two-headed dog with a wet and very sensitive nose that won't go away. Every time we try to push him away, say he's not right, he comes back even more persistently—he can smell you and knows you're hiding something.

You've heard all the standard explanations about the whys and wherefores of sex and violence's allure. Wonder why they still leave you doubting? That's because no one has really got this number pinned—not the shrinks, not the cops, not the media executives. They're equally desperate to keep the lid on, with their various punishments, medications, and dubious statisical reports. Whatever their lid is, their supression has become one of the most important elements in proving the power of sensation's appeal.

The erotic combination of sex and violence has this in common: they both assume an entrance into our body. Before sex, before a violent act, our bodies are closed, there is no tear in the fabric, we are intact—a safe, but impenetrably blank, place to be. It's only when a thread comes undone, when we unravel, that our peril and pleasure spill out: the come, the blood, the tears, the shit, the cries. We can't not be affected, and of course, our real bodies can only spill so much. In our erotic storytelling, though, we spill over and over, on a vicarious level that we can't live without.

Finally, we have the smudge mark of Cynicism, the black humor in erotica that I find so prevalent in all fiction these days. Cynicism begs the question "Ask me if I care?" and the thing to pay attention to is not the question, but the begging. My favorite book title this year was *The New Fuck You: Adventures in Lesbian Reading* (from which I've excerpted "Morning Love" by Linda Smukler, in this volume), and I can't help but smile every time I pass it on my bookshelf. It's irresistible, that punk, never-mind-the-bollocks-it's-the-sex-pistols kind of attitude. Only this time, my sex pistol is in my own pocket, loaded, ready to squirt at all the lies and delusions I'm asked to digest on a daily basis about what is great literature, great beauty, great politics, great religions. Mainstream propaganda has reached surreal proportions. Who honestly believes that supermodels are the essence of feminine power, or that the White House is the leader of democracy, or that Christianity is about the righteousness of one man over another? The eye of that biblical needle is just as slim as ever, but the fat man is still putting out a press release saying that he slipped through. Our literary cynicism is a necessity—because the gap between the advertisement of our culture and what's really going down is so gigantic that all we can do is free-fall, laughing and bellowing all the way down.

SOME corners of our erotic minds are still soft and precious. In a story like Bonny Finberg's "Light," the erotic experience is about being so innocent, so new in the world, that all love is erotic, all body is sensuality, there are no definitions yet. Sometimes erotic love is the tender and exquisite part of nature, as in Bob Zordani's "A Fish Story" or Cecilia Tan's "Pearl Diver." Yet even there, someone gets caught—you always have to think about the drowning.

Erotica does have the capacity to be timeless; it's eerie that way. That's what's so confusing about trying to spot new trends when doing a yearly series. You can pick up a stroke book today and find the same pizza delivery boy, traveling salesman, nympho housewife, farmer's daughter that you found twenty years ago. In fact, commercial porn purveyors are well acquainted with the fact that the smut that sells the hottest today is the material that is nostalgic.

Fin de siècle sensationalism that thrills and titillates members of the current generation will undoubtedly nestle in their groins twenty years from now . . . it will just be more sentimental and cherished than we can ever imagine now. I'm no good at predicting the future; I can't tell you exactly what erotica in the year 2000 will look like when I'm still reeling from 1996. I'll tell you this, though—and you won't find it in any national advertising—after death comes only one thing: reincarnation. Erotica is dead. Long may she live.

—Susie Bright

Eric Albert

THE
LETTERS

"DEAR MR. DAVIS," Megan typed, "I would like to suck your dick."

She paused and considered whether the idea needed further explanation. No, better to keep it short and sweet. She inserted a blank line, typed "ME," saved the file, and sent it to the printer.

The "ME" part was clever. Mr. Davis would think the letter writer was hiding behind the anonymity of a first person pronoun, but in fact it stood for Megan Elizabeth. Megan Elizabeth Bryant, in full.

Megan was used to feeling clever.

She took the letter off the printer, folded it precisely in thirds, and slipped it into a long envelope. She neatly wrote "Mr. Timothy Davis" in block capital letters. Her printer had an attachment for printing on envelopes, but she'd never been able to make it work. Everyone's capital letters looked pretty much the same, anyway.

Should she stick on a "LOVE" stamp? She was a big fan of irony. But maybe Mr. Davis wasn't. She sighed and held the letter in her hand, balancing it. Three minutes later she was on her bike. Spring had finally arrived, and the late afternoon sun made her feel extra alive. As if the stuff that ran in the veins of Greek gods—ichor?—coursed through hers too. She turned her head for a second and let the wind blow her warm hair across her face.

Mr. Davis's house was only a dozen blocks away. Megan coasted past, making sure his car was not in the driveway. She braked to a stop, walked purposefully up the brick path, and pushed the letter through the slot in the door. Then she headed back to finish off her homework.

That night she lay in bed, another math problem set successfully conquered, and pictured her letter's reception: Mr. Davis coming home. Mr. Davis seeing the envelope on the floor. Mr. Davis picking it up, opening it, reading it. Mr. Davis's thing getting hard in his pants.

Megan put her hand between her legs and found she was much wetter than usual. The letter was definitely a great idea. She flopped over on her stomach, both hands underneath her. Again and again she flashed on Mr. Davis, her letter in his hands, the front of his pants poking out. "That's my boner," she thought. "I gave it to you, and it is all mine."

When the orgasm came, it was one of the good ones, emptying her out and leaving her cheeks tingling.

The next day was Wednesday, which meant U.S. history and Mr. Davis at 11:00. Megan was in her seat up front at 10:58. Mr. Davis entered the classroom exactly two minutes later.

For fifty minutes he talked about Theodore Roosevelt's accomplishments as mayor of New York. For fifty minutes Megan watched him, seeking some sign of change. She watched him pace the area around his desk like a big cat. She watched him illustrate his sentences with sweeping strokes on the blackboard. She watched his crotch. Nothing.

The bell rang. Megan felt the sting of loss, sharp as when her father had grounded her the weekend of the canoe trip. She stood quickly and walked to the door, pausing to let Kirsten Wallace catch up. Kirsten languished in the back row of Mr. Davis's class, doomed to separation from her friend by the tyranny of the alphabet.

Over English-muffin pizzas in the cafeteria, Kirsten began dishing out details of last weekend's big party. Like Megan, Kirsten was only a sophomore, but she was a sophomore on the swim team, and that earned her a place on the periphery of the high school's movers and shakers. Megan the math whiz had resigned herself to living in some parallel world which Kirsten would visit, bringing news from the planet of the popular.

In fact, it was Kirsten who'd relayed the rumor that Mr. Davis's wife had left him after he found her in the arms of another woman. Megan had been skeptical at the time. "Is this from the same source that said Peter Green's kid brother was abducted by aliens?" But the idea had stuck in her head.

"Earth to Megan."

Megan blinked. Kirsten was waving a hand. "How many fingers am I holding up?" she asked.

"I'm sorry," said Megan. "My mind went on vacation. Kirsten, did you notice anything different about Mr. Davis today?"

"Sure. That tie was a joke. He really needs someone to coordinate his clothes."

"No, no. I mean, the way he acted."

Kirsten contemplated the question for a few seconds. "Don't think so," she said. "Why?"

"No reason. I just thought he might have something on his mind."

"Nothing 'cept Teddy R." And with that, Kirsten was back to who kissed whom when the lights were out, a subject so complex that Megan had to skip dessert to make Mr. Thorndike's trig class.

That night, Megan lay in bed and stared at the ceiling in frustration. Mr. Davis had read her letter, she was sure of it. And that was all she'd wanted. Right? Right.

But now she wanted something more. She felt scared and slightly sick, as if she'd sipped one drink and woken up an alcoholic.

What is enough?

She would lose everything if this got out, all the perfectly typed papers, all the extra-credit work, all the endless activities amassed like gold pieces for her college hoard.

What is enough?

"Not this, not yet," she thought.

So she converted it into a math problem. "Given that Ms. Bryant wants an explicit, sexual response from Mr. Davis, and given that Ms. Bryant in no way intends to reciprocate, and given that Mr. Davis may under no circumstances learn her identity, show there exists a procedure to obtain this response in a manner that preserves both Ms. Bryant's chastity and her anonymity."

That was better. "Now use your brain," she said softly to herself, calling her well-worn homework mantra into service. "Use your big brain." Time passed. She waited. And the answer appeared, a red apple hanging from a black bough.

Tension slowly eased from Megan's body. Already her brain had moved on to her regular fantasy of the past few weeks, unreeling the images before her eyes in a mental videotape. There was Mr. Davis coming home early from a meeting. There were his wife and another woman, sprawled on the bed. The women's actions were vague and indistinct. Mr. Davis's reaction was not.

He ran out of his house into the comfort of the night and stumbled to his car. He drove for hours, aimlessly, then parked on a small, secluded back street. His head was full of the scene at home, the women writhing on the bed, the sounds and smells. He was getting big. He fought his desires, then broke down and unzipped his fly. Tears leaked from behind his closed eyelids.

Megan, face-down and panting, let the movie work its magic once again.

"Dear Mr. Davis," Megan typed, "I look forward to having you in my mouth. In the mailbox at 47 Grove Street you will find a token of my seriousness. If you too are serious, please accept the item with my good wishes. Leave in its place a letter stating your desires. ME"

She reread it twice. It sounded a bit Victorian, but she consoled herself that the Victorians were pretty kinky underneath it all. She spell-checked the file, sent it to the printer, and took off her jeans.

All through the school day she'd been aware of the panties against her skin. They were hot pink, cut bikini-style, and unlike anything she'd ever worn. They were also two sizes too big. Mr. Davis, she was sure, would want a woman with hips.

Megan wondered if she'd left her scent. Images appeared unbidden: Mr. Davis examining the panties, running his fingers over the silky material, holding them up to his face. Something thrummed inside her. She wanted to lie on the bed in the late afternoon sun and touch her suddenly wet self slowly, melting into the day.

She checked her watch. There wasn't enough time to also deliver the panties and letter before dinner. "Maturity is the willingness to postpone pleasure," she reminded herself as she stripped off the panties. Then she giggled. He'd certainly smell her now.

That night, Megan lay in bed and struggled to recapture the excitement of the afternoon. But that still, sweet moment was gone, lost somewhere in the day's nonstop activity. It had taken her forty-five minutes to get to Grove Street and back, about what she'd estimated. But it had taken a full hour to drop off the letter at Mr. Davis's house, and that was just ridiculous.

She hadn't expected his car to be there. For forty minutes she'd lurked around his property before convincing herself he was either out or asleep. In the next sixty seconds she'd managed to trot to the front door, jam the letter through the slot, race back to her bike, mount it, and ride madly for three blocks, only to screech to a stop a second before wiping out Mr. Davis and his Scotch terrier.

She'd almost lost it then, but she'd managed to apologize splendidly and explain she was late for supper, which she was. Mr. Davis had barely acknowledged her. She'd made it home unscathed and gulped down her meal, then plowed through two hours of English homework before doing some last-minute memorization for the French test tomorrow.

Things jostled and jangled in her head. She shifted about uneasily, then rolled onto her stomach. Sometimes the position itself would call up the pictures that brought release, the release required to disconnect her mind so sleep could carry her away.

Instead, she saw the Grove Street mailbox. And then she was standing on one foot in the middle of her moonlit room, pulling up her jeans. She dressed to be unnoticed: dark blouse, sneakers over bare feet, hair tied back from her face, a windbreaker. She slipped out the front door and closed it quietly behind her. Her parents, asleep in their separate rooms, did not stop her. In that moment, she understood that they would never stop her, that this leaving was a rehearsal for a later one.

Mist kissed her face. It was raining gently, and her thoughts dissolved in delight. She heard her mother's voice calling her across the years, "Meg, come in, you're getting soaked!" But she would not come in, she would run through the rain in a world deliciously her own.

On her bike, drops spattering her forehead and cheeks, she said out loud, "You can only get so wet," and felt that same extraordinary freedom. She was sailing through the watery streets, the tires hissing beneath her. Street lamps drifted by, haloed in the damp night air.

Mr. Davis passed this way, she thought, dry and warm in his car, eagerly anticipating his prize. Joy boiled up in her and she squeezed the hand brakes hard. The rear wheel caught, choked, and began to skid out, just like a thousand times before. She squeezed harder and let the bike heel sharply, squeezed harder still, flirting with gravity. She let go. The rear wheel bit into the pavement, the bike jerked wildly, she grabbed the handlebars and yanked. She was upright, in control again. She rolled into her old neighborhood smiling.

It had been two years since they'd moved, leaving the brown monstrosity behind. She passed her old street and took a quick glance. Sixth house down on the right, but all she could see was the rain. Eight more blocks and she turned onto Grove. She coasted half a block, dismounted, and laid her bike under the massive rhododendron as tradition required. She followed the crack in the sidewalk past two more houses, and she was there.

Number 47 was a middle-period Victorian, set back a full forty yards from the road. It had remained unoccupied for almost a decade, an innocent bystander in some legal battle Megan had never understood. The long narrow path to the front porch split the yard into two enormous rectangles. Ragged dogwoods lined the path, and other ornamental trees were scattered about the yard as if planted by some drunken Johnny Appleseed. Japanese maples clustered in a grove on the left, thirty feet in, while three ancient crab apple trees formed a scalene triangle halfway back on the far right. A privet hedge, long untrimmed, extended out from both sides of the house, then ran down the sides of the yard to form a wall to keep out neighbor friends and foes alike. The house itself was beat up and boarded over and basically unchanged from when she and Michael had first discovered it.

Michael. What was he doing now, anyway? His family had moved to Arizona three years ago, and he had vanished from her life. Did he ever think about the innocent messages they used to exchange here? Had he learned how to spell "rendezvous"?

Megan found herself on the large porch that wrapped around the building like a blanket, running along the front and right side of the house. A battered mailbox was bolted to the railing, a single seven hanging on its side. She stared at the mailbox and longed for X-ray vision. Would she see a pile of pink cloth, limp and pathetic? Or had her offering been transmogrified into something rich and wild?

"This is stupid," she thought. She yanked open the box, the hinge squealing, reached inside and pulled out an envelope.

Her eyes got wet. She felt like that guy in the poem when he first saw the mountains of the New World. She took a breath. This was just too good not to share with someone. Kirsten? They'd barely talked about sex, two horses nudging each other from separate stalls. But in the spaces of their conversation, sex often hid. Yes, Kirsten.

One peek first.

She tore the envelope open. Inside was a single sheet of lined paper. It was blank.

"You jerk," she said, and she was off the porch. He was coming from behind a crab apple tree. Megan dove between two dogwoods and tore away across the lawn, the marshy ground trying to steal her sneakers. Five yards past the end of the house she turned right sharply, sprinted to the privet hedge, stopped short and sidestepped neatly through the dead spot. Then she was running again, along the big bow of the living room, under the kitchen windows, around the rear corner of the house, across the flagstones to the corner where the big porch began.

Megan could hear him thrashing around in the privet, trying to bull his way through. She dropped to the ground and pulled herself under the broken latticework with a single move that Michael would have applauded. She was beneath the porch. She scampered on hands and knees along the side of the house and turned the corner. She went twenty more feet, then stopped and huddled, the mailbox almost directly over her.

"Jesus," she thought. "How long has he been here?" It was a truly awesome image: Mr. Davis standing in the rain hour after hour, waiting for her to show. She forced herself to take slow, deep breaths as she held her body still. There was a scrape along her shin and she was wet clear to the bone. Now Mr. Davis was clomping around on the porch. "Who are you?" he called into the night. "I just wanted to talk. Please come back."

Three feet below him, Megan lay slowly down on the muddy ground and stuck out her tongue. "Got you," she mouthed, grinning widely. "Got you!"

Friday's history class began with Mr. Davis launching into an account of the McKinley and Roosevelt presidencies. Megan listened for a while but couldn't pull the meaning from his words. It hardly seemed to matter. He specialized in knowledge of the past, while she could tell his future. She would tell him in a letter.

"Dear Mr. Davis," it began, "You broke the rules and I am quite angry with you. You will have to do penance before you can be in my good graces and my mouth. Please perform the following actions precisely as described . . ."

She realized he was staring at her. She tried to replay his last few words, but they were gone.

"I'm sorry, sir," she said. "I seem to be having trouble concentrating today."

The final ten minutes of class crawled by as she struggled to look attentive. Kirsten caught up with her in the hall.

"What happened to that famous bulletproof brain? I've never seen you space like that."

"I didn't get much sleep last night."

Kirsten raised one eyebrow, showing off another physical skill that Megan lacked. "Care to talk about it?"

"Not right now. I'll explain everything later. In the meantime, I need to borrow some equipment from you. Actually, from your Dad, but he can't know about it."

"Fabulous. And let me guess. You'll explain that later too."

"You read my thoughts like they were written on a blackboard."

"Yeah, yeah. You're going to owe me big, best friend o' mine."

. . .

IT was Sunday afternoon. Megan pressed PLAY for the fourth time and the clearing in the woods appeared once more. A minute passed while nothing happened. Then Mr. Davis, punctual as always, entered stage left. But it was a different Mr. Davis, hesitant and uneasy. He stopped, then turned slowly, hoping to catch a glimpse of his unknown audience. "Give it up!" Megan called to her TV. "I'm not a moron." For a moment, Mr. Davis stared straight at her. Then his gaze moved on. He was looking for a woman, not a camcorder wedged in a tree.

Megan fast-forwarded, scanning for her absolutely favorite part. There! Mr. Davis, her teacher, had followed instructions perfectly. He stood in the middle of the clearing, half-facing the camera, his pants bunched at his knees. He was jerking off. Back and forth his hand moved, gliding slowly, almost absent-mindedly. Megan stared, feeling the hypnotic pull. "Bet you wish that was my mouth," she thought, and just like that she was ready again.

She put the remote down and leaned back in her beanbag chair, squirming to get her bottom comfortable on the vinyl. She licked her fingers. Soon she was matching the urgency of his hand with that of her own. She managed her excitement expertly, balancing on the edge of orgasm. Mr. Davis crouched forward a little. His thing, his cock, stuck straight out in the spring air. Megan knew he was getting close, knew exactly how close. She refocused on his face, slightly fuzzy yet still intensely human, serious and sad and pained and a little lost, and there were his eyes, the lids shut tight, and there, Megan was just about convinced as they came together, were his tears.

THAT night, Megan lay in bed. She felt completely wired. Video frames flickered endlessly through her head, like a catchy chorus she was sick of but couldn't stop humming. It was nine hours at Disney World all over again.

What is enough?

She got up and walked to the bathroom. Sexual tension lingered in her body like a low-grade fever, but she was too tired and too tender to do anything about it. She soaked a face cloth in cold water and draped it across her neck. That was better.

What is enough?

She padded back to her room and sat at her desk. "This is enough," she thought. "This is enough of Mr. Davis." She clicked the switch and was suddenly silhouetted in the glow of the computer screen.

"DEAR Mr. Thorndike," Megan typed, "I would like to suck your dick."

Katya Andreevna

THE
PERFECT FIT

IT WAS ONE OF THOSE DAYS. I spilled coffee all over my desk. The copy machine broke down. While I was receiving a twenty-three-page fax, the paper kept jamming and the machine printed the same page over and over. As soon as the church bells next door struck six, I was out the door and headed, where else, but to Macy's, the largest department store in the world.

My feet slapped against the pavement as I overtook slow-moving commuters. I dipped into the street to cut around a pack of them, all smoking, and slipped into a moving revolving door. Inside, the cool air and the perfume enveloped me. I charged past some dazed tourists to the escalator and jogged by several women with shopping bags and a kid drooling on the handrail.

I hit the designer shoe section and, slowing, breathed deeply. I started cruising at the far end, keeping the truly expensive shoes for my climax.

A pair of oxblood pumps drew me. Too preppy, I thought, but the warm color of the leather made me stroke them and hold them close to my face so I could take in their rich scent. Then a pair of blue suede loafers caught my eye. I checked to see that no other shopper was looking and rubbed their soft skin against my face. The delicate perfume filled my head. I closed my eyes and drank in the leather-laden air.

I felt someone looking at me, but I didn't turn to confront the eyes at my back. Probably just some store detective, I thought, and kept moving toward the even more expensive footwear.

Then I saw them. The heel was probably higher than I could comfortably wear, but it was exquisitely crafted. Chunky and solid, yet elegant, the heel, which arched toward the instep just slightly, would leave a half-moon print behind the delicately pointed toe. The rich burgundy leather called out for my touch.

I approached slowly, studying the play of light on the subtle sheen that complemented this pair. I leaned toward them as if greeting a dog that I didn't know, hands at my sides, ready for re-jection. I could feel my heart beating in my sex as I moved a hand to meet them. I caressed the heel with one finger and gasped. The leather felt as smooth as fifty-year-old port, as soft as wet labia. My hand closed around the heel gently. Realizing I was still being watched, I lifted one shoe, as if to read its designer label, and inhaled deeply.

"What size would you like to see, Ma'am?" a husky female voice asked me from behind.

"Seven, please." I smiled at the salesgirl, a tall brunette. Her eyes pried into me, but she acted cool.

"Would you like to see anything else? You know, we're closing soon." Her dark eyes held mine. I shook my head, still clutching the curve of the heel.

The salesgirl was back before I knew it with a glint in her eye. She directed me to a seat and opened the box with a flourish.

Slightly larger than the display pair, the shoes looked bolder and more powerful. I slipped out of my flats.

The salesgirl lifted one burgundy shoe out of the box and, with her other hand, took my arch. The firmness of her fingers made the pulse between my legs grow stronger. She slid my toes inside and smoothed the shoe over my heel, allowing her cool fingers to linger briefly at my ankle.

I gazed at the perfect shoe on my left foot. The salesgirl stepped back, wiping curly hair from her forehead. I followed her lead to the mirror near the cash register. She held the other shoe out to me. As I reached for it, she pulled away. A slight smile played across her chestnut-colored lips. Again I reached. And again she withdrew.

"Tsk, tsk," she said, holding the shoe out. "Patience." I stood my ground. She moved closer. My eyes focused on the shoe, but I saw her high breasts rise and fall with her breath. My bare foot on the carpet seemed glued to the spot. My eyes climbed, cautiously. Her face was utterly still, but I detected movement behind her deep eyes.

Slowly, she directed the shoe at me. She touched the tip of my breast with the toe and began to circle around my nipple. I closed my eyes as my nipple hardened and poked through my silk top. She pinched it firmly through my shirt and led me into the storage area. I was surrounded by shoes, boxes and boxes of them emitting their opium. She applied the toe of the shoe to my other breast.

Air rasped through my lungs. I clutched a metal shelf, my knees were so weak. Where had this woman been all my other visits? I kept my eyes closed for fear she would stop. I heard a register across the floor beginning to cash out.

I reached down and took the shoe from my left foot. I cradled it to my face, pressed it against my cheek. This leather had an unusually sweet bouquet that went right to my head. The salesgirl's cold fingers covered my hand, loosening my grip from the burgundy prize. All the while she held my right nipple firm.

"No. I want it," I whined as she dragged the shoe from my cheek.

"Show us how much," she said.

She held the shoe around the middle, just in front of my mouth. I leaned forward and kissed the delicate leather, then unleashed my eager tongue. I licked the toe as she moved her hand downward. I ran my tongue along the side and dipped it into the crack where the upper meets the sole.

"Yes, baby," she hissed through closed teeth as I squatted to the floor. I lay down on my stomach and thoroughly explored that crack, tracing it with my tongue from the point of the toe to the back of the heel. Her breathing grew deeper and more rapid above me.

Kneeling in her short skirt, she rubbed the crescent of the heel along my bottom lip. Momentarily I wondered if another salesperson might see us, but then the shoe in front of me absorbed my attention. At first I caressed delicately with just my lips, but soon I began swirling my tongue around the heel, pondering the slight metallic flavor of the inner part of the heel and its contrast with the rich burgundy leather that wrapped its curved back. She moved the heel deeper into my mouth, then drew it away so my lips could barely reach its tip.

"Down," she said as I turned over and moved to sit up. She moved my hand from where it had drifted between my own legs. "Lie still," she commanded.

My cunt absorbed her words and burned with them. I lay flat on my back and closed my eyes. All was quiet for a moment, so still, in fact, that I wondered if she had disappeared from my side. I held myself down on the floor, my mind racing, anticipating what was to come.

She laughed slightly, a rich, throaty sound. The heel caressed under the arch of my foot and across my instep. I felt my toes parted. She ran the heel between my first and second toes, back and forth, and I gasped.

"Sh-sh," she replied and began to trace the bones around my ankle with that heel. She moved up my calf slowly, then teased at the back of my knee. I twitched on the floor, trying to keep my body still as she had commanded.

"You want it, don't you?" she asked in a low, steady voice.

I moaned. "Y-yes," I stammered. My heart beat fiercely in the damp space between my legs.

Abruptly she pulled up my skirt. She played the heel over my knee then moved up, stroking my inner thigh. She rubbed my groin with the whole shoe and my hips rose involuntarily. She passed the shoe across my belly, along the bikini line. I was afraid to look at what she was doing; afraid if I did she would stop.

I moaned loudly as she dipped the heel under the waist of my panties. She brushed my bush hairs one way, and then the other. She slid the heel slowly down till it was just at the edge of my slit. I shifted my hips so I could feel its slight pressure on my clit.

"Please," I whispered hoarsely, looking up at her. My face was flushed and I felt sweat breaking out all over my body. I had never been so excited. "Please," I repeated.

She pushed on the heel a bit, making my clit, and my whole being, jump. She ripped down my panties. The sole grazed my bush, exciting every hair follicle. She ran the delicious shoe between my thigh and outer lip. The soft leather felt perfect against my delicate skin. I thought I would either come right then or die from arousal.

"Yes, now," I pleaded. My burning inner lips parted. The crescent heel slipped between the folds of my waiting flesh. Then withdrew.

"Do it. Do it now," I croaked. I couldn't stand any more.

"Certainly, Madam." She laughed again. And then it was inside of me, that perfect leather-covered heel. Something in my chest loosed and my limbs flopped on the floor as if a spring that had held me together had finally come undone.

She pumped the heel into me. My head rocked from side to side. She placed the shoe's mate in my hand and I held it against my cheek.

"Deeper," I cried, and she plunged. The sole of the shoe massaged my clit, while the heel pressed ever inward.

The words "yes yes yes" poured from my lips as I sucked in the scent of the shoe's mate. This time, as she slid the heel deep inside me, she twisted the shoe and pressed it hard against my G-spot.

"Harder," I whispered.

She rammed the heel inside me, holding at the top of the up-swing. Her speed and force increased and all I knew was my smell, the pulsing between my legs, and the shoe, the perfect shoe inside of me where it fit so well.

My body had begun to tense and tremble. The air entering my lungs came in short gasps. I raised my head slightly, gazed at the salesgirl's face intent on her work. Beyond her a mirror held the scene: I lay, legs parted, the heel of the perfect shoe disappearing into me. I watched the heel slide out and then plunge. All my muscles jerked, my spine arched up, my head fell back.

The heel still inside me, I drooped against the floor, turning my flushed face to the other shoe. My ears began to ring.

She slowly pulled the shoe from between my legs. Patting my bush with one hand, she placed the shoe next to its mate on the floor. She stood, towering over me, smoothed her skirt and straightened her employee name tag.

"They're a perfect fit," she said.

"Yes," I croaked, scrambling up from the floor. "The heel's not too high?"

"They look great . . ." she paused, "on. They suit you."

"Yes," I said, smiling and pulling out my credit card. "Yes, they do."

Lars Eighner

THE
TRADE

It's really too early in the day, Bruce thought.

A fly buzzed around the Dumpster at the corner. In the August heat, the Dumpster stank. Bruce pecked around the corner. The trade was still there, leaning against the wall near the entrance of the alley.

He sure looks like trade, Bruce thought.

Bruce had walked past the man twice. *I should make my move or forget it*. Bruce walked slowly toward the man. Bruce slowed even more as he came near the man—the man with the hard hat, the athletic T-shirt, the greasy jeans.

The man was not going to speak first. Bruce was almost past him.

"Got a light?" Bruce blurted out, too suddenly.

"In the alley," the man growled as he grabbed Bruce's arm.

Bruce pulled back instinctively from such a violent

move. It made no difference. The man was much stronger than Bruce. Bruce was dragged into the shadows far down the alley.

"Look, how much?" Bruce asked. "I don't have much money at all."

"You know how to suck dick?"

Bruce didn't know what to say.

"Hey, it's free. You don't have to pay me," the man explained. "But, like, I'm straight. I don't do nothing back."

Bruce nodded.

The man's hand closed on the back of Bruce's neck. "Well, get to it. I got a dick that will change your life." The man's hand pushed Bruce to his knees. The man's button fly was just an inch in front of Bruce's face. Bruce unbuttoned the man's fly.

When the man's cock was free of his jeans, Bruce scarcely had time to look at it before it was forced into his throat. It was big, rock hard, and shiny. *Not,* thought Bruce, *so great that it's likely to change my life. Straight men are so vain about their dicks.* But it was good hard cockmeat, and the man was hot and forceful without hurting Bruce.

Bruce tried to get a hand free to open his own fly. But the man was already pressing Bruce against the wall. The man's powerful legs were driving the hard, hot cock into Bruce's mouth, fucking Bruce's mouth. Bruce could move only just enough to rub his dick through his jeans.

Already the man was gasping and grunting. Bruce wanted to make it last, but he could not move.

"Here's my nut, cocksucker," the man said between his teeth.

Bruce's mouth was flooded with hot, sour cum. His own cock throbbed, and a sticky stain spread down the right leg of his jeans. Bruce swallowed. He swallowed again and began licking the man's cock tenderly.

"That's it, cocksucker. You got it all." The man pulled his cock out of Bruce's mouth. "I don't do nothing back."

"That's okay—" Bruce was about to explain that he had cum in his pants.

"Don't matter whether it's okay. I don't do nothing back. I'm straight. Hey, cut it out. None of that love shit!"

Unconsciously, Bruce had laid his cheek against the greasy jeans on the man's thigh and had begun stroking the man's flank with his dry hand. None of the trade had ever objected to that before. At least not in the minute or two after they had cum.

The man stepped back, out of Bruce's reach. He milked the large limp cock a couple of times, but there wasn't a drop left in it. "See ya around, man. I gotta fly."

And then the man was gone. Bruce sat on his heels for a long time, leaning against the wall. *I have got to stop doing trade*, he thought. *That one could have killed me as well as anything.*

Bruce snapped back to reality when a fly landed on the huge cum-spot on his jeans. The spot spread from halfway down his thigh almost to his knee. There was no way to cover it up. Bruce just had to hope that no one would notice before the stain dried in the August heat. He shooed the fly and stood up.

ALAN looked out the window. A September storm was brewing over the bay. There would be just enough time to get to the gym before it started to rain. Already it was dark enough so that Alan could see his reflection in the window. Alan forced a smile onto his face.

"Bruce, come on. Let's go to the gym." Alan bounced into the living area wearing his chartreuse silk gym shorts, a blue and green soccer shirt, and his green Reeboks.

"You go ahead. I don't feel like it."

Alan looked at the TV that Bruce was watching. "You said that the last three times. It's not like you."

"It's just so boring working out. And I hate the smell of the gym."

"I don't believe my ears! What's wrong, Bruce?"

"Nothing. Get out of the way. I can't see the TV."

"Something is wrong. You say it's boring to go to the gym. You say you don't like the smell of the gym. You haven't worked out in two weeks. Come to think of it, you haven't made love to me in three weeks. And look—here you are, watching commercial television. Is the cable out of order?"

"No. The cable's working fine. I just happen to like this show."

"You like watching *The Wheel of Fortune?*" Alan reached to feel Bruce's forehead. "Are you ill?"

Bruce realized that he had pulled back involuntarily to avoid Alan's touch. Bruce looked puzzled for a second. "No. I'm fine. I never felt better."

"Fine? The perennial hypochondriac? Bruce, you used to give someone a medical history if they asked, 'How do you do?' Now you tell me you're fine. You've never in your life said you were feeling fine."

"Well, now I feel fine. All right?"

"Bruce, I think I better take you to see Dr. Jim."

"Hey, I don't need a doctor."

"Yes. Yes, Bruce, I think you do."

"Okay! Okay! If it will get you off my back. Jesus, I can't take this constant bitching. Now get out of the way. I can't see Vanna White."

"YOO-HOO! Anybody home? It's Mona." Mona peeked through the door at Bruce and Alan's tasteful living area. Mona coveted the Picasso sketches although, as Alan always explained, they hadn't been so very expensive.

"Mona? Come on back. I'm in the kitchen."

Mona entered the apartment. He found Alan rolling croissants on the marble slab. Mona sat at the bar. "Mind if I have a drink?"

"Oh, no. Help yourself. Oh, let me get you some ice."

"Never mind. I don't need it." Mona poured four ounces of rye into a highball glass and downed it, Alan noticed. That drink seemed a little excessive, even for Mona. Alan shooed a fly away from a buttery corner of the slab. "Is something on your mind, honey?" Alan asked.

"Yes, well. First let me ask you. How are things between you and Bruce?" Mona poured himself another rye, but he seemed content to sip this one.

"Not so good, now that you ask. Why do you ask?"

"Honey, darling, dear. I don't want to be the one to break it to you. I don't know how to soften the blow. I was downtown in high drag, you know."

"Yes. Go on." Alan put down the rolling pin and looked at Mona. Mona had not quite managed to get all of his eye makeup off.

"You'll think I'm just flattering myself."

"Out with it, Mona."

"Your husband tried to pick me up." Mona downed the rest of the drink and poured himself another one. "You don't seem to be especially surprised to hear that."

"I'm not especially surprised to hear that. He hasn't touched me in weeks. And he's been doing all kinds of strange things . . . Oh, my dear, I didn't mean that the way it sounded."

"No. Strange is right. I told you I was in high drag. The strange thing is, he didn't recognize me. I almost think . . ."

"What? Go on."

"It sounds crazy. I almost think he thought I was an RG."

"A real girl?"

"Exactly."

"Hmmm."

"Alan, what does it mean?"

"I don't know, Mona. I thought he was ill. We're supposed to go back to Dr. Jim's this afternoon for the results of the tests. Pour me one of those while you're at it."

The front door slammed.

"What in the hell is this shrieking?" Bruce bellowed from the living area.

"What shrieking?" Alan called.

"This goddamn shrieking on the stereo."

The sound of a needle skating over a record came over the kitchen speakers; and in a moment, from the living area, the little snap of vinyl bent past the breaking point.

"Oh God, Mona," Alan whispered. "It is—it was *Don Giovanni*. His very own record. His favorite."

THEY had been in the waiting room for a long time when Dr. Jim came to the waiting room. It was part of Dr. Jim's person-to-person style of medical practice that he came to the waiting room himself.

"Bruce," Dr. Jim called. "And Alan, you'd better come, too."

Bruce and Alan followed Dr. Jim, not to an examining room, but to his office. Alan was surprised to see another man waiting for them.

"Bruce and Alan, this is Professor Tom. I asked him to join us. There are some things I want him to explain to you himself."

"A professor? Professor of what?" Alan asked.

"Of a kind of biology," Professor Tom replied.

Alan looked suspiciously at Professor Tom. "What kind of biology?"

"Professor Tom is a virologist," said Dr. Jim.

"A virologist? Then it is—"

"No. It's not any of the sexually transmitted diseases we tested for." Dr. Jim tried to look reassuring, but it was the piercing blue-eyed, encounter-group stare that always put Alan's teeth on edge. "Professor Tom, why don't you take over."

"Oh yes. I need to know if the two of you have been completely monogamous. It's important."

"Yes," said Alan immediately.

"Well, practically," Bruce said slowly.

"Practically?" asked Alan.

"I thought so." Professor Tom laid out a series of photographs on the desk. They looked like pictures of pairs of strange, banded kinked-up snakes. In each picture, the pairs of snakes were numbered one through twenty-two, and then there was a pair of mismatched snakes. "These are karyotypes. They show pictures of a person's genetic makeup. This one is from an old sample from Bruce. This is Alan's current sample. This is Bruce's current sample. And these are from a group of completely heterosexual men, each of them straight as a board. Now, see this little bump on the X chromosome of Bruce's current sample, and over here on the control group we—"

"Skip the shit!" Bruce said. "Give us the bottom line."

"You see I've been working on this theory—"

"I said skip the shit."

"I think you've caught a retrovirus of a kind we've never seen before. Your genetic makeup is being altered. It's a million-to-one shot, but it's being altered in a way that produces an extra kink on the X chromosome. Otherwise we wouldn't have a clue as to what was happening. You see I've been working on the theory—"

"I said the bottom line. What's happening to me?"

"You're developing an extra kink on your X chromosome. It looks very much like the same kink—"

"We hope we're wrong," said Dr. Jim. "But think hard. Did you do some trade? Say, maybe in the last two or three months?"

"Well, yeah, I guess I did." Bruce remembered the man's words. "I got a dick that will change your life."

"We hope we're wrong," said Professor Tom. "But it looks like a kink I have found on the X chromosomes of only one type of man. See, the kink isn't on your old karyotype. And see, it's not on Alan's."

"Yes, go on," Alan said.

"We've found it only on the chromosomes of straight men, Kinsey zeros. So far. It doesn't necessarily mean anything. There could be lots of other explanations."

Alan thought about what Mona had told him. "You mean—"

"He means he thinks I'm going straight. What bullshit! That's what you mean, isn't it, professor?"

"We think it's one possibility."

"Bullshit!"

"Maybe so," Dr. Jim said. Professor Tom looked a little hurt. "We are dealing with the unknown," Dr. Jim went on. "As scientists we must not jump to conclusions. But we think it's definitely likely to be catching."

"Definitely likely? What's that mean?" asked Bruce.

"It means, until and unless we know more, only safe sex. Okay?"

"Sure. Sure," said Bruce.

Alan thought, *It's not the safe sex I mind, it's the no sex at all.*

BRUCE toyed with the thing on his plate. Finally he brought the fork to his mouth. He got it past his lips. He forced himself to chew. He tried to swallow, but his throat began to close up. He felt like he was going to choke. He spit the chewed yellow mass back onto his plate.

"God, Alan! I can't eat this shit! Why can't we ever have steak and potatoes? Why does it always have to be this foo-foo stuff?"

Alan seemed frozen for a moment. Then the shuddering icy finger of terror raced up his spine, snapping him back to reality.

"Bruce, you spit that out on your plate."

"So?"

"So your napkin is perfectly handy. But look. There it is on the table. You haven't even unfolded it in your lap. You just left it there under your silverware."

"So what? Even Miss Manners must have an occasional lapse."

"It's not just an occasional lapse, Bruce. Look at your hand. What's that in your hand?"

"My fork."

"Your *salad* fork, Bruce." Alan was on the verge of tears. "You tried to eat your quiche lorraine with your salad fork."

"Hey, a fork's a fork."

"No, Bruce. You never used the wrong fork before. Don't you see? Can't you tell?"

"Tell what?"

"Like your fingernails."

Bruce dropped his fork on his plate and looked at the back of his hands. He saw. He tried to hide his hands in his lap. "So? My nails are a little dirty."

"No, Bruce. Not a little dirty. Greasy. Your fingernails are greasy. Tell me, your car needed a tune-up. Does it still need a tune-up?"

"No."

"Bruce, where did you take your car for a tune-up?"

"I don't know. What difference does it make?"

"You know. You know what difference it makes. Why doesn't your car need a tune-up anymore?"

"Because I . . ."

"Yes, Bruce. Go on."

"Because I tuned it up myself. All right? That's what you wanted me to say. I said it. I'm just getting a little more butch as I get older."

"No, Bruce. Not just a little more butch. Like when you scratch your balls."

"What about when I scratch my balls?"

"When you scratch your balls, you don't put your fingers up to your nose and smell them afterward."

"So?"

"So, Bruce, every gay man in the world smells his fingers after he scratches his balls. Butch numbers do it most of all. You're not getting butcher. You're . . . you're going . . ."

"Yes?"

"You're not getting butcher. You're going straight."

Bruce jumped up and overturned the dining table. *"No! No!* You're just jealous. You're jealous because you're just a mincing little fairy who wishes she could pass for butch. Get out! Get out of my apartment!"

ALAN was appalled. The Picasso sketches were gone. In their place were three paintings on black velvet: one of Elvis; one of wild horses; one of a leering devil offering a cocktail glass, a pair of dice, and a curvaceous blonde. Alan could see only the back of the recliner. The recliner faced the television, which was tuned to a football game. On the mantel, in place of the art deco clock, was a tiny black-and-white TV, tuned to a different football game. The room was littered with beer cans. A wave of dread passed over Alan. His voice cracked as he said, "Bruce? Bruce, are you here? I came as soon as I played back your message on the answering machine."

A deafening belch came from the recliner.

"Yes, Alan. Come in. I didn't want you to see me this way. Now I think you better. You were right. I am changing. I am changing into . . . into Straight-Bruce."

"Oh, no, Bruce!"

"You were right. I've stopped denying it. Pull up the chase lounge."

"You mean the *chaise longue?*"

"Straight-Bruce calls it a chase lounge. Just a second, the game's almost over."

Alan moved the *Road & Track* and the *Hustler* off the chaise longue and pulled it next to Bruce's recliner. Only after he was seated did he dare to look at Bruce. Bruce had changed. The stubble on his face had grown much past the fashionable three days' growth, yet it was not a beard. Bruce was wearing a stained and greasy white T-shirt. The beer belly was now very evident, completely obscuring Bruce's gym-built abs. Then there were the orange-and-blue-plaid Bermuda shorts.

Bruce lifted a leg and farted.

"Wanna brew?" Bruce's hand plunged into the icy water in the Playmate cooler by his recliner.

"Do you have any white wine?" Alan asked, noticing on Bruce's forearm the fresh carbon tattoo of a dripping dagger.

"Naw. Not unless there's some you left here. Come on, god-damn, let's have that instant replay! God did you see that call! It *wasn't* fucking interference, he was going for the ball. Come on, show the goddamn replay! Well, you want a beer or not?"

"You don't have any light?"

"Jesus! Of course I don't have any light. Can't you see? You no-ticed it first. Can't you see what's happening to me?"

"Yes, Bruce. I can see. Bruce, how are you living? I mean, what are you doing for a living?"

"Oh. You know that after you moved out, they fired me from the salon."

"Yes, I know. What else could they do?"

"Nothing I suppose. Well, they could have found something for me. Maintenance, janitor, something. It's okay. I found a job at an auto-parts store. It's a great bunch of guys. Only . . ."

"Only?"

"Well, it's only that you and I were buddies for so long—"

"We weren't buddies. We were lovers. Lovers for seven years."

"Five . . . four . . . three . . . two . . . one! That's the game. God-damn Wildcats. Goddamn. Dropped a hundred bucks on them last week, too. What was I saying?"

"We were lovers for seven years."

"Oh, yeah. We were buddies for so long. Well, you know, in my situation, old pals are hard to come by. Look, I got some stag flicks at the video store. Let me put one in the machine." Bruce staggered a little as he got up and went to the VCR. He pulled a tape from the stack and slipped it into the machine. Then he threw himself into the recliner. He picked up the remote control.

After the FBI WARNING came the title: *Sorority Snatch*.

"This one's pretty hot," Bruce said as he began to squeeze the lump in his Bermuda shorts.

The opening shot was exterior, at night. A man in dark clothes crawling into the bushes outside a building. Then, through the blinds, a well-lit room, college pennants on the wall, a teddy bear on the bed. A woman, possibly younger than forty, entered the room. She pulled a collegiate sweater off over her head. She bent and, reaching behind her back, began to unfasten her bra. Reverse angle of the man's eyes through the blinds, sweat forming on his brow, and the muscle of his neck showing that somewhere below, out of view, his hand was moving frantically. Back to the woman. Alan had to look away from the screen.

Bruce had unzipped his Bermuda shorts and was pulling at his long, hooded cock. He noticed Alan looking at him.

"Hey, come on. Look at the flick."

"I can't stand it."

"Yeah, I know. Just don't be so obvious looking at my dick until I get going good. But, you know, we can still get off together, like this. I mean I'm real drunk."

The sight of Bruce's cock getting hard overcame the repulsion Alan felt. Alan unzipped his own trousers slowly.

"Hey," Bruce said. "This wouldn't happen if I wasn't real drunk. But we've been buddies for a long time."

"Lovers, Bruce. We were lovers."

"Straight-Bruce has to call it 'buddies.' Hey, don't stare. Look at my dick out of the corner of your eye if you have to. But pretend you're watching the flick. So you know, we were buddies for a long time. And I had a lot of respect for you."

"You loved me."

"Had a lot of respect for you. And now I . . . well, you know we had some good times together, and I . . . I . . ."

"You're lonely and you miss me."

"Let's just say everybody needs friends. Hey, I love my girlfriend. But she's pregnant now, you know. Oh, I guess you didn't know." Bruce spit on his hand and stroked the length of his cock.

Alan's own cock was hard now. He couldn't help himself. He watched Bruce's cock out of the corner of his eye. He tried to block out the picture of the woman on the TV screen. He began stroking his own cock.

"Anyway, so I watch the videos for the time being."

"Because you're afraid that if you fuck your girlfriend, you'll dent the baby's little head. Straight men always think that."

"They do? Well, it does seem to me that my cock is even bigger than it was. I measured it and it's not. But my cock just seems huge now. I guess that's part of getting to be Straight-Bruce. Anyway, I'm real drunk, or this wouldn't be happening. I'm real drunk and horny. So, look, why don't you just suck my dick a little while I watch the video."

"Bruce!"

"Come on, Alan. You've done it before. I don't get much head these days."

"Bruce, you know the doctor said it was catching."

"He wasn't sure. And they don't know everything. You know you want it. C'mon. Please. I may not be this drunk again."

Alan stopped pulling on his cock. His erection was beginning to wilt. "I get it now. You want me to catch it. You want me to be just like you."

"It won't be so bad. C'mon. You'd love to have my dick again. Look, my girlfriend has a sister. It won't really be so bad. Like we can go fishing together. I'll show you how to work on cars. Maybe when the girls go to see their mother, maybe we could get drunk together, maybe real drunk. Maybe things would be like old times."

Alan's eyes widened with horror. "No! It wouldn't be like old times . . . You . . . you want me to be just like you!"

Bruce hadn't stopped jerking on his cock. When the tip poked out of the foreskin, it was very red. A pearl of precome formed at his cockslit. He peeled the foreskin all the way back.

"Ick! God, Bruce! It's—it's smegma! You haven't been washing!"

"Headcheese. Gives it flavor. You'll love it."

"No, Bruce, no!"

"Enough arguing. Suck my dick, faggot!" Bruce's hand caught the back of Alan's neck.

"No, Bruce! No! How can you do this to me?"

"Yes, yes. C'mon. Join me. I need a buddy. C'mon, I'm about to get it. Drink my cum. Swallow my straight cum, cocksucker!" Bruce drew Alan's head closer. Alan's eyes glazed over with fear. "We'll be together this way, Alan. We'll be buddies. C'mon, take my wad."

Alan tried to pull back, but he could not take his eyes off the cock, Bruce's huge, hot, throbbing cock. He couldn't look away. Bruce's hand pulled Alan's neck.

"No, Bruce, please don't make me!" Tears began forming in Alan's eyes.

"I'm so lonely. Take it, take it, and then we'll be friends. You'll be my brother-in-law. C'mon, hurry. Don't you know how hard it is for Straight-Bruce to have friends? Eat me, faggot, eat me!" Bruce's balls clamped up close to the base of his cock.

Alan couldn't pull away. His lover was still somewhere inside of Straight-Bruce. He couldn't help himself. He opened his mouth. Bruce's cock aimed at his mouth, coming closer and closer. Bruce's balls began to jump.

"How long has this been going on!" Mona shrieked as he stood at the open door in full drag.

Alan looked up.

"Oh, no!" Bruce's cock pumped out its wad, four, five spurts arcing into the air and splatting against the TV screen.

"Nobody answered me when I knocked," Mona explained. "So I didn't think anyone would mind if I let myself in."

"Oh, God, it's wasted! You wasted my wad, you little cock-sucker."

"Help! Mona, get me out of here!"

"Run, Alan, run! The Volvo's downstairs. I left the motor running."

Alan broke free and ran toward Mona and the door.

"No. Come back. Come back. I can get it up again. It will only take a second. Oh, gee, if only I weren't so drunk." Bruce staggered to his feet, pulling frantically at his limp cock.

"Ta-ta, Bruce!" Mona waved. "Sorry we have to run. I guess you're so drunk that you won't remember this in the morning, will you?"

AS the Volvo pulled away from the curb, Alan noticed that his trousers were still unzipped. He zipped them.

"Thank goodness you came by when you did, Mona. He was about to . . . about to . . ."

"There, there. I know. The professor is one of my afternoon callers. He told me all about it. You just have to stay away from here for a few more weeks. Bruce has bought a house in the suburbs. By the time he moves, we think the transformation will be complete."

"You mean . . ."

"Yes. He'll be a Kinsey zero. He won't even want to try something like that again."

Caught in the Volvo, a fly buzzed past Alan's cheek. Alan began to sob softly.

David Shields

GIRLS WHO
WEAR GLASSES

WOMEN WEAR GLASSES on chains, like metal dogs on a leash. They whip them around in the air like a lasso. They bite the earpiece of the temple, than which simply nothing is more suggestive. They lay their glasses down on the table, allowing the whole world to go fuzzy on them, while they rub their eyes. They crawl around on the floor, looking for their glasses, which they can't find because they're not wearing their glasses. They find their glasses and hug you in a frenzy of unblurry relief. They clean their glasses with your T-shirt. They read in bed. They place their glasses on top of their head like deep-sea divers emerging from the deep sea. They push them halfway down their nose so they can neither see you nor not see you, so you can neither see them nor not see them. They remove their glasses, exposing the little red indentation across the bridge of their nose. They smash their glasses while making love to you. They tuck their glasses carefully in a case, like putting a baby to bed.

A woman recently riding the crosstown bus struck me as extremely beautiful, if in a rather traditional, all-American way; without glasses, she would have been a statue, a mannequin, a doll, a cartoon: her beauty would have been too too. Her simple red tortoiseshells eroticized her to an almost intolerable degree. They drew me in and stood me off. They said, "You can look at me all you want, but you can't see me in public. You have no idea what I look like or am like. You have no idea how interesting things get when I take these off. I'm so sexy I need to wear these as a buffer."

The way her glasses worked against her beauty was exactly what made her more beautiful: more human. Glasses insist upon the constant simultaneity of body and mind; the beauty of a woman's face is deepened and complicated by the antiglamour scholasticism of her eyewear. Superman without Clark Kent would be perfect, completely unconvincing, boring.

Glasses have the spectacular virtue of suggesting that there is everything left to imagine: only someone in special circumstances will see the veil removed, the gate opened, the cage unlocked— her naked eyes. Only I get to see her without her glasses; only I get to see the beauty behind the barrier. Glasses make completely explicit the relationship between eyes and I, between love and trust. Glasses, mask of masks, allude to the difference between how a person appears in public and how the same person might perform in private, and thus suggest the bedroom. The arrogance implied in believing that one's beauty can afford to be concealed is entrancing. By contrast, people not wearing glasses sometimes seem preposterously accessible, uncomplicated, unmysterious, trampy.

What is so sexy about glasses is that they block the male gaze and return it redoubled; they transform the woman from viewed to viewer, from looked-at to looker. *Men seldom make passes at girls who wear glasses*—Dorothy Parker's aphorism tells us much more about her particular brand of self-loathing than it does about eyewear. "Smell me, touch me, but don't look at me": needless to say, this is a tantalizing message to send.

When a woman wears glasses, she is—to me, anyway—displaying her woundedness. (In the wild, a wounded animal doesn't get courted.) She seems both very vulnerable—I could remove her glasses, causing her to be disoriented—and very brave—choosing not to conceal her defect in the most vital of the five senses. One sense is diminished; another sense (touch? taste?) must, in order to compensate, be particularly acute.

In high school I read Philip Roth's *Goodbye, Columbus*. The book opens like this: "The first time I saw Brenda she asked me to hold her glasses. Then she stepped out to the edge of the diving board and looked foggily into the pool; it could have been drained, myopic Brenda would never have known it. She dove beautifully, and a moment later she was swimming back to the side of the pool, her head of short-clipped auburn hair held up, straight ahead of her, as though it were a rose on a long stem. She glided to the edge and then was beside me. 'Thank you,' she said, her eyes watery though not from the water. She extended a hand for her glasses but did not put them on until she turned and headed away. I watched her move off. Her hands suddenly appeared behind her. She caught the bottom of her suit between thumb and index finger and flicked what flesh had been showing back where it belonged. My blood jumped." Immediately I was deep into Brenda.

"Now what can you do?" I once asked a lover who, in bed, had just removed her glasses and who without glasses was legally blind. I thought I meant "How well can you function without your glasses?" but my question clearly implied another question—concerning mattress acrobatics. I wanted her to put her glasses back on so I could tear them off.

Is anything more unnerving than to be asked, in the middle of a lovers' quarrel, "Why won't you look at me?" The eyes, as the Renaissance never gets tired of telling us, are the windows of the soul. What glasses say is: "My soul is not so easily accessible."

The terms for frame parts are about the distance between me and you, between here and there—rim, bridge, hinge, shield. Some temple parts: bend, shaft, and, um, butt portion. Is everyone aroused by looking at diagrams of glasses, or is that only me? I love how the long thin temples screw into round liquescent lenses. In the interest of full disclosure: absolutely nothing could possibly be more erotic to me than the subservient-yet-unreachable paradox embodied by a woman performing fellatio while wearing glasses.

I must acknowledge that some things about glasses just don't work. All sunglasses, for instance, which are striving so strenuously to be mysterious that they work zero magic on me. So, too, the cat's-eye, which is much too obvious in its female = feline, Cat Woman = Bitch Goddess equations. Movie stars at the Academy Awards wearing horn-rims in order to read the TelePrompTer do not suddenly seem deeper and more widely read. Pornographic photos—intended to excite the bookish gentleman—in which glasses are perched on the tip of the model's nose as a totally alien accessory are not very exciting. Glasses can't be a self-consciously sexy accoutrement; the joke can't be explained; the contradiction can't be resolved in favor of overtness: glasses are sexy precisely to the degree that a woman's sexiness appears to emerge despite her attempt to hide it.

My wife needs glasses only to drive at night and read subtitles in movie theaters. As often as possible, I tell her I'm not sure I know the way home—would she mind driving? As often as possible, I suggest that we sign up for, say, the Fellini retrospective at the Grand Illusion.

And yet, finally, no one, as I've learned all too well, wants to hear: "I love how you look in your glasses; I think you look even better with them on." The sexiest thing about glasses is that they come off. The sexiest thing about glasses is that the first time you kiss, she lets you take them off and then blinks once, trying to focus.

Cecilia Tan

PEARL DIVER

I BREATHE. As I lie still in the bottom of the boat, the sea breathes with me, rising and falling. There is just enough room for me in my little wooden shell, the oars tucked against each side. Droplets of seawater glisten on my bare skin, and I watch my own chest as I breathe, touch my stomach with my hands. The time is coming, and I am almost ready. The moon is still climbing up the sky, and I wait for it to reach its peak. It must, because that is the way things are and have always been, the moon and the sun circling forever above without cease, just as the waves must rise and fall, and the rains to follow the dry time. Tonight is not just any moonrise, though, not just any night upon the water. Tonight is the night of the pearls.

I sit up in the boat and peer over the edge. The water is dark, but the sand and the stones are almost white. Below me the silvery flash of fish in the moonlight catches my eye—but I know it is just fish, not pearls. I will know the pearls when I see them. When the moon is at its height. I have been prepared for this moment since my breasts first began to swell; for years I have prepared my body for this, to be a pearl diver.

The elders in the village say the pearls fell down from the skies; some say they are stars out of the heavens, some say *we* came down from the heavens, that we came long ago from another place where we were not the only people, where there were people with pink skin and yellow hair, that we traveled on the water in boats like my little shell, and some say that when we die we will go back to that place and others say that when we are born that is where we come from, and in any case the only thing we do all agree on is that the pearls are magic and precious, and if there is a link to our ancestors, gods, or afterlife, it is through them.

I lie back down in the boat. The moon is taking its time. I let my feet hang over the edge on either side, warm water touching my toes as the shell rocks into a small swell. The night breeze rustles the dark cluster of hair between my legs and the lips sigh open. As they taught me, I lick my finger and let it rest there, rocking my hips as each wave passes, slow as a sleeper's breath. Just as I had been taught, I gather the magic around me, and I can almost see myself beginning to glow as I resist the urge to press my finger harder and let the energy burst and dissipate. It surges through me as I go on touching what we call the *woman's pearl*, the nub of flesh now grown hard like the treasures I will be seeking.

My eyes have slipped closed but I must keep watching the moon. I open them to find it is almost above me, looking down on me like an eager lover, who will now finally be allowed into my virgin flesh. I slip over the side of the boat and into the warm embrace of the sea. Bubbles rise up and catch between my legs, and I want to keep my hand there, but I will need both of them to swim. I lower myself under the surface of the water and as sounds grow dim, my vision grows sharp. I am a pearl diver and I know how to see through the shadows and murk. But there is nothing to see, yet. I let go of the boat and float face down on the surface, my legs hanging free below me and open. I tense the muscles inside me, and feel the energy shoot through me again. Soon those muscles will do what I have practiced so long to do. The elders chose me out of all the others to do this task. All the girls of my age had been taken aside and trained, the old women rubbing our women's pearls with oil until we learned to do it ourselves, reaching fingers inside of us, first one, then, two, then three, as they exercised us until we had the strength that was needed, and holding our breaths until sometimes it seemed we did not need to breathe at all . . .

And now I see why. The moon must be over my head as the shadows have all shrunk as small as they can be, and I see at first faint but then as bright as the nighttime stars, the pearls. Glowing from the bottom. They are invisible and dead as rocks at any other time, but now they glow. Maybe, I think to myself, they fell not from the stars but from the moon itself, and they glow only when the moon draws so near. I take the last breath that I will ever draw as a girl and with wide strokes I dive toward my womanhood.

The first pearl I find is small, no bigger than the end of my thumb, and I lift it from its bed of sand and turn it in my fingers to convince myself that what they told me is true, it is smoother than anything I have ever felt, much smoother then the wooden beads we used for practice. Curling myself into a ball with my head between my knees, I open myself with one hand and slide the pearl inside me, using my muscles to draw it as far up inside as it will go . . .

The shock of the first vision almost makes me lose my air, a tiny silver bubble rises toward the moon as I see in my mind's eye the moon, the stars, not spread out above me like a roof but hanging all around me like a school of fish in the water, and I know that I feel my place among them.

My legs together, I stroke with my arms to the next glowing spot, and lift out of the sand a pearl the size of my eye. It feels warm, warmer than the blood-warm sea water, and with one hand I slip it inside.

This time I am ready when the vision comes: I am moving through space like a swimmer, circling down toward a planet blue with oceans, and thinking HOME! HOME! and already I am spiraling toward the next pearl, this one bright as it protrudes above the sand, almost too large to fit in my closed hand. I press it against my opening, but it does not slide in like the others. I cannot breathe to help me relax, and I do not have time to waste with only one breath of air inside me. While I take the time to do this I float toward the surface and it will be more work to get back to the bottom. As my hands work at my opening, they brush my woman's pearl and I feel something inside me blossom open like a flower, and take the white orb in.

I am swimming, turning and tumbling, as the planet below revolves in its dance around the sun, the moon its partner swinging round, and all the close family of others moving stately through the sky, and beyond, and beyond, and beyond . . . and a voice, not my own, in my head, saying "the seeds of life, scattered."

I realize my vision is getting darker and my air is almost done but I make for one more pearl nearby. This one I lift in two hands, it is the size of my fist. Some part of me thinks I cannot hope to take it in, but one hand is already rubbing hard at my own pearl while the other is pushing the huge thing against me. It goes partway in and then slips back out and if I could I would be gasping for breath but there is only water all around me as I thrash, I need this last pearl more than all the others, I am hungry for it, the energy and magic flowing in and out of it as I push my fingers inside myself, trying to open the way wide enough, and then it is going in, it moves in my hand into me bit by bit, up to its widest point, and then, as my other hand presses hard on my woman's pearl, I swallow it whole.

The universe breathes like giant wings beating, I see people infinitely small in a band across the face of the stars, I see white glowing star stuff spread like webs across the void, I see embryos bursting into life inside mothers' wombs, I see the *man's pearl* dripping from the tip of his finger, I see all of creation. I cry out as the magic bursts through me and my bubbles race out of me like a flight of startled birds. My hands are between my legs, one keeping the pearls in place and the other holding my own pearl which throbs and ebbs, and my head breaks the surface . . .

and I breathe. I lie on my back in the water with the moon shining upon my breasts and I cannot take my hands from between my legs as I burst the bubble again and again, fingers furiously working as the sensations wash over me, and under the moon's watchful eye I know I will return to the shore, bearing the wisdom of ages.

Susanna Moore

From

in the cut

I STOOD ON THE STREET, smelling the diesel from the trucks on the West Side Highway and the odor of brine from the Hudson River, too faint to be really pleasing, and that particular New York smell, at least in summer, of urine.

It was not far to Washington Square, an easy walk, but as it was one o'clock in the morning, I decided to forgo my usual habit of walking up Broadway and walk along West Broadway instead. Broadway, although well lighted, would be deserted. At least West Broadway, despite the odd turn that it takes near Lispenard Street and three rat-stricken blocks, has a few restaurants that I knew would be open to light my way.

As I walked north, cars shooting past now and then like noisy comets, I decided that I would not mind excessively the seeing of a rat (Pauline once saw hundreds of them pour out of a Con Edison hole at the corner of Desbrosses and Hudson and undulate in ripples across the cobbled street and then undulate back again, diving into the hole as if the Pied Piper himself had summoned them back), but I would not be very happy to *hear* a rat. The sound fills me with particular dread. It is a high, beseeching call, like that of newly hatched birds, and it causes my hair to stand on end. I imagine that it causes the hair of most people to stand on end. I would almost rather a rat trot across my feet, as happened to a friend pushing her baby in a carriage in Central Park, a friend who not coinciden-tally left for Los Angeles the next morning, than *hear* a rat.

So I was on the lookout, if I can use that word in regard to lis-tening, jingling my keys, swinging my arm so that the charm bracelet would sing its metallic song, giving any smart rat time to change his mind before leaping out of the vacant lot at the end of the block. Andrea, one of the more opinionated and thus more in-teresting students in class, once asked me why I had corrected the phrase "listened out of the corner of her ear" in one of her stories, and I had struggled for a few minutes, citing the mixed metaphor rule and other stylistic rigors, all the while thinking to myself that of course she was right to object. Fiction is just that. Well, I'd said, teasing her a little, if you can make it a magical ear, a Borges ear, perhaps you will convince me.

I walked along, having myself a time given the possibilities, given the fact that just that week a rubber hand had been left in my front hall. I had not mentioned it to Detective Malloy when I spoke to him on the phone. I could add it to a list of things that I seemed to be keeping from Detective Malloy. Questions that I was surprised I had not asked him. I wondered if he knew that I was the girl in the dark basement room. I wondered if, in some way that I did not understand, he was using that knowledge to presume an intimacy between us, as if we shared a secret that was exciting because it was dangerous to both of us: A woman with red hair had been on her knees with his red cock in her red mouth a few hours before having her throat cut and her arms and legs pulled from their sockets.

I walked north on West Broadway, a little drunk, harking for rats, wondering if he liked the way she sucked his cock, when I heard the sound of footsteps behind me, beneath the distant swish-sound of the trucks. I looked over my shoulder. There was no one there. Which frightened me. Because I could hear him.

I was not far from Canal Street. There was a café on Canal that would be open. I would go inside. I had just enough money to order an espresso, New York waiters being difficult about women smelling of mescal rushing in from the street shouting that they are being followed. I smiled at myself. For a moment, I had even imagined that I could hear breathing.

There was the sudden sound of a car alarm and it made me jump. I looked behind me.

Clothed not in the black suit of an undertaker, not even black-skinned, but in some black and shiny material like plastic or, more terrifying, rubber, an arm wrapped casually, easily around my neck. My head was yanked back, my neck pulled taut, a hand over my gaping mouth.

He wore a black stocking mask, black holes for eyes. There was a strange odor on his gloves, like glue or acetone. Formalde-hyde.

He moved me forward with his legs, my feet dragging on the ground. There was a car parked in the empty lot ahead and I realized that he was not going to kill me. Not kill me there on West Broadway. He was going to take me someplace else. And kill me.

I jammed my feet into the pavement and threw back my head, grabbing at the mask, convinced that if I could see him I would at least know that he existed, that he was not an incubus, a hoodoo sent from the depths or even from Samarra to take me away.

The keys were in my uplifted hand as I caught hold of the bottom of the mask. He pressed his chin deep into my shoulder. I dragged the keys across his neck, hurting him, and in the instant of his startled recoil, he let go of me and I fell away from him, onto the pavement. A taxi rounded the little bend at Walker Street as I rolled into the street. The car stopped with a streak of brake and the stink of slopped gasoline, and veered onto the curb.

I looked behind me.

He was gone.

THE driver, a nervous young Pakistani who thought that I wished to harm him in some way with his employer, his wife, the consul general, allowed me into the back of his car and took me home, promising the whole way that there would be no charge, no charge, the meter was off. Just for me. No charge.

I dialed his beeper number and he called me back five minutes later. I'll be right there, he said when I told him. Are you okay? I'm on my way.

I put on my glasses and ran downstairs and sat on the top stair of the stoop, leaning back against the front door, waiting for him, jumping up and then sitting down again, watching the last drug dealers walk round the corner of the park and back again, working late. This must be the shift they give the new men, I thought, drug dealing being a candidly hierarchical arrangement.

He was there in ten minutes. "I was near here," he said, coming quickly up the stairs.

He took me by the arm and helped me to my feet and we went inside.

"Near here?" I asked.

"That gambling club above the Red Turtle. The one a friend of mine owns," he said. "The ex-cop. I mentioned it to you once before."

I shook my head.

"You don't remember."

We went into the kitchen and I asked him what he wanted and he said, "Bourbon."

I gave him the drink and he sat down in the living room. My hands were trembling.

"That's good," he said, tasting it. Looking at me.

I walked back and forth.

"Tell me what happened," he said quietly.

I told him, grateful not to be scolded, trying to keep it simple the way one learns to do, not telling your doctor or your pharmacist or your police officer everything that has pained you in the last two years, and he listened without interruption, only stopping me to ask, had I seen the man's face? could I identify him? He asked me twice.

When I finished, he put down the drink and said, "It sounds like someone just trying to take your money. Take your purse. That's what it sounds like. What about your friend, what's her name, Pauline? Did she get a look at anyone?"

"She wasn't with me. She lives above the bar on Chapel Street."

"She lives alone?"

I nodded.

"On the second floor?"

"Third."

"Is she careful?"

"Careful?"

"More careful than you? I'm surprised only one guy tried to jump you. Walking on West Broadway."

"I do it all the time."

"Well, don't."

"Where was she killed?"

"Who?"

"That girl with the red hair. The girl who was killed in the Red Turtle."

"Who told you she had red hair?"

"Your friend."

"My friend?"

"The man with the water pistol."

"My partner. You mean my partner."

"He showed me a photograph. In the car that night when you questioned me."

It was suddenly difficult to breathe. I closed the windows and turned on the air conditioner.

"She wasn't killed in the bar," he said slowly. "You're confused."

I could see one of the drug dealers from the window, standing under the Hanging Elm, looking up at me. "What is disarticulation exactly?"

"I told you."

"Tell me again."

"It is when an arm or a leg is pulled out of the joint, not cut, not sawed, but pulled out. Probably with a foot placed on the shoulder or hip. For leverage. It makes a funny sound."

"That girl was killed that way?"

"No."

I waited for him to go on, but he was silent.

"How was she killed?" I asked.

"With a straight razor." He stopped. "It seems to me like maybe he was trying to take the head and something happened. Maybe he wasn't too good at the cutting part yet. He was trying to fit her into something. A bag, maybe. A box."

"The cutting part?"

"Somewhere between the fifth and sixth cervical vertebrae."

"And?"

"And what?"

"Is that all?"

He didn't answer.

"What else?" I turned to look at him. "You said there were two murders."

"Did I?" He ran his hand through his hair. "A disarticulated body, cut the same way, was found six months ago. Well, parts of a body. We don't know yet if it's connected to the DOA last week. They don't think so. Richie don't think so. But I think so." He stood up. "Why don't you come over here and sit down."

I shook my head.

"What was her name?"

"Whose name?"

"The girl in the Red Turtle. The DOA, as you call her. The girl with the red hair."

He was silent. Waiting. Then he said, "Angela Sands."

"And it was the same killer."

"We don't know yet." He spoke slowly, deliberately. "I personally think it's the same killer. But I can't prove it. Not yet. I can't even explain why I think it. Richie thinks I'm crazy. A dismembered female body was found last January along the river. She was wrapped in sections of the Sunday *Daily News*." He paused. "This happens all the time," he said. "You know what I'm saying?"

"What happens?"

"Murder."

I was silent.

"That's the thing about it. It never stops. Never."

"Why do you think it's the same killer?"

"Because something was taken from the bodies. Something was missing." He spoke reluctantly. "A souvenir. What's called a souvenir. The slashing is the same. He cuts a certain way."

Yes, I thought, I know that. The difference between male and female perversion. The action of the man is directed toward a symbol, not himself. The woman acts against herself.

"Souvenir? You mean, like a memento?"

"The killer gets to do it over again whenever he wants. You know. Fantasize. In private. Like jerking off."

"Like jerking off?"

"Jerking off."

I nodded. I was suddenly afraid that if I seemed too upset or afraid, too crazy, he would stop. "What did he take from her?"

"You really want to know this shit?" he asked, frowning.

"Someone," I said, "left a rubber hand under my mailbox."

"When was this?"

"Last week. Tuesday. Monday."

"Why didn't you tell me?"

"Does he take hands?"

He stood, the chair still startling him a little, even though he'd sat in it a few times by then. "Tell me again," he said. "What happened to you tonight. Go over it once again. Come here. Show me."

He came up behind me and pulled me back against him, my head against his shoulder. I took his right arm, bending it at the elbow, and laid it across my neck. I could feel his breath against the side of my face.

Like this, I said. Like this.

He let his arm fall from my neck, down across my chest, until his hand was on my breast, his fingers finding the nipple. He pulled me back against him. He had an erection. I could feel it.

"All right," I said. "All right."

He followed me into the bedroom, taking off his clothes, having trouble for a moment unbuckling the ankle holster, laying the revolver on the mantelpiece.

I looked at him. He had a long scar down the right side of his stomach. He was high-waisted. Strong. Black hair on his shoulders. More than I like. He had no shamrock tattoo. In fact, he didn't have much of anything on his ass.

He lay on his back on the bed, hands folded behind his head, and watched me as if it were his habit. His due.

I took off my glasses. I took off my blue and white striped dress, watching myself through his calm, shrewd eyes, standing alongside the bed, still wearing underpants.

"Take those off," he said.

I shook my head.

He sat up quickly and pulled down my underpants, and with one hand at the small of my back pushed me face down on the bed while he put his other hand between my thighs, spreading me apart, opening my legs for his mouth.

He put his tongue inside of me, in my vagina, in my ass, and then he lifted my hips and turned me so that I was on my back, my legs over the side of the bed, bent at the knee, and he kneeled on the floor, his fingers inside of me, too, hooked deep inside, the way a man carries something hooked on a finger over his shoulder, and he sucked my clitoris into his mouth.

There was nothing intervening. Not a nightgown. Not even a penis.

"Come all over me," he said.

LATER when I couldn't sleep because I kept going over and over what had happened in the street, over and over in that way of time attenuated, slowed down and exaggerated, he said, "There's nothing to be afraid of."

"I was wondering about you," I said.

"Don't," he said.

"Don't you want to know?" I asked. "What I was wondering?"

He sighed in that way men do when they want to sleep, not angry, only exasperated, tolerant, even affectionate. As if it gave him a little pleasure to indulge me. "What?"

"What you did to me," I said.

"What I did to you?"

"I want to know how you did it to me," I said. "Just in case I don't see you again. So I can do it to myself."

"You'll see me again."

"Someone taught you. An older woman."

"Get the fuck out of here," he said, laughing. For the first time, he sounded shy.

"Tell me," I said. "It will make my head stop for a minute."

He was silent. I waited, not knowing if he was asleep, men having the ability to fall asleep even when the conversation is about themselves. And then he said, "The first time I ate a broad, it was the Chicken Lady."

"I thought so."

"Get the fuck out of here. You know the Chicken Lady?"

I lay very still, arms at my sides, afraid that he would stop if I moved.

"I was fifteen. I worked at Bill's Butcher Shop on St. Nicholas Avenue delivering chickens. Her husband was a teacher at the Hebrew school on Saturday afternoons. It was summertime. She invited me in. She gave me a drink of water. We talked a little. I was up against the sink, drinking the water, and she came over and stood in front of me and took hold of my dick. I just stood there. I was scared. Nervous. She said, does this feel good? She asked me if I'd ever been with a woman, never taking her hand off my dick. She took me into the bedroom and started to undress me, kissing my chest. I kept asking if she was sure her husband wasn't coming home. She went right down and started to blow me. She got up and took her clothes off and I thought how big she was. She had a great ass. She was womanly."

"Did you like it?" I asked. I realized that I was whispering.

"Like it?"

"That she was womanly."

"I came to like it, but I didn't like it in the beginning. She was a mother. I mean, she was probably only twenty-seven, twenty-six, but I didn't know anything. I laid on top of her and I screwed her. I'm sure I came quick. I gave her a good hump, but I knew even though she didn't say nothing that it wasn't like banging a girl. When you bang a girl, they're not too experienced either, they keep their clothes on, they're embarrassed. But with her I knew she wanted more. There were things I knew I didn't do right. Things left undone. When it was over I felt empty. It was the first time it wasn't about me. It was the first time I realized there could be something better. She never said a thing. She never got up. I got dressed and she laid there nude. She knew her body was beautiful. Wide hips, nice small breasts. They stood out by themselves. White soft skin. She was good. Dark hair, black hair. Tight wiry pubic hair from thigh to thigh. I had never seen so much hair. Like Spanish girls, thick and coarse. She made me come over to her and she kissed me. She said, did I want her to show me what women like. I said yes. It was hard to get my hand inside of her. She had a meaty, fat pussy. You had to go all the way down to the bottom of her snatch to get your finger in. It was so strange once you got your finger in, it was like sticking your finger in the ocean. If she was sitting on me, I used to think she pissed on me. Hot liquid on my balls. I swear she used to piss on me. She told me to hold women when they come, to hold them in your arms. She taught me how to unhook a bra with one hand. She said it would come in handy someday. She asked me if I'd ever kissed a woman down there, and I said no. I may have lied to her. I might have done Margaret White at Rockaway. I don't remember. I asked her if women liked to have their asses licked and she said yes. She asked me if men liked to have their asses licked and I said no, and she licked me, and yes, I liked it. She never put her clothes on. I thought that was the coolest thing. She put a robe on to take me to the door and she gave me two dollars which I thought was fucking unbelievable. A six-pack cost maybe a dollar-three, and she said you can buy some beer and you can keep a dollar for yourself. The second time, I told her I basted the chickens extra long. Something stupid like that. She got the best fucking chickens in New York. What a dickhead I was. I'd clip the chicken snatches closed with little metal clips and baste them all morning. The second time I saw her I was more nervous. I thought about her all week long. I walked past her house. I looked for her on the street. She grabbed me and kissed me and told me she missed me. She told me I was a natural kisser. She laid on the bed without clothes on and we kissed for a long time.

We only had forty-five minutes. She'd walk around, ask me if I wanted a soda, stand in front of me, her hands on her hips. I never saw her disheveled, or angry. The one thing she didn't teach me because I was always in a rush was to stick around. I was always getting laid on the run. Later, too, when I was a cop. Always on the fucking run. I told my friend Bozo about her and he didn't believe me so I took him to Fort Washington Avenue and we waited for her to come out, and she come out with a baby carriage. Oh, God. She said hi to me, very friendly, and I introduced her to Bozo. He still didn't believe I was fucking her. It went on for a year and a half, every Saturday. Years later, actually a couple years ago, I asked the other guys who were delivery kids at Bill's—the guy before me and the guy who came after me—I asked them both if she'd ever come on to them. And they said, no, as a matter of fact, she was a shit tipper. It made me feel good. I came one Saturday and she told me they were moving. She was upset, but I wasn't smart enough to know it then. She gave me thirty dollars and told me I would be a good man. Now go, she said. She kept saying, go. I'd always get halfway down the hallway and she'd call me back, saying Jimmy, Jimmy, come back, and she'd kiss me. The day I saw her the last time, she didn't call me back."

We were silent, both of us thinking.

"You know, she'd be sixty years old now. Jesus. Fuck me. Her son is thirty-two years old now. Fuck me. How cool is this. He's thirty-two."

"What was her name?"

"Annette, I think. I'm not sure. Annette."

"I'm in her debt."

He laughed. "Yeah. Well. We'll see."

He sat up, his stomach tucked in a fold, accommodating itself to his scar. "She reminds me of you a little," he said. "I mean, you remind me of her. Small back. Nice hips. Only her tits were small. She had great tits. Once when she was pregnant, I fucked her from behind on the bed on her hands and knees and I saw it in the mirror. It was weird, stomach hanging down, tits hanging down. I asked her if I'd made her pregnant and she just laughed."

"It must have been like sleeping with a goddess," I said.

"Yeah, she was gorgeous."

"I mean in another sense, too. In a mythic sense. In a ritual sense. It must have made you feel powerful. And powerless."

"Get the fuck out of here," he said. "Powerless?"

"Yes."

"*No.* Why would I feel powerless? How do you get me into these fucking conversations? You think too fucking much. It wasn't no myth."

I reached across his hip to touch his scar. He leaned away from me, pushing aside my hand. "I don't like it," he said. "If you touch it."

"I'm sorry," I said.

"You didn't do nothing," he said in surprise.

"I can be sorry even if it's not my fault."

He looked at me as if this were a new idea for him. He rubbed a red mark on his throat. "Look what you did," he said.

"I did not," I said, surprised.

"You don't remember? It was that good?"

I reached up and touched the red scratch across his throat. He pulled away and turned on the light to look at his watch, a gold Rolex, then turned it off again. It was three o'clock.

"I got to go," he said. "Mr. Sweeney the plumber's coming at nine. She works. I got to be up."

He was anxious to go, reluctant to go. Ready to go. "Who gave you that little ring?" I asked.

He looked at it. "My wife," he said.

"Your ex-wife."

"Yeah, my ex-wife."

"Does it matter?"

"What?"

"What time you come home?"

He wound the watch. "Mr. Sweeney might mind," he said, "but she don't care. She'll be asleep."

"Good," I said.

He looked at me, suddenly wary.

I put my hand in his lap and lifted his cock from his thigh.

He took my hand away and laid it across my stomach, patting my hand. "I'll never get out of here if you start," he said.

I didn't like that he had patted my hand. I sat up, my legs under me, and leaned back on my heels in that way that makes me think of the collection of pornography I once discovered in my father's library, in particular a print of a geisha with the heel of her bare foot in her vagina. Something I have never mastered. Something I've never even tried to master. I leaned over and drew him into my mouth.

He resisted for a moment, laughing, nudging aside my head with his hip, and then with a heavy sigh, as if I were leading him to his doom, he leaned back on the bed, elbows bent, and watched me.

He was soft, tasting like salt. He got hard very fast, and I realized that I was moving my head in the same slow dipping way that the girl with the red hair had moved her head, wondering if he had taught her, knowing that he would have liked it a certain way, just the lips, not too hard, slower, a finger in his ass, no hands, no time, all the time in the world.

He reached behind and pulled a pillow under his head, settling in. He put one hand between my knees, between my legs, between my ankles, and pulled hard on me, the labia in his closed fist, swollen, loose, open.

He sat up and put an arm around my waist, turning me over and pulling me toward him so that I was on my knees, my ass high against him, his hand at the small of my back, holding me to the bed. My face pressed into the bed. My arms stretched above my head. He pulled my arms to him and took my two hands and placed them on my ass, and then with his hands on top of mine, he pulled me open, apart, exposed to him with my own hands, arched, spanned, and with a low moan he entered me with such ease, such presumption, that I began to come the moment he was inside of me. He said, "That's right, that's right." He ran his hand down my back, reaching beneath me to lift my swaying breasts, running his thumb between my buttocks, stopping for a moment at my opening, wetting it from my vagina, teasing, threatening. Then he let himself slide out of me and I turned on my side, hands between my legs in some girlish prolongment of pleasure, and he put himself roughly in my mouth, and I forgot about the girl with the red hair, the dead red girl. Opening my mouth, his balls in my hand, tracing with my finger the soft fluted ridge between anus and penis, back and forth, wetting it with my tongue, and then in that gesture I had seen him use once before, he put both hands on my head, slowing me down a little, keeping me steady, letting me know, and with a small shudder, a tender arch of back, he came in my mouth.

His orgasm was short, doubled and tripled with a quick convulsion, so private, so disciplined that he made no cry, no whisper, no exhortation. In case the Chicken Lady's husband walked in unexpectedly, his yarmulke held in place with two black bobby pins.

Bob Zordani

A FISH
STORY

MY WIFE insists on watching me fillet
the fish I catch. She brings her lawn chair
out back while I hose off the concrete slab
I use to clean them on. She watches me intently,
making sure to say how good I am with knives,
how easy I separate the flesh from bone
and slice the skin away. She likes for me
to open up their stomachs and pull
the contents out—half-digested crayfish,
minnows, bugs, bait, and even plastic worms.
If the stomach is empty, she tells me
to turn it inside out so she can see
the ridges which, to her, look like a brain.
When I finish one, I hand her the fillets.
She sprays them off, lightly, so they won't tear,
and leaning down so I can see her cleavage,
places them in the bucket. Then she fills it,

swirls the water with her free hand, and talks
to the fillets, telling them how nice they are,
telling them to swim. She is serious,
all the while looking straight at them and chanting
her words. She gets sexier as she goes.
By the time I finish, her cheeks flush
and burn, but I just go about my business
like nothing's happening. I watch her pull
fillet after fillet from the bucket
and shake each one until it's dry enough
to carry in the house. I bury all
the bones and guts and skin and take my time
cleaning off the slab and putting up my gear,
placing my rods along the cellar wall
and straightening my tackle boxes.
I smoke a couple cigarettes and close
the cellar door behind me when I leave.
The house is silent when I enter.
The first uncooked fillet rests on a plate
smack in the middle of our foyer,
and next to it, her shoes. I take the plate
and follow her nylons up the stairs
to the second plate. Two fillets, her blouse.
I pile the fish on my plate. Down the hall,
three fillets, her skirt. I pile the fish.
The final plate's outside our bedroom door.
Four fillets and her favorite lace panties.
By now I'm sure she knows I'm standing there.
She starts to coo and rustle on our bed
while I kneel down and heap the last fillets
on my full plate. I touch her panties, feel
the moisture soothe my fingertips, and rub
my nails back and forth against the door
as gently as I can. She gets louder

and wilder. I crack the door enough
to watch her work. Her hands are skimming
across her breasts, rippling her skin like wind
over water. I feel faint and almost drop
from excitement. Holding my plate,
I swing the door wide open with my foot.
I stare, I gawk, I ogle over her
until she calls me in. I go to her
and set the heaping plate between her legs.
My clothes are sticking to my skin. I itch.
She strips the top fillet from the pile,
draws it down one leg, up the other,
then up her stomach, around her breasts,
her shoulders, and her neck, brings the meat
to her mouth, kisses it, and licks it clean.
It glistens in her hand. She puts it back,
and I lift the plate and put it on the floor.
I fake a cast, pretend to bump
an orange Salty Craw across the bed.
She doesn't hit. I fake a cast and touch her
with my hand. She quivers once and strikes so hard
I think my arm will snap. I pull back hard
and try to horse her home, but she won't come
that easily. I have to work my way
around the bed while she, with her hands
around my wrist, rolls back and forth.
When she's tuckered out, I pull that slick
and gorgeous trophy in and look at her.
She sighs a little, so I ask her what
I ought to do with her. Now I've caught her,
now she's mine. I grab her by the arms,
holding them tight enough to settle her.
I make her answer me. She says,
I'll do you favors if you let me go.

Like what, I say, and watch the color
rising on her chest. She says she'll fan
my spawning bed with her tail and keep
the bluegill and the crayfish out.
I tell her that's not good enough.
She breathes in deeply, and then it comes:
she offers to fulfill my wildest dreams.
I start to tell her that I love her,
but she's all over me in nothing flat.
Her mouth's on mine, and I can taste
the fish she licked a little while ago.
She pulls my T-shirt up above my head
and yanks it off, and soon enough
I'm naked to the bone. She says I've got
the kind of worm she needs and takes me
in her mouth. I fall back on the bed
and tell her what a fish she is.
She keeps on going, bobbing her head,
twisting it until I'm ready to scream.
And then she stops. *I want to spawn*, she says,
climbing up beside me. I let her roll
on top of me and tell me that she's lonely,
that sexy fish like her are really sad
and spend their days swimming by themselves
in all the darkest coves which they can find.
I kiss her neck and squeeze her to me.
She kisses back. I tell her now, for real,
that I'll swim with her through anything
the years throw at us, through weather bad
and good, through indifferent days and months
when the whole sky is gray and overcast
with doubt. I tell her that I love her,
that I wouldn't let her swim alone
through this lake's dark and tangled coves.

We taste each other's grit and decide
to go do it in the tub. We bring the plate
and set it on the sink top just for luck,
then turn the shower on and step in the tub.
I grab a bar of soap and lather her down
until she's slicker than a channel cat.
She does the same for me, and we rub up
against each other in the rising steam
and let our lather mix like fish spunk
as it swirls down our legs and drains away.
Moaning like catfish, our bodies quaking,
she lets me work my way into her.
We go until we're spent and tangled
together against the bathroom wall.
The closest hand will shut the water off,
and we will come apart eventually.
But it's good to stand here, flesh to flesh,
where we'll come clean in the easy water
and make a plan for how to cook the fish.
Maybe we'll bake or fry or broil it,
serve it with a garden salad, potatoes,
fresh beans, a bottle of chardonnay.
I admit I like it spicy best of all
because that's how I like to think of her:
the way she tastes and feels, the way she moves
when I come home and show her what I've caught.

Steven Saylor, writing as Aaron Travis

THE HIT

THE HOTEL WAITER is surprisingly young. And blond. And very, very nervous, all dressed up in his blue monkey suit and black bow tie. Earlier, watching him wheel the breakfast cart into the suite, Vince wondered what the kid would look like naked.

The waiter is pouring his coffee now, holding the china saucer and cup in one hand and the small porcelain pitcher in the other—jangling the cup against the saucer, splattering a few drops onto the deep green spread that covers the serving cart. The kid's lips move soundlessly, forming a curse and then suppressing it. He glances quickly at Vince, then at the hair-matted cleft of muscle exposed between the flaps of Vince's robe, then quickly away. The more nervous he gets, the cuter he looks.

Vince takes a drag off his cigarette and exhales the smoke through his nostrils with an audible rush, letting the kid know he's impatient for the coffee. He spreads his legs beneath the cart and leans back in his chair, letting the robe open another inch or two across his chest. The heavy silk drags sensuously over his thighs, and Vince feels the stirrings of an erection. He bought the robe the week before, during a job in Kansas City, at a fancy high-priced men's shop. In his line of work, at the age of thirty-one, Vincent Zorio can afford to treat himself to the very best.

"You always take this long, kid?" Vince mutters the words softly, but the boy jerks and almost loses the cup.

"No, sir." The kid looks him in the eye for an instant and swallows nervously. He holds out the cup. It jangles in his hand. "Your coffee, sir?"

"Yeah, my coffee. If you're finished spilling it all over the tablecloth."

"I'm sorry, sir. If—"

"Just set it down on the cart."

"Will there be anything else, sir? I mean, if you'll just sign the check . . ."

"Sure." A silver pen lies beside the green-bordered slip of paper, both stamped with the hotel's crest. Vince studies the check for a long moment, feeling the kid's nervousness, feeling his cock growing longer, unfurling warm and thick against the inside of his thigh.

"Is something wrong, sir?"

Vince signs the check and sits back in the chair, holding the pen between his thumb and forefinger, studying it.

"How old are you, kid?"

"Sir?"

"I said, how old are you?"

"Nineteen. Almost twenty."

"Kinda young to be working this job, in a hotel like this. I'd figure you for a bellboy maybe. Or a maid's helper."

Vince glances up. The kid is actually blushing. He'll be biting his lip next. Looking blonder and cuter than ever.

"I've been at this job almost two years, sir, ever since I got out of school. I've never really had any complaints—"

"Shit, they hired you right out of high school? You must have connections."

The kid looks down and shrugs. The uniform jacket stretches tight across his chest. His body is lean and broad shouldered, slim hipped, with intimations of smooth muscle inside his tight blue uniform. "Well, yeah, I guess. My uncle Max is head chef—"

"Yeah, figures. What's your name?"

"Kip."

Vince nods. He always likes to know a kid's name before he dicks him. And, in the last two minutes Vince has made up his mind that the least he'll be getting from cute little Kip is a long and very thorough blowjob.

Vince puts the pen down beside the check. "I guess you expect a tip." He pushes his chair back and stands, walks to the dresser and returns with his wallet. His cock pushes up against the heavy silk, tenting the robe and swaying as he walks. He catches the boy staring, then looking away. Blushing darker than before.

Vince sits. "You have breakfast this morning, Kip?" The kid looks puzzled. "Uncle Max feed you down in the kitchen? Maybe a big juicy sausage, with a couple of eggs?" Kip flinches; Vince has aimed at a nerve and struck it, dead center. He pulls out a fifty and lays it on the cart beside the check. "Still hungry?"

The boy stares at the fifty, uncertain. As green as they come. Vince likes that. He picks up his fork, spears one of the fat link sausages on the gold-rimmed china plate, watches the grease erupt. He says the words again: "You still hungry, Kip? Maybe Uncle Max didn't feed you enough sausage this morning."

The kid looks him straight in the eye. Blushing. Breathing unevenly. Swallowing.

"Push this cart out of the way."

The boy moves to obey automatically. Vince loosens the sash

around his waist and pushes aside the flaps of his robe. The boy turns back and sucks in his breath.

Vincent Zorio is a big man. Massive shoulders and chest, huge biceps and thighs, hard muscle without a trace of fat. A big booming voice, intimidating even when he speaks softly. Extra-large feet and hands—a strangler's hands, or a butcher's, meaty and thick. And a cock to match. It snakes beyond the edge of the chair, heavy and thick, balanced atop the plump cushion of his testicles.

Vince sits back in the chair, sliding his hips forward, spreading his thighs apart. He narrows his eyes. His dick grows into a fat, swollen truncheon of meat, curving outward and up, pointing straight at the boy's face. Kip's eyes are lowered, his lips parted. No longer looking Vince in the face, but staring at the cock. Waiting to be told.

"Go ahead, Kip. Put your mouth on it."

Kip fumbles toward him. Drops to his knees. Stares at the cock for a long moment. Then he looks up at Vince's chest, and his eyes glaze.

Vince smiles. Christ, you got a great body, mister . . . that's what the last kid told him, the cute little brunette with the bubble butt back in Kansas City. But that one Vince picked up on the street—a common little gutter whore, shameless with his mouth. Little Kip is a different story. With Kip, Vince will do all the talking.

Kip's eyes return to the cock. He stares. His chest rises and falls inside the tight blue jacket. He lets out a little moan, then closes his eyes and opens wide, moving forward blindly to take it in his mouth.

Vince butts the palm of his hand against the kid's forehead. "Not so fast, cocksucker." He squeezes his cock at the base and aims it at Kip's mouth, hunching forward until he can feel the boy's warm breath on his dick. Kip stares at it, cross-eyed. "First you kiss it. You look me straight in the eye like a good little cocksucker, and you give my dick a nice, sloppy kiss."

Kip looks up. Eyes hungry, pleading. He seems to hesitate, then presses his lips against the fat bulb of flesh.

The contact electrifies him. Kip shudders and his face burns bright red. The muscles in his neck twist and contract. His Adam's apple twitches; the bow tie does a dance. Vince settles even deeper into the chair. It is all decided now.

"Yeah, kid," Vince croons. "Now wrap your lips around the head and give my dick a deep, wet French kiss."

Vince stares at the connection: the long, thick shaft leading like a tube into the boy's mouth, the wide-open lips stretched taut around the crown, the boy's hollowed cheeks and glittering eyes staring wildly back at him. His scrutiny is so blatant that Kip finally shuts his eyes tight, embarrassed; but his tongue never stops squirming against the swollen knob of flesh.

Vince studies the boy attached to the end of his dick. Kip is on all fours, his butt sticking up behind him, pressing firm and round against the seat of his pants. Both hands grip the thick cream-colored carpet—no move to touch himself. Everything centers on his mouth and the knob inside it, and the nine-tenths of Vince's cock still waiting to be sucked. A natural submissive. Vince knows the type, inside and out. Cock-hungry boy. Born to be dicked. Vince sized him up the moment he walked in the door, and Vince is never wrong.

"Good boy." He pats Kip's hollowed cheek, at first gently, then harder, almost slapping him. "Good little cocksucker." Vince grabs a fistful of silky blond hair. "Now we feed you the whole thing." Kip's face flashes alarm, and he grunts in protest—and then the grunt turns to a gurgle as his throat is filled with Vince's cock.

Kip heaves and chokes, spewing a mass of saliva into the pubic hair against his lips. He struggles to pull his head off the cock, but

Vince holds him tight—then jerks the boy's head back, wrenching the cock from his mouth. It snaps against Vince's belly, then ricochets meaty and wet against the boy's stunned face.

Vince's eyes are heavy-lidded with lust. He purses his lips. "Mmm. That felt good, cocksucker. Let's do it again."

Before Kip can react, Vince yanks him back onto the cock, spearing it all the way down his throat. Gagging him with it. Listening to him sputter, feeling him heave. Screwing Kip's face into the wiry pubic thatch and savoring the deep-throat convulsions. After a long moment, Vince jerks the boy's head back and empties his mouth again.

Kip's face is drawn into a long silent howl, like a deep-sea diver breaking surface and gasping for air. Vince grips his cock at the base and spanks his face with it, keeping him off base and dizzy. Kip squeals and tries to say something—but then the cock is lodged deep in his throat again.

This is the way Vince likes it—dominating a kid with his dick. Force-feeding him. Bludgeoning his throat. Punishing him with it and watching him open wide for more. Vince rides the boy's face, holding him by both ears, grinding his head into his lap and screwing it like a cored melon. Yanking his meat out of the kid's mouth and spanking him with it. Rubbing it huge, wet, and slick all over his face, until Kip is drunk with cock.

Vince croons. Beneath him Kip whimpers, gasps, makes strange mewling sounds of desire. The kid is into it now, wanting it bad. Wanting to join in. He balances himself awkwardly on one hand and gropes at the hardness cramped inside his pants. Vince kicks his hand away, and the boy submits, reaching instead with both hands to steady himself against the hard wooden legs of the chair while Vince begins a fresh volley of thrusts down his throat.

Suddenly Vince kicks him away, sending him sprawling against the floor. Kip looks up at him, confused and hurt. Then hungry again, staring up at the huge cock as Vince stands and steps toward him. Then abruptly alarmed, shrinking against the door as the big man looms over him. Vince towers like a giant above him—the broad muscles of his thighs foreshortened, the big cock thrusting upward from his groin, slick and bloated from fucking Kip's throat. His big balls are pulled up tight against the base of the shaft, silky smooth and as swollen as his cock.

Vince smirks. He pinches the base of his cock between his forefinger and thumb and spanks the air with it, watching the boy's eyes as they follow the beat. The kid is his now. He could pull him up off the floor, strip him, run his hands over that smooth, naked boyflesh—see what little Kip looks like bent over the bed naked with a big cock up his ass . . .

Vince glances at the clock on the dresser—a quarter to nine. Already running late. The best will have to wait.

"Up," he growls, beckoning with his cock. "On your knees, kiddo." Kip scrambles to rise. Too slow. Vince grabs him by the hair and pulls his face to crotch level. Kip's eyes are closed, his mouth already open. A natural.

"Cocksucker," Vince whispers, hitting hard on the consonants. He pushes into the waiting hole—between the glistening lips, beyond the clenching sphincter. Deep in Kip's throat, his cock starts to twitch like a snake on hot asphalt.

Kip chokes, caught by surprise. Then his throat begins an automatic undulating caress around the cock, milking it as it empties itself into his belly. Vince throws his head back and growls, twisting Kip's face into his groin, burying his cock another few inches in the boy's neck. His hips shudder and convulse, and Kip's throat spasms in response.

After a long moment, the orgasm peaks, then slowly subsides. Vince keeps his cock lodged deep in the boy's throat, savoring the afterglow and the warm, clenching heat. Finally he pulls himself free.

Below him, Kip squats on folded knees, both hands pressed between his thighs, desperately kneading the bulge in his tight blue trousers. Vince smirks and reaches down, scooping the boy up by his armpits. He brushes Kip's hands away from his crotch. The boy moans in frustration. He clutches Kip's wrists, pins his arms to his sides, and runs his tongue over the boy's face—across cheeks slick with saliva, over lips wet and shiny with semen. He covers the boy's mouth and kisses him—harsh, demanding, sucking Kip's breath away and then forcing it back into his lungs.

Vince breaks the kiss. He pushes Kip against the door and pats him roughly on the cheek, then turns and walks to the chair, stretching his arms above his head, belting his robe before he sits and draws the cart back in front of him.

Kip stands at the door, dazed, breathing hard, reaching up to wipe his mouth with the back of his hand.

Vince looks at him sharply. "Clear out, kid. Uncle Max'll be missing you down in the kitchen."

Kip hesitates, then turns and reaches for the doorknob.

"Hey, kid." Kip turns back, glancing guiltily at Vince for an instant before returning his gaze to the floor.

"Better take the check. And your tip."

Kip bites his lower lip and walks slowly to the cart. He reaches for the tray with trembling fingers, staring at the fifty on top. Vince catches him by the wrist, reaches for his wallet and adds a twenty.

Kip accepts the money in silence. He walks shakily to the door.

"Hey—cocksucker."

Kip freezes. He looks over his shoulder. Vince is sitting back in his chair, smoking a cigarette and smirking at him. "You take it up the ass, pussyboy?" Kip blushes. "Yeah, sure you do. What time you get off work?"

"I—" Kip clears his throat. His neck feels swollen and bruised inside. "Seven."

Vince nods. "Be here at eight sharp. That'll give you time to grab some dinner. Eat light. And don't bother to change—I like the little bow tie. Not that you'll be wearing your monkey suit for long." Vince takes a drag off his cigarette. "I wanna see what you look like naked."

Kip clears his throat again. "I—don't know . . ."

"And keep your hands off your dick. Understand? You just keep that little boner tucked up and twitching inside your pants all day, and think about what I got waiting for you here between my legs."

Kip stares at the doorknob. He grips it tight to keep his hand from shaking. "I don't know," he whispers hoarsely. "I have to go now." Without looking back, he opens the door and slips away.

The coffee is cold, the food lukewarm. Vince doesn't mind. He wolfs down his breakfast in two minutes flat. A blowjob in the morning always makes him hungry.

After breakfast he dresses quickly, choosing his black suit and suede overcoat; the day is hardly chilly enough for it, but the bulk will help conceal the gun strapped across his shoulder. He checks himself in the mirror mounted above the dresser, and glances at the clock. Nine sharp. An instant later, he hears Battaglia's telltale knock at the locked door that joins the separate bedrooms of the suite.

It will all be over by five o'clock. Until then, he and Battaglia will be walking on glass every instant. The job is going to be a bitch. But once it's over, Vince will be twenty grand richer.

Besides, he has an evening with Kip to look forward to. There's always a chance that he's spooked the kid, but Vince remembers the look in Kip's eyes when the boy screwed up his face to kiss the fat knob of his cock. The way he opened his throat for it, like a holster to a gun. Action speaks louder than words, and a big dick speaks loudest of all to a cock-hungry kid like Kip. There isn't a doubt in his mind that the boy will come knocking at his door exactly on time, blushing and biting his lip, looking blonder and cuter than ever.

Vince will have some surprises for him.

Ten till eight: Kip steps into the service elevator off the kitchen and presses the button for the fifteenth floor.

All day long, he has thought of Vince Zorio's cock, and nothing else. The way it filled his mouth. The way it stung his face when the man dredged it shiny and wet from his throat and beat him with it. The taste, overpowering and musky, when Vince packed it all the way home and started shooting.

Big. Big enough to choke him. Bigger than Uncle Max—and Max never uses his cock on Kip the way Vince did. Max never pushes him around, never calls him a cocksucker. Max is always happy to suck Kip off in return. Vince wouldn't even let him touch himself.

Kip has been with relatively few men, despite his looks and his eagerness. A couple of jocks used to let him suck them off in the locker room, but it never amounted to much. Kip is naturally timid about sex and embarrassed by the things he thinks about, naked and alone at night, beating his meat and imagining another man above him—always above, never beneath or beside. Shameful things—like the things Vince Zorio did to him.

Max was the first to fuck him. It was never said outright, but that was one of the conditions of the job: that Kip would do certain favors in return for Uncle Max's help. Kip seldom admits it to himself, but this is what turns him on most about sex with Max— the dirtiness of it, the way it makes him feel soiled and small.

Sometimes he wishes that Max would push harder. Usually it's nothing more than a hurried exchange of blowjobs, or a quick fuck in one of the vacant rooms. But when he lies naked with his fantasies, with his cock in his fist, Kip likes to imagine Max turning mean and ugly . . . calling him names, ordering him around . . . touching him in front of the other employees, letting them all know that he whores for his uncle. But Max will never be the man for that, and Kip is too shy to ever share his fantasies aloud.

Sometimes he has sex with guests at the hotel. They are always older. They always pay. As often as not, they simply want to suck him off. Kip gives them what they want, even though he wants it the other way around. He prefers the ones who want him to do the sucking. Best of all are the men who pay to fuck him. Kip never refuses, even if the man is old or ugly or fat. There is something intoxicating about pulling down his pants and bending over to let a stranger use him. They always rave about his beautiful ass . . .

But in two years of working at the hotel, two years of whoring for Max and the men passing through, Kip has never met a man like Vince Zorio. He first saw him the previous afternoon, checking into the hotel with another man, older and bigger and equally well dressed. Later, Kip sneaked a look at the register: Vincent Zorio, Leo Battaglia, Suite 1505, home addresses in New York. When the breakfast orders arrived that morning, he spotted Zorio's room number and took rounds for the fifteenth floor. It caused an argument with Walter, the headwaiter—the top floor always tipped the best. Max stepped in to settle it, and Walter was out of luck.

As soon as he entered the suite, Kip had gone weak in the knees. The sight of the man wearing nothing but his robe unnerved him; Vince Zorio was darkly handsome, with wavy black hair and strong, blunt features, and an impressive physique that had been obvious even in a business suit. And even before the man showed him his cock and told him to suck it, somehow Kip knew it would be a big one.

But there was something beyond the man's sheer physical appeal that made Kip turn to jelly inside. The sex was like a dream, unreal and out of control, pulling Kip helplessly along; but the fascination went beyond even that. There was something dark inside Vincent Zorio, powerful and frightening. Kip had glimpsed it. He had responded to it; submitted to it; craved it—but exactly what it was escaped him, and he was not sure he wanted to know.

Somehow Kip managed to get through the day. Late in the afternoon there was an echo of excitement from the hotel lobby—a headline two inches tall on the front page of the evening paper, something about two executives shot to death in an office building only a few blocks away. But to Kip, everything was tedium. He worked in a haze, replaying the incident in Zorio's room over and over in his head. His cock stayed so hard inside his pants that it hurt, his balls felt swollen and full; but he did as the man had told him to do, and kept his hands away from the day-long ache between his legs . . .

Now, ascending in the elevator, Kip begins to feel loose and weak between his legs. Vince Zorio intends to fuck him. The man as much as told him so. Vince is going to fuck him, in his room, only minutes from now. Not a quickie, with Kip's pants pushed down around his ankles. I wanna see what you look like naked— that's what the man said. Vince is going to make Kip strip. Vince is going to fuck him naked.

The man will be rough—Kip knows that. Fucking his ass the way he fucked his face. It will hurt. It always hurts some, at first, even with smaller men. Kip wonders if Vince will let him touch himself while he's being fucked. It wouldn't hurt as bad that way; but it doesn't really matter. Kip liked it, somehow, the way the man denied him this morning, as if his own big cock was the only thing that mattered, as if Kip's cock wasn't worth the effort and didn't deserve to be touched.

Perhaps Vince will let Kip suck it before he fucks him with it. Or maybe the man will make him wait until afterwards, making him lick the big cock clean after it's been up his ass, calling him cocksucker and pussyboy and slapping his face. Maybe he will make Kip beg for it. Kip will beg. He will crawl on his hands and knees naked and beg for the privilege of sucking Vince Zorio's dick . . .

FIVE minutes to eight: Kip knocks at the door to suite 1505. His hands are sweaty. His mouth is dry. He listens to his heartbeat pounding in his throat while he waits for Vince to answer the door.

The doorknob turns; the door swings open. The first thing Kip notices is the heavy shadow of stubble across Vince's jaw, then the smell of alcohol on his breath.

Vince gives him a cool smile and nods. "Come on in, kid."

Vince walks to the dresser. He still wears the black suit, but the collar of his shirt is undone, the thin black tie loosened around his neck. The room is lit softly. On the dresser stands an empty glass, and beside it a half-empty bottle of expensive bourbon.

Vince lights a cigarette. He reaches for the bourbon and pours himself a drink. He stares at Kip in the tall, wide mirror above the dresser. The cigarette hangs from the corner of his mouth.

"What are you waiting for, kid? I'm not paying to watch you model your monkey suit. Take it off."

Kip hesitates. With the other men there is usually a drink first, mention of money, some talk to feel him out. But Vince isn't like the others. That is what had brought him here, after all.

He reaches up to undo his tie.

"The bow tie stays," Vince says sharply. "Take off everything else."

Kip's fingers shake as he unbuttons his jacket and shrugs it off his shoulders. He takes off the stiffly starched white shirt, then peels off his T-shirt, wet with perspiration in the armpits. The re-frigerated air is cool against his skin; his nipples turn to goose-flesh, but his face is burning hot.

The patent-leather shoes. The black nylon socks. Then his blue trousers, always hard to get out of. Max ordered them a size too small. Max likes them tight. Kip almost trips stepping out of them. He is naked now, except for a bow tie and black nylon briefs. He hesitates, suddenly self-conscious and uncertain.

"That's far enough," Vince says. He holds the glass of bourbon in one hand. The cigarette hangs from his lips. He stares at Kip in the mirror and motions with the glass. The ice cubes swirl and tinkle softly. "Turn around."

Kip turns and stands rigid. He can feel the man's eyes on his ass, burning hot. He hears the sound of Vince swallowing, then the clink of the glass being placed on the dresser; then Vince's breathing, close behind him.

"Well, well. You dress up special for the occasion—or do all you bellboys wear panties under your outfits?"

Kip flushes. His skin prickles in the cool air. His briefs are sheer black nylon, skimpier than any bathing suit. They ride high in the back, digging into the crack of his ass and exposing the bottom curve of each cheek. In front they narrow to a snug little pouch that cramps his genitals even when they're soft. Max ordered a half-dozen in assorted colors from a mail-order outfit in Hollywood. The catalogue called it the Cupcake Thong—for the young male beauty with his assets in the rear.

"I asked you a question, Kip." Vince's breath is warm and moist in his ear, heavy with booze. "You always wear panties?"

Kip's voice is small and hoarse. "Yes."

"Umm. Cute." Vince cups his hand over one of the boy's firm buns, feeling the smoothness of the nylon against his palm and the even silkier flesh against his fingertips. He slides his middle finger under the hem, over the curve of Kip's ass and into the cleft. He strokes the tightly puckered hole, and Kip sighs in response. "Oh, kid, fucking your hole is gonna be a dream. Yeah. Now be a good little girl and take off your panties for me."

A trickle of sweat runs from Kip's armpit down the side of his chest. Vince is already taking him places he has never been, even in his fantasies. He slides the black panties over his hips and bends to peel them down his thighs.

Vince purses his lips. Sucks in his breath. The kid's ass is flawless. Smooth and white as ivory. Plump but firm, superbly shaped. A real bubble butt, perfect for screwing.

Kip stands, arms at his sides, eyes downcast. Vince slowly circles him, nodding approval. The boy's sturdy little cock stands straight up. The bow tie adds a sluttish touch, like a stripper's prop, flaunting his nudity.

"You work out, kid?"

Kip can hardly speak. "There's a gym in the basement. And a pool . . ."

Vince nods. The kid's body is even better than he had hoped. Lean, muscular limbs, sharply defined under porcelain skin. A flat belly, gently ridged with muscle. Slender hips. A natural posture that pulls his broad shoulders up and keeps the small of his back arched stiffly, making his ass jut out hard and round behind him, lifting his pectorals up for display.

And it's the boy's pecs that Vince can't help staring at. The kid lifted weights to get a pair like that, did a lot of swimming. It shows—big, thick pectorals, pumped-up and round, glazed with a thin sheen of perspiration that makes them shine in the dimly lit room. So big they look lewdly out of place, top-heavy above the sinewy slenderness of his torso, extending a blatant, passive invitation to be cupped and fondled. Capping the smooth mounds are nipples an inch wide, standing out puffy and pink, ripe for plucking.

Vince likes big tits. On his women. On his boys. Twin handfuls of smooth, pliant muscle he can reach around and grab hold of when his cock is buried balls-deep in ass. Nipples he can pull on to make that ass do a grinding dance around his dick.

Vince takes a swig of bourbon. Then he takes an ice cube from the glass. Slowly, watching the boy's reaction, he touches it to the tip of each protruding nipple. Kip flinches and sucks in his breath. The icy contact makes his nipples crinkle and stiffen, erecting them into elongated little nubs of flesh. Vince toys casually with the effect, drawing a gasp from the boy each time he flicks the wedge of ice against the sensitive, swollen tips.

Kip is astonished at the sensation. His tits begin to sting and burn. He closes his eyes and moans. His nipples feel enormous, throbbing with each heartbeat. The frostbite claws into them, filling them like pincushions with sharp needles of pain. His whole body trembles, but Kip keeps his arms at his sides, clenching fistfuls of air. His cock stands up rigid and shiny red.

Then the ice cube is gone, melted away. Vince's forefinger and thumb choose a nipple to pick on, plucking and pulling at the scalded tip.

"You put out for a lot of guys, don't you?"

The question slides into Kip's consciousness, taking a long muddled detour around the ache in his nipples. "No. Not really—"

"Don't bullshit me, kid. I don't like pussies who lie to me. I saw the way you got down on your knees for it this morning. Couldn't wait to get your mouth all over it. You've gone down before, plenty of times."

"A few . . ."

"Oh yeah?" Vince savagely twirls the nipple between his fingernails, making him yelp. "Sucking off the hotel johns for a little cash on the side. You bend over and let those guys stick it up that tight little hole? Or is that just for Uncle Max?" Vince slaps him smartly across the face.

Kip recoils and cringes. "No—I mean, sometimes. But usually, most of them"—he stammers, trying to defend himself—"usually they just . . . want to suck me off."

Vince laughs. "You shitting me, pussyboy? Pay to suck this little weenie?" He runs the chilly surface of his glass against Kip's cock, making him gasp. "Must be a pretty desperate bunch of old toads—paying good money to slobber over your stiff little nub." He raises the glass to his lips and swallows. "You know what I think, Kip? I think you're a cocksucker. And a liar. I thing you're nothing but a cheap little slut, working the hotel johns to get a stiff dick up your pussy."

Kip tries to answer, but his lips and tongue are suddenly shapeless. Instead he only groans. Then yelps, as Vince slaps him across the mouth.

And then Kip is alone again, blushing nude and erect in the center of the room. Vince has returned to the dresser to pour himself another drink.

"Get your pussy over here, slutboy. On your hands and knees."

Kip drops to all fours, suddenly dizzy and glad to be on the floor. He crawls across the carpet, face stinging, nipples throbbing, until he reaches the heels of the man's shiny black shoes. He stares at them for a long moment. Vince turns around. Kip raises his head slowly.

Above him, Vince looks down and smirks. A fresh cigarette hangs from the corner of his mouth. His fly is open. His big, nude cock hovers over Kip's upturned face, softly swollen and impossibly thick. The dizziness returns. Kip clutches the carpet and moans.

Vince takes a long drag on his cigarette and laughs. "See something you like, pussyboy?"

Kip moans louder, and licks his lips. He stares mesmerized at the massive tube of smooth, naked flesh, displayed luridly before his face. So beautiful. So brutally big. Heavy and blunt, corrugated with veins beneath the sleek, taut wrapping of flesh. Pulsing and growing thicker before his astonished eyes. Suddenly he seems to see the scene from somewhere else in the room: the nude blond boy in a bow tie on his hands and knees; the big man in the business suit above him, lewdly exposing his oversized sex. The man smoking a cigarette casually, taking his time—the boy itchy and hot between his legs, hungry to have it in his mouth. Kip puts on a show for the voyeur in his mind: wiggling his ass, breathing hard, biting his lips. Naked pussyboy, craving cock.

Vince finishes his cigarette and snuffs it out. He leans his ass against the dresser and spreads his feet apart, framing Kip between his legs. The plump, waxy-looking head of his cock hovers inches from the boy's parted lips. Kip feels the heat that radiates from the cockflesh. He watches Vince's heartbeat in the long thick vein that pulses lazily down one side. His nostrils are filled with the odor of the man's sex. He can almost taste it on his tongue.

But instead of cock, Vince feeds him liquor. He uncaps the bottle of bourbon and lowers it to Kip's mouth, pushing his head back and telling him to swallow. He slides the neck of the bottle into the boy's mouth and pours the booze down his throat in long, burning draughts, tilting the bottle up and lowering it, listening to Kip gurgle and cough. Trickles of amber bubble from the corners of Kip's mouth and run in rivulets down his undulating throat, into the hollows of his collarbone and over his shiny, pumped-up pecs, stinging his swollen nipples. Kip's glazed eyes are riveted on the naked shaft, watching it thicken and slowly grow erect along-side the bottle, wishing it were the big cock that Vince was emptying over and over again into his throat.

The bottle is empty. Vince sets it aside and pulls the boy to his feet. Kip moans, wanting to stay close to the big cock. Then hands are gliding over his naked flesh, pulling him close, crushing him against the man's big chest. The hands glide down the small of his back and onto his ass, pulling his buttocks apart—then a finger penetrates his hole and slides knuckle-deep into his rectum. He gasps and looks up into Vince Zorio's smoldering eyes.

"Ummm. Now I think I'm ready to have some fun with you, pussyboy."

HALF past nine: Kip kneels on the hard tile floor of the bathroom in Vince Zorio's suite. His trembling body glistens with a sheen of cold sweat. His legs are folded beneath him. His ass rests on his heels. He is naked, except for the bow tie wrapped snugly around his neck, and the black silk tie that binds his hands behind his back. His throat is filled with Vince's cock. His ass is filled with the enema Vince gave him earlier and the cruelly thick buttplug that holds it inside.

Vince sits on the toilet. He has removed his shirt and jacket. Tufts of wiry black hair sprout above the neckline of his undershirt. His pants and boxer shorts are pushed down to his ankles. His bare feet are planted on either side of the toilet, propping his knees wide apart. His dick is buried deep in Kip's throat.

Kip's jaws ache from sucking cock. His shoulders and arms are stiff and sore from being pulled so tightly behind his back. He cannot seem to stop shaking. The enema rumbles in his guts, making his bowels spasm and knot into wicked cramps. His hard-on would have vanished long ago, except for the thin leather cord tied cutting-tight around his cock. Kip is miserable, on the verge of crying.

He pulls his face from Vince's crotch, letting the cock slide free from his throat. It snaps upward from his lips, ramrod stiff and glossy with saliva. It seems to Kip that he has been sucking on Vince's cock for hours. The big dick never goes soft, never shoots. It towers before him like a harsh rebuke, unsatisfied and demanding to be sucked again.

His bowels are knotted with cramps. He shivers uncontrollably. Beads of sweat erupt across his forehead and trickle down his nose. He stares up at Vince's face, looking for relief, but the big man only smirks.

"Please," Kip begs hoarsely. "Please—take it out of me. Out of my ass. Oh, please. I can't hold it anymore."

Vince smiles. And shakes his head. "You know the rules, pussy-boy. You blow me till I come. You suck the cream out of my big, fat dick, and then I pull the plug." Vince grabs the base of his dick and waves it like a billy club, cock-proud and horny. He tilts it down, pointing at Kip's mouth, and rubs the head over the boy's pouting lips. "Well, pussyboy?"

Vince is playing a cruel game with him. Kip knows he has sucked the man to the verge of coming several times already—he can tell from the quickening of Vince's breath, the way his body draws taut, the way his cock expands abruptly and throbs in his throat. But every time Vince shoves his mouth away at the last minute and sits gasping on the toilet, letting the orgasm recede, waiting until his twitching dick has cooled before beginning the game all over again.

Kip sobs. Tears well in his eyes. He has promised himself he will not cry, but he can no longer help it. He opens his mouth, whimpering, and leans forward to suck.

Just as his lips make contact, Vince pulls the cock up and out of reach. He looks at Kip thoughtfully. "Uh-uh. I think I want you to suck on my nuts for a while."

Kip groans. Vince pinches his mouth open and stuffs the big balls inside. He sits back on the toilet and spreads his legs wide open. Kip's cheeks are outrageously bloated. The plump, heavy scrotum fills his mouth. The testicles are alive, twitching and jerking inside the sack. Vince laughs. "You look like a little chipmunk, pussyboy. Don't just hold 'em. Use your tongue." Vince strokes his cock slowly and gives himself over to the exquisite sensation . . .

KIP'S mind is so jumbled that he can hardly recall a time when he has not been in bondage on his knees, sucking cock and enduring the enema. Vaguely he remembers how it began—in the other room, long ago, when Vince removed his tie and told Kip to cross his wrists behind his back. Kip was slow to respond, partly from the booze, partly out of fear, but as Vince wrapped the silk cord tight around his wrists, placing him in bondage for the first time in his life, he flushed with an excitement that made him shake. To be standing naked and erect and helpless in the man's room, while Vince slowly circled him, pulling on the big, nude cock that jutted from his open fly and appraising Kip like a newly purchased toy—as if a deeply buried fantasy had somehow erupted into the real world and taken on a dangerous life of its own. Kip was excited. Kip was frightened. Kip was a nude, helpless pussyboy with his hands tied behind his back and his cock standing up stiff between his legs, and Vince Zorio was going to fuck him.

Then the man began to humiliate him, gradually escalating the abuse. Vince liked to use his big, meaty hands. Pinching Kip's swollen nipples. Slapping his face. Punching his belly. Squeezing his ass, hard enough to leave bruises. Stinging his sturdy little erection with hard open-handed slaps.

Vince seemed especially to enjoy abusing his cock. Tying it at the base so that it stood up shiny and red. Swatting it with his hand. Raking his fingernails up the length and pinching the tip. Humiliating it—telling Kip he had a little weenie between his legs. Cradling the weenie in his hand and spanking it with his own huge truncheon of meat, driving home the difference between them. Humiliate a boy's hard cock, Vince had once told Battaglia, and just watch the way his hole opens up for anything you wanna put inside.

When it came time to clean the boy out, Vince opened the dresser's middle drawer and pulled out an aluminum briefcase. Kip caught a glimpse of the contents and raised his eyebrows in alarm. A yellow enema bag and a coil of tubing. A huge black rubber buttplug. A confusion of items he couldn't name, made of leather, rubber, chrome. And at the back of the briefcase, buried in the tangle but catching the light with the unmistakable glint of cold black steel, a gun . . .

A quarter past ten: Vince has decided to come. It seems a shame. Kip is doing such a fine job on his cock. Hard, relentless, deep-throat cocksucking. Nonstop. No sissy-kissing or tongue-lapping. No idling while the boy stops to catch his breath—getting Vince off is infinitely more important than that.

The dark-headed hustler back in Kansas City sucked with the same enthusiasm. So did the blond bitch in Dallas. So have all the other cocksuckers in all the other towns who have found themselves naked on their knees in a hotel john with Vince Zorio, with an enema up their butts and their hands tied behind their backs. Guaranteed incentive to make certain Vince's cock gets the loving, undivided attention it deserves. A sure ticket to the best blowjob in town—and Vince always treats himself to the best. A UCLA gymnast he picked up at a bar in West Hollywood holds the record—a little over ninety minutes of desperately fucking his face on Vince's big cock before Vince gave him the load he was begging for and pulled the plug from his ass. Of course, the gymnast had the added incentive of the alligator clamps Vince had attached to his nipples and the tip of his penis.

Vince is up for breaking the record. Kip has worked him up stiff as a girder, and Vince could stay that way all night; he is in no hurry to shoot. But little Kip, for all his natural talent, obviously doesn't have that kind of stamina. The boy is covered with sweat, shaking like a leaf. Whimpering and gagging himself nonstop, his head bouncing up and down like a piston about to blow.

At one point the boy even pissed himself—let go with an uncontrollable spray that jetted straight out of his hard, bound cock and spattered against the front of the toilet. Kip flushed cherry red, but never stopped sucking. Vince has seen it happen before.

Remembering excites him. Vince grabs the base of his dick and whips it out of the kid's mouth.

Kip sobs and groans, thinking Vince is teasing him again. "No," he croaks. "Let me. Put it back—"

"Let you what?"

"Let me suck it." Kip is whining now. Begging. Babbling. "Please—come in my mouth. Oh please, put it back—in my mouth—let me suck." The kid is raving, delirious. "I can't—I can't—Please. Fuck me. Fuck me!" And he opens his mouth almost frighteningly wide, scrunching his features up against his forehead, making his whole face into a gaping, hungry hole.

Vince is impressed. And almost tempted to prolong the torment. Kip looks so desirable that way. Down on his knees, cringing nude in a pool of his own sweat and urine. Big tits heaving out, tight rump sticking up behind. Blond hair plastered against his forehead. Tears running down his cheeks. Every muscle taut and glazed with sweat. Turning his mouth into a pussy that begs for Vince's dick.

The least Vince can do is shove his cock into that hole and come. Instead, he leans back on the toilet and aims his dick at Kip's wide-open mouth. He breathes deep. Two quick strokes and he's there.

It's a hefty load—after so much sucking, Vince's balls hang heavy as a pair of lemons. He thrashes on the toilet seat, shuddering from the force of the climax. His cock is like a hose, spraying semen all over Kip's gaping face and chest.

He takes his time catching his breath, then slowly gets off the toilet, pulls up his pants, tucks in his undershirt. He leaves his fly open. His emptied balls contract to their normal size, but his cock thrusts out the opening as stiff and ready as if he had never come. Finally he pulls Kip to his feet and grabs the base of the buttplug. He has to screw and tug—it's a tight fit. Then he steps aside, laughing, while Kip scurries crablike onto the commode . . .

MIDNIGHT: Kip lies on the bed. The sheets are wildly rumpled, soaked with sweat. He is hog-tied, wrist to ankle—arms pulled down alongside his body, legs folded beneath him, knees apart. He began that way at the foot of the bed, with his ass hanging over the edge, an easy target for Vince's dick. Now he is jammed sideways against the headboard, neck bent, face pressed against the wood. Over the past two hours, Vince has ridden him up and down and across the bed a dozen times.

Vince stands at the side of the bed, facing Kip's ass, naked except for his undershirt. The thin, ribbed cotton is almost transparent with sweat, clinging to his broad chest and back. His satisfied, rubbery cock droops heavily from his crotch, coated with shiny mucus and oozing semen from the tip. In his hand he holds a wire coat hanger, untwisted at the top and crudely straightened like a long, thin shepherd's crook.

The wire hanger has done a good job. Vince was lucky to find it. The hotel hangers are all made of wood, but high on a shelf in the closet, left over from a previous guest's dry cleaning, he came across the tool he was looking for.

He would have preferred using his belt. But belts are noisy.

So are boys in the process of having their asses whipped. Which is why the buttplug that earlier held his enema inside is now stuffed into Kip's wide-open mouth, held in place by a bandanna made from his own nylon panties. Kip's face is red from the strain and wet from crying.

Kip's ass is pushed outward and up, taut as a drumhead. So wide open that the deep cleft between his cheeks is flattened and his hole rudely exposed, completely vulnerable. The pale, silky bottom flesh sizzles with thin red welts. The bud of his anus is equally red and chafed, distended and swollen like a bee sting, the tender lips rubbed raw by long, relentless fucking.

Vince reaches for the phone on the bedside table and dials the switchboard. While he waits, he prods Kip's ass with the blunt, hooked end of the coat hanger. Kip's grunt is muffled by the buttplug. Vince snakes the hanger between the boy's thighs and hooks his cock, pulling it backward between his legs. Still hard as a rock.

"Yeah, operator. Suite 1505. I want you to ring the phone in the adjoining bedroom."

Vince pulls the hanger upward and back, seeing how far the stubby shaft will bend. Another inch and it snaps free, slapping up against the kid's belly. Kip moans.

"Leo—I saw the light go on under your door a while back. Getting in kinda late, aren't you? Yeah. So how were the chicks down on pussy boulevard? No such luck, huh? You're a crazy sonofabitch to be out on the streets tonight anyway, not with all the heat. Yeah, tell me about it—always horny as hell after a job. Especially like the bitch we pulled today."

Kip turns his head, realizing only gradually that Vince is speaking to someone else.

"Nah, stayed in all night. Found my piece on the premises. Yeah, you know me. Sure, come on over."

Kip stiffens, suddenly understanding.

Vince is in the bathroom, pissing, when the door to the adjoining bedroom swings open. Pressed against the headboard, Kip can see nothing. But he feels the stranger's presence in the room, somewhere behind him, drawing closer; then hears the toilet flush, and Vince returning.

"Jesus, Vince, you sure did a job on his ass." The voice is deep and detached, faintly sarcastic; delivered from the corner of the mouth, with a more pronounced New York accent than Vince's.

"Yeah." The sound of a striking match—Vince lighting a cigarette.

"And such a pretty ass it is. So what does the rest of him look like?"

Vince seizes Kip by the hair and twists him around.

Above him stands a giant of a man. Thick featured, rumple faced, with a broad, flattened nose. Heavyset and balding. He wears a long purple satin robe and smokes a cigar. A gold necklace hangs from his bull-like neck, almost buried in bristling black hair. Rings glitter on both hands.

Leo Battaglia looks down at the bound boy with the buttplug in his mouth and the bow tie around his throat. He sneers and shakes his head. "Ah, Vincent, you're gonna burn in hell for this kind of shit. You and your boys. But I gotta admit—you know how to pick 'em. Pretty as a girl. And such big titties. You always go for the blonds with big tits, no matter what they got between their legs."

Vince shrugs, smiling faintly. "What they all got between their legs, Leo, is a nice, sweet hole."

Leo snorts. "So where'd you find the little cocksucker—in the hotel, you said?"

"Room-service waiter. Delivered a blowjob with breakfast. Came back for more. Just a hustler, really. Works the hotel johns."

Leo cups the boy's chin. Kip meets his stare for an instant, and shudders. Leo runs his thumb in a circle around the rim of the buttplug, grazing the boy's puffy, swollen lips.

"Good mouth?"

Vince kisses his fingertips. "Perfetto. Try it on for size."

"You sure we oughta pull out the gag? What if he starts yelling?"

"No sweat. He's plenty softened up by now. Besides, he's got a sugar daddy on the staff. Uncle Max might just about shit his pants if he could see you now—right, Kip?"

Leo nods. He unties the sash at his waist and lets the robe fall.

The utter corpulence of the man's nudity overwhelms Kip. At one time, Leo Battaglia possessed a magnificent physique; in his youth he must have been godlike. But there is nothing beautiful about his body now. Leo is an awesome wreckage of a man, still muscular but long gone to seed. Enormous slablike shoulders, powerful arms. Big, fleshy tits and a hard, overhanging belly. Swirls of kinky black hair carpet his stomach and chest. His body exudes a crude, intoxicating aura of overpowering maleness; virile, overripe sensuality oozes from every pore. Beside him, Kip feels small and ridiculous, trussed up naked and dribbling saliva around the plug in his mouth.

Kip looks down, between Leo's legs. His eyes widen in alarm. He had hoped Leo might have a small cock, at least smaller than Vince's, easy to accommodate and satisfy. But Kip is out of luck. And the night is just beginning . . .

FIVE o'clock in the morning: Kip lies on the bed, on his side. His mind and body are exhausted. He can hardly move. But he is no longer bound. He might leave now, escape from the room. But Kip is going nowhere. Because Vince is inside him. The man lies behind him on the bed, pressed against Kip's back, joined by a glue of sweat and semen. His cock is lodged deep in the boy's ass, holding him impaled like a fish on a hook. He nuzzles the back of

Kip's neck, grazing it with his lips, nipping gently with his teeth.

They are alone, and the room is dark and quiet, except for the low mewling sounds that Kip occasionally makes, like a puppy whimpering in its sleep. Leo has come and gone. Come twice: once in Kip's ass, once in his mouth.

Kip's mind is neither awake nor asleep, but motionless, running in place. The eternity of the past few hours replays itself over and over in his head. Leo's huge, gnarled cock in his mouth. The wire hanger slashing out of nowhere against his already-punished ass—the memory makes him flinch—and the vibrations of Kip's muffled scream coursing through the man's dick, making it tingle. Leo liked the effect. Vince obliged, wielding the hanger with his strong right arm. They traded places. Leo whipped even harder than Vince.

Then they moved on to another game.

Leo seldom fucked ass. At least not boyass. That's what he said. But Kip was the exception. Vince and Leo double-dicked him like seasoned partners, one of them screwing his mouth, the other his rear, pulling out to trade places again and again, until Kip hardly knew which man fucked him and which man he sucked. His body was a long continuous tube, plugged with thick cock at both ends. Eventually they untied him. Leo said something about getting his gun to make sure the kid didn't bolt. The words hardly registered on Kip's exhausted brain, but Vince snapped at Leo to shut up. "You're gonna really fuck us up one of these days, Battaglia. You're always too fucking careless with your mouth . . ."

But his anger cooled quickly as they returned to using Kip. To satisfy Leo, he retied Kip's hands behind his back. They put him on his knees, then took their places at opposite ends of the room and made him crawl stupefied from cock to cock. When one of them had finished with him for the moment, he would shove the boy away, and Kip would shuffle awkwardly to the other, scraping his knees against the carpet until they were raw. Depending on the hole preferred, he would bow his head to suck, or else turn around and stagger to his feet, squatting back to take the waiting cock up his ass while the man across the room watched and pulled on his own freshly serviced dick.

When Kip suddenly came to a standstill in the middle of the room, unable to go on and begging them to let him rest, Vince reached for the hanger. Kip continued to crawl, miles and miles without ever leaving the room.

At some point, hazy in Kip's memory, Leo finally left, returning to his own room, leaving the taste of his oily semen warm and fresh on Kip's tongue.

Then the evening wound down and contracted to a single spot, concentrated at the point where Vince's cock is now snugly lodged inside the boy's well-worked hole . . .

The cock is deeply rooted—almost motionless—but Kip's ass is so tender that the least movement sends twinges of sensation through his crammed bowels. He can feel each beat of Vince's heart from the veins that throb against his rectal walls.

Vince plays his passive body like an instrument, making him whimper and squirm. His caresses are slow, calculated, tender—but Kip's raw flesh is so acutely tuned that even the most delicate touch courses through him like the crack of a whip. Vince runs his fingertips over Kip's nipples, down the ridges of his belly. The boy quivers in response. He squeezes the swollen head of Kip's cock gently, and strokes the shaft once with his forefinger and thumb. Kip shudders, on the verge of coming. Vince flicks his finger against the boy's balls, seizes a hair, and slowly, slowly plucks it—Kip's rectum convulses around the man's cock. Vince runs his hand over the boy's hip, onto his ass, and plays his fingertips across the welts, like a blind man reading braille. His other hand, circling Kip from below, finds a nipple to twist gently. Kip writhes in the man's embrace and squeezes his ass around the big, inexhaustible cock with a slow, steady rhythm.

For Vince, this is the best of all fucks. The final screw. A tenderized hole that throbs around his dick. A boy who quivers like a bowstring in his arms at the least whisper of a touch. It has taken all night to bring Kip to this point. The effort is always worth it.

A pale blue light shows through the heavy drapes. Dawn, and soon Vince will have to end it. Kip is the best he's had in months. He could easily spend a week working the kid over, or a month, grinding him harder and harder beneath his heel seeing just how deep the boy's hunger dwells. But Vince has an early morning flight to catch; and now that the job is done, there is no reason to stay and every reason to leave.

Soon he will come in the boy's ass, for the final time. And then, to milk the last few drops from his cock, he will finally bring Kip off. The boy's cock is primed to bursting, and has been for hours. A single stroke will do it—a glide of his fingernail down the underbelly of Kip's cock, and the stubby little erection will give a twitch and suddenly explode.

And then—

Vince hears a noise.

In the hallway. Muffled steps. Someone walking up the hall. Not someone—the noise is too complicated to come from a lone walker, or even two. A group of people coming up the hall. Vince goes rigid, wide awake.

A sound at the door. Not the normal jangling of a key in a lock, but quiet, methodical—a stalking, covert sound.

He is off the bed in an instant. He takes Kip with him, keeping his cock in the boy's ass as he bolts toward the dresser and fumbles in the open briefcase for his gun. Kip squeals in protest—the swirling movement dizzies him, the sudden jogging of the cock in his ass threatens to send him over the edge. The gun flashes in the corner of his eye and he stiffens in fear, groggy and confused, but coming rapidly to his senses.

The door to the room bursts open, ripping the chain lock from the wall. Almost instantly the overhead light flashes on, blinding after the darkness, as they rush into the room—a man in plainclothes and behind him uniformed police, at least five of them, more in the hallway, all holding guns.

There is a frozen moment of shock on all sides.

Vince's arm is locked across Kip's chest. His cock is still in the boy's ass, throbbing with a jackrabbit pulse. He holds the gun to Kip's throat.

"My, my." The plainclothesman finally speaks. The room seethes with tension, but the man sounds bored, covering his agitation with studied finesse. He shakes his head. "We knew you was a killer, Zorio. But I had no idea . . ."

Kip's whole body prickles with heat. He cannot escape. There is no way to hide. He feels the eyes of all the men rake over his naked body, hoisted to tiptoes on Vince's cock. He hears them murmur in shock and derision. Pussyboy, caught in the act. His cock juts stiffly from his hips for all to see, quivering and closer than ever to coming.

The plainclothesman speaks slowly, deliberately, getting down to business. "Come on, Zorio. There's no way out of this hole. We got half the department down in the lobby. And the rest are taking a coffee break across the street. Come on. You don't wanna hurt the kid."

Vince stands stock-still, breathing hard. His heartbeat pounds like a fist against Kip's back. And then it happens. Kip cannot stop it. He tries desperately to cover himself with his hands, but his arms are pinned to his sides. His cock twitches and bobs in the air, and then begins to shoot—long, spiraling ribbons of stored-up semen that jet halfway across the room, landing with a dull splat on the carpet before the plainclothesman's feet. He writhes helplessly in Vince's hold, jerking weirdly like a puppet. The ordeal seems to go on forever. The officers stare speechless. One of them mutters, "Holy shit!"

Behind Vince, the door to Battaglia's room bursts open. Vince whirls halfway round. A confusion of sudden movement and shouting—"Watch out!"—then the deafening blast of pistol fire, three times in rapid succession.

With each shot, Vince convulses in a horrible parody of fucking Kip's ass. He staggers forward, his weight bowing Kip's shoulders, then falls back. His softening cock pulls out of Kip's bowels with a loud, liquid fart. His body slams the floor with a thud that reverberates into the soles of Kip's feet.

Kip swings around, his cock still twitching and dribbling. For an instant he sees the motionless hulk of Vince's body, lying flat on his back with a strange surly grimace on his face, his eyes wide open. Then the cops are everywhere, a swirling sea of blue, and the plainclothesman is on him, grabbing Kip by the shoulders and steering him toward the door to Battaglia's room. "No," Kip whispers dully, looking over his shoulder, "no . . ."

There are more cops in the other room, and Leo, standing handcuffed in his purple robe, his big ugly face made even uglier by the unexpected tears gushing over his rumpled jowls. The cops, flushed with triumph, are startled at the sight of Kip, then rally with whistles and jeers. "Can it," the plainclothesman says. He yanks the spread from Leo's bed and wraps it over Kip's shoulders.

With the bedspread folded around him, Kip stands mute and numb as a refugee, shivering uncontrollably. The plainclothesman speaks softly, asking him something, but Kip does not hear. He turns and stares into the other room. Through the narrow frame of the doorway, he can see only Vince's legs and feet. Then a blanket descends, and only the feet are visible. And then, as the policemen swarm, even the feet are lost to sight, obscured by a maze of blue trousers and shiny black boots.

Bonny Finberg

LIGHT

INSIDE THE CRIB LOOKING OUT. Only her eyes
are free, reaching through the slats into the speckled
night. Crying, calling. Does no one hear? They hear better in the daylight. Night absorbs her sounds like a
sponge on spilt milk. The night is speckled with her
cries. She touches the wooden slat, sobs convulse from
heart to hand in a shocking wave. She hears the T.V. in
the living room, envisions its light flickering in the dark,
her sisters on the floor in front. They must be taking
turns shining the flashlight on their faces from under
their chins to look like the man on T.V. A head with a
voice that comes low and deep from inside his invisible
body. It's scary, but her sisters make a giggling game out
of it, let her have a turn. They put the flashlight into their
mouths and their cheeks glow red. When she puts it into
her mouth red pours in around the edges of her eyes.
They shine the light into their palms, between their fin-

gers, making their hands glow soft and rosy like dolls' hands. She doesn't hear them giggling now, but what if she falls asleep? She doesn't like being left out, had come in the middle of things, had catching up to do. Why won't her mother come? She rarely did, but she might come now. Maybe this time she'll come, smile at her, pick her up, take her outside with the others. They could all sit and smile together, children on the floor, mother and daddy on the couch.

In the morning she wakes with her eyes stuck closed. Her mother comes with a warm wet wash cloth and gently wipes away the crust of dried tears defeated by the night. She opens her eyes and sees the new day in the brief vision of her mother's face, then her mother's back returning to the place where she has supplies of wash cloths and running water, the labyrinth of rooms where the others move at will, unafraid; where her mother moves from table to stove to sink, moving things, making things; the uncooked dough she gives her sometimes to put into a miniature pie plate made of tin. Under the kitchen table she fills her mouth with its moist fleshy taste, her mother filling the room with the warm oily smell of the oven, making daytime sounds with dishes and pans, the water running in the sink while she sits under the table eating dough.

This night thing is a dead thing. Once a pressing from inside woke her up. She didn't want to wet the mattress so she climbed out of her crib and walked through the dark, constellations of dots all around her, sad memories of the light that had come and gone. She made it to the bathroom, reached to push the light switch up. This made the darkness go away. The dots all melted together and overpowered the darkness. The black and blue tiled border gleamed above her. She peed and ran back to her room. She didn't remember too much else about that night.

Doesn't she hear her? Doesn't she know how much she wants her to come? Isn't she making herself understood? What else can she do? Is there something else? Some thing that will make her come? If she watches them even more closely will she understand what it is? Some secret thing they aren't telling her, an understanding, a definition of the world, a bond stretching back to before she came here, from wherever it was she came from, a different origin. But they are all she knows and there is something indefinable linking her to them. Crying is all.

She rolls onto her stomach and begins pushing her hips forward. She tightens her thighs around the feeling. She must have been rolling around on the floor or something when it first happened. Just a wordless body groping around for whatever felt good. There was the floor all around her, a vast lover, hard and steady to bounce herself against, until the world funneled down into an imploding eddy at the center of her being, giving her the power, not merely between her own small thighs, but at the core of all the universe which was her, in a nameless explosion at the beginning of space and time. All this without hands, fingers or small objects. Just the flat surface of the big world against which she could pleasure herself.

Her father found her this way one evening when he returned from work, or wherever it was he went when he went out there. She looked up from her garden of earthy delights at his disapproving face framed by the brim of his gray hat, tilted like a movie star newspaper man, his finger pivoting up and down, eyes glaring a warning, "Don't do that." But this couldn't stop her. It felt so good. She just took it into the dark.

Lying in darkness now, she sees no one, hears no one, she is invisible. The springs of the crib scream, the frame threatening to fly in all directions as she rides ecstasy like a dark stallion, breath steaming from flared nostrils, a stream of burgundy double galloping through her veins, heating the room beyond the season.

She rolls over onto her back and looks up at the ceiling, thick with warm stars. They move imperceptibly, shift position. The darkness between takes shape. There she is again, the lady looking down on her. She visits at night, darkness falling like clay on the potter's wheel, spinning vessels for dreams. Her breasts hang down like glowing clouds, her nipples like round light bulbs. She is smiling, her hair falling down her back through her arms and over her shoulders. She is reaching down to her, fingers long and tapered, palms large and smooth. Children steal her hands and put them under their pillows, listening to their secrets.

Smiling up at her from the crib, she feels herself rise like the steam from her mother's pies, a sweet humid rising up, up, up, expanding as she rises, until she is part of the air itself, forgetting where she comes from, leaving the tart sweet world below, painful in its deliciousness, too tantalizing in what might lie under its crust. She takes the lady's nipple into her mouth and feels herself aglow. A moist fleshy taste fills her mouth. Daylight penetrates her closed eyes.

Estabrook

there's more to
that state trooper
than meets
the eye

the trooper eyes me like troopers always eye you even though I was doing the speed limit in fact a little bit under as I passed on by some construction the road-builders at it again and she had her brown Smoky the Bear hat low down on her forehead standing with her arms crossed over her chest like troopers always stand and as she eyes me I'm tempted so very tempted to wink at her seeing as she is kind of cute with her arms folded across her ample chest rather nice hips too I can't see her legs of course but my hunch is they're white and smooth and strong and sweet I bet those legs of hers smell so good and taste good too and I'm thinking how I'd love to lick her from behind her knees up the backs of her thighs to that precious patch of female heat and moisture and I bet even her seat her cute little trooper seat smells really good and tastes good too but I don't wink at her coward that I am figuring she wouldn't like it that much probably

chase me down give me a citation for winking or for not wearing
my seatbelt tight enough so I don't wink even though (damn me!)
I'm fantasizing like crazy that she pulls me over on some deserted
back road says I can avoid this here ticket if I'll simply stick my
tongue into her musty dark private parts no kissing on the mouth
mind you "I simply want you to lick me lick me lick me clean"
and she's already got her trooper pants down her panties off her
luscious white smooth legs spread wide open up over the seat and
she doesn't have to tell me twice no sir I always obey the law the
long legs of the law and my face is down in there and I'm doing
what I've been told to do I'm licking and licking working my
tongue all around in her pussy gently sucking and kissing at her
clit and my face is all wet from her luscious pink snatch and after
a while of her moaning and sweating and swearing and twisting
around and wriggling all over the damn place she says "I'm the
law and I order you to work on the other side my pussy needs a
break" and she pushes me away from her delicious snatch and
rolls over and arches her back and her ass my God it's sticking up
perched there in front of me and it's just so perfect and beautiful
and smooth and white and musty sweet smelling and I spread
open her ass cheeks ever so carefully with my trembling hands
and press my face down into there push my tongue into there as
deep into there as I can get it and by God but it is so delicious hot
sweet musty sweet and I lick and lick and lick her clean just like
she's ordered me to and she's arching her back more and more
"deeper please push your tongue into there deeper oh it's so good
it feels so good deeper please don't stop I've never felt anything
so good in my life" and I am I am and she's actually coming as I'm
licking her ass as I'm stretching like crazy working my tongue in
as far as I can get it then I slip down to her pussy once again
which has had time to rest which is still wetter than hell and I
begin these long sweeping licking movements from her pussy up
to her tail bone and back down again and up again and back down
again and man oh man is she wriggling around now wriggling like

crazy and panting and drooling and sweating and moaning and finally she disengages her delicious self her delicious beautiful female parts from my feverishly working mouth "but I'm not done
yet, oh please" I beg her I can't seem to get enough of her taste
her smell her eternal wetness I can't get enough of eating her but
she's the boss she's the trooper and before I know what's up she's
fumbled my pants down nearly tearing my underpants off and she
has my thick throbbing cock in her mouth and she's sucking and
after a couple quick strokes the whole thing is over and she's smiling up at me my withering cock still in her beautiful hot red
mouth then she lets me loose and says "like to see what happens
if I catch you speeding?"

Doug Tierney

THE
PORTABLE
GIRLFRIEND

"HEY, WIREHEAD, wake up." Jack Bolander felt the vibrations through the floor as his roommate pounded on the bedroom door. The sunrise coming through his window turned the yellow painted-over wallpaper a sick orange color, the color inside his head when he wired in without any software in the 'Face. Ron pounded the door harder. "You're going to be late for work again, asshole. If you get fired, I'm kicking you out in the street."

"Yeah, yeah, I'm up." Bo had been lying awake for a while on his bare mattress, staring at the water-damaged ceiling, drawing pictures with the rusty brown splotches, and trying to forget his dreams. Unconsciously, he stroked the inside of his left thigh, but he stopped when Ron kicked the door again. "I'll be out in a minute."

"I'm leaving in two minutes, with or without you."

"I said I'm coming." He dressed without looking down at his body, without glancing down at the lacework of shrapnel scars that ran from his right leg, across his crotch, to his left hip. He stuffed the 'Face and wires into his rucksack along with a couple disks before he pulled on his boots and his field jacket. He didn't bother to tie the boots; he'd do that in the car. Stepping out of his room felt like stepping into someone else's house. Ron had furniture and house plants and cats. Bo had a mattress on the floor, piles of clothes, and milk crates of software. Sometimes he slept in the closet when he couldn't stop dreaming about the war.

In the car, Bo pulled out the 'Face and wired the first disk he pulled from his bag without looking at the title.

Do you want me? The woman, a brunette with huge conical breasts that defied gravity, appeared where the dashboard had been a moment before. She gave Bo a heavy-lidded look of lust with her wide brown eyes. Through her left nipple, Bo saw the hubcap of a passing truck. He popped out the disk and saw that it was a piece of AIC barterware he'd picked up in trade a few days before. Cheap, low format, look-but-no-touch kind of thing, even slightly transparent. Masturbation material, if you kept the lights down low.

For the second disk, he made sure he picked his only MASIC tri-disk. Full-sensory including tactile, capable of carrying on a conversation, it remembered you from one session to the next. The sim—called "Carson," for Kit, not Johnny—lived on a thick black-and-green MASIC wafer chip sandwiched between magneto-optical disks. The startup reminded him of the prairie, the sound of wind in the grass and the smell of rich black coffee and dirt. Across the bottom of his vision, the 'Face captioned in bright red script:

Warning: License period expired. Three (3) days remaining in renewal window. Proceed at your own risk? [n] He chose to go ahead. Bo had gotten the Kit Carson sim free with the 'Face, but like everything, it's only free until you're hooked. The renewal would cost most of his savings, and he'd planned something else for the money.

Hey, pardner. You got an upgrade code for me? Kit shimmered into existence in the back seat of the Saab, dressed in red plaid and dusty chaps. He smelled of gunpowder and horse, chewing tobacco and leather. Kit slapped Bo on the shoulder, a warm, friendly gesture they'd both grown accustomed to.

"No, I guess not. I just thought you might want to bullshit for a while," Bo offered. Ron sat in the driver seat, oblivious to the silent conversation taking place beside him. Bo turned to see Kit better, and the sim shuddered when Bo jerked the power cord between the 'Face and the battery pack. "Heading to work, and the yup's not speaking again."

Well, ol' pal, I'd like to stay and talk. Kit flickered, and suddenly he wore a business suit and tie. *But as you know, it's against the law to access unlicensed MASIC media.* He blinked back into his chaps and cowboy hat. *So until you get off your cheap ass and pay the renewal fee, I've got nothing to say to you, low-down, software-rustling loser.* He flicked Bo's ear with his finger, an electric shock that ran down his neck to the shoulder. *Cheapskate son of a bitch, pay for your software.* Kit's fist almost connected with Bo's jaw before he popped the sim out without powering down. The cowboy dissolved with a squeal, and Bo tossed the disk out the window.

"What was that?" Ron snapped, looking back.

"Bad disk," Bo said and rolled the window back up. He considered throwing the AIC vixen after the MASIC hombre. Then he thought about how short he was on licensed softsoft, and decided against it. He knew where he could get a black box to defeat license protection, but if he had that kind of money, he'd go ahead and buy the house and the Ferrari instead.

Ron dropped him off at the gate of the auto plant, where he worked for just above the minimum outrage, running a robot welder. His workstation sat like a slick green throne in the middle of a scrubbed concrete assembly-line floor. The whole building echoed with its own between-shifts silence while Bo inserted the manipulator probe like an IV into the socket in his right arm and keyed the machine to life with the magnetic tattoo on his thumb. The work was on the level of autonomic, barely a conscious effort in the whole process, just a well-practiced dance of fingers flexing, pointing, gripping, rolling, until all the parts were fixed together. Unable to read or wire up while working, he'd once tried masturbating and had arc-welded the trunk lids shut on three sedans by mistake. He could only sit and doze and wait out the shift, gripping a soft rubber ball in the working hand.

Everyone got paid at the end of the shift, and Bo wired up to check his bank balance. With the automatic deposit, minus his rent, he finally had enough. He'd saved up his money for months, socking away spare change, skipping meals whenever cigarettes alone would get him through. It was time for Jack Bolander to go downtown to find himself a date. Not just any woman, though. He had someone special in mind.

The last several weeks, she was all he'd lived for. He rode the bus into the growing Boston gloom, knowing he'd have her soon. The excitement of it was an electric pulse down the inside of his thigh all the way to the knee. When he noticed he was tapping his foot, he tried to stop, tried to be cool, but it didn't last.

The dark seemed to flow up around the windows of the sick yellow and stained white bus as the driver pushed his way through traffic to the core of the city. Darkness seeped up from the sewers, slicking the sides of the glass and concrete towers, turning the streets into a sodium-lamplit tunnel. The bus hit a pothole so hard the windows jarred, and Bo nearly fell off his seat.

"Fuckin' streets," the driver muttered. "As much money as this city makes offa parking tickets, you'd think they could repave this place once in a while." He hit another crater, so hard it could only have been intentional. "Like fuckin' Beirut."

"It's more like Goradze." A suit next to Bo spoke, a comment meant to open a conversation.

"Before or after the Ukes carpet bombed it?" he asked. The other man either missed or ignored his sarcasm. Bo checked the guy over and didn't know which to hate more: the euro-styled hair or the entrepreneurial smile. Bo decided on the smile.

"During," the man said. He pulled back his mop of blond hair and revealed a teardrop-shaped scar running from the corner of his left eye back up over his ear. He'd had an ocular enhancement removed. Another wired-up vet. "Forward observer."

"Three-thirty-second Mobile Artillery," Bo replied. He peeled back his sleeve, a ritual showing of scars. "Gunner. Still wired. You probably called in fire for us."

"Many times. That was the shit, wasn't it?" He shook his head. The bus's brakes squealed a drunken scream Bo felt in the base of his spine. The man pulled out a business card and passed it to him. "I'm Scott Dostoli. Listen, I'm starting up a consulting firm with a couple other wired vets. The pay isn't great, but it's better than that workfare bullshit the VA keeps pushing."

"It beats jacking off a robot all day."

"Without a doubt," he said and stood up. "I get off here. Give me a call, okay?"

"You got it." Bo smiled and threw him a lazy salute. When the suit stepped off the bus, Bo threw the card on the floor and went back to watching out the windows. "Fuckin' Spyglass Johnnies," he muttered. Several minutes later, the bus turned onto Essex Street.

"This is my stop," Bo said. When the bus didn't slow down, he yelled, "Hey, asshole, this is my stop." He stood up, catching himself on the worn aluminum pole as the bus swerved to the curb. The brakes sounded even worse up front, grinding metal on metal. Bo shouldered his green canvas rucksack and brushed his greasy brown hair from his face.

"Ring the fuckin' bell next time." The driver cranked the door open and yelled, "Essex Street! Change here for the Orange line."

Essex stank of rotting fish and urine in the gutters. Bo had forgotten how bad it could be in July. The summer heat blew up the alleys from the South End to mingle with the thick brown smell of the Chinatown dumpsters, the bready reek of stale beer, and the Combat Zone's scent of lust and cigarette ash. Bolander breathed in short, tight breaths through his mouth as he shuffled down the street, trying to look as if he were going somewhere else, shoulders hunched, weaving between refuse, trying without success not to make eye contact with the dealers and junkies haunting the corners.

"Hey, my man, you look like you're after a date." The pimp stood a head shorter than Bolander, but his arms were thicker, his chest broader. Muscle didn't mean much on the streets anymore, not when any punk or junkie could afford a gat or a taser, but it never hurt to look the part of the tough. He wore a tight black Bruins T-shirt and a black Raiders cap, and he smelled like cheap musk cologne. "Got a nice Asian girl, big ol' tits, just waiting for you. Guarantee you'll like her."

"Not interested." He tried to push past the pimp or to outpace him, but the man stayed with him, shouldering him toward the plate glass door of a cheap hotel with red and gold Chinese screens in the lobby. The sign over the desk advertised hourly rates.

"You like a white girl, izat it? Stick to yo' own kind?" He angled so he was chest-to-chest with Bo, backing him toward the doors once again. As Bolander spun right, away from the hotel, away from the pimp, the greasy yellow light of the streetlamp glinted orange off the metal stud on the back of his head, between his brown hair and the gray collar of his fatigue shirt. The pimp saw the wire port, and Bo saw the pimp seeing him. "Oh, so that's how you play. Hey, I can set you up with some softsoft, good shit, straight from Japan."

"Not interested. Back off." Something in Bo's voice, a hot edge, like bile in the back of the throat, made the pimp take several steps back, hands raised, the pale palms ghostly and disembodied in the shadows and uncertain light.

"Hey, wirehead. You just gotta say so." He stepped back a few more paces before turning his back to Bolander. "You a wire freak," he muttered, still loud enough to hear. "Don't fuck wit' no wire freaks."

Bo pulled his collar up over his port and covered the rest of the distance to the shop in strides lengthened by both adrenaline and anticipation. He glanced around once to make sure no one was watching before he ducked through the door of Abbe's Cellar. As far as it went, the Cellar was about the norm for the Zone, the usual stacks of porno movies and erotic magazines in their stiff shrink-wrap, glass display cases of adult toys of every improbable shape and size, a lot of B&D leather and masks, as the store's name implied. Unlike the other places on the street, though, it was a little darker, quieter. It had more atmosphere, and their prices kept the lowlifes out. Instead of being a poorly lit supermarket for human lusts, they catered to the desires, the fantasies. Their clientele were businessmen on their way home to someone, picking up a gadget or a piece of silk that would repaint the faded colors of a lover's smile and restore the sharp-edged, naughty gleam in a wife's eyes, the look that used to say, "my parents are going to be out all night . . . I'm so glad you stopped by." Abbe's also took pride in being on the cutting edge. Softsoft, ROMdolls, network services.

Bo didn't bother to sift through the collections of paraphernalia in the front. He didn't even consider the bulletin board where swingers posted their parties. What he wanted—who he wanted—was in the back room, waiting, sleeping, ready to wake up to his gently insistent kiss on the back of her neck. Maybe she'd been waiting as long for him as he had been for her. The further back he went, the less the Cellar looked like a shop. It came to resemble a basement or a lonesome middle class attic full of boxed history and old thoughts, faded and threadbare as the clothes that hang in the back of a closet. The leather harnesses and silk bonds didn't glare with the orange and blue scanner-coded tags like they did up front. Some didn't even have tags at all, hanging like personal mementos in the owner's den.

It was hotter in the back, where the air conditioner didn't quite reach. Bo shifted his pack from one shoulder to the other as he shrugged out of his mottled gray and black field jacket. He knotted the sleeves around his waist, feeling self-conscious of the hardware and of his small tank-gunner's frame. He felt bigger with the jacket on.

"Help you find something?" Abbe came out of the store room, a can of diet something in his hand. He was a bit shorter than Bo, about five and a half feet, close to two hundred pounds, give or take, balding on top but he made up for it with facial hair. He wore a white silk bowling shirt with red trim and sweat stains under the arms. His name was embroidered in red over the pocket, and somehow, he smelled clean. Not clean like showered, or clean like the Boston air after a summer thunderstorm when the sun finally comes out. It was clean like skinny-dipping in an icy spring-fed pond in the hills. His smell made Bo comfortable and took the nervous edge off their conversation.

"I've got something particular in mind."

"Okay, that's a good place to start." Abbe dragged a wobbly barstool from behind the curtain and offered it to Bo. When he declined, Abbe grabbed a magazine from the shelf and tossed it to the floor to prop up the short leg. "What exactly is it you'd like, and we'll see if we can hook you up." He struggled up onto the chair, still not quite on eye level with Bo.

"I'm looking for a girl." Bo was surprised to realize that he was embarrassed. He'd been chewing his lip, and his voice caught like dust in his throat. "I'm looking for a particular girl."

"You look like a smart kid," Abbe said. "You go to Tech?"

"No," Bo said, looking around at the low glass cases that lined the walls. Somewhere, in there, she was waiting for him. "I'm not in school anymore." He wondered if he should really be so nervous. His knees felt warm and weak. "She's on MASIC format."

"Tri-disk. I figured you for the high-end type. That's Mil-Spec hardware, isn't it. Not that cheap Japanese entertainment-only shit. Hold on, Colonel." Abbe leaned back through the door to the back room and called to someone named Janet. Bo couldn't hear her reply, but her voice was like speaker feedback. "Just get out here and help this boy. When I want your opinion, I'll start paying you for it."

"You watch your mouth, you old bastard." Janet stepped through the curtain, and the first thing Bo saw was her eyes, huge and brown and slightly bulging. With her combed-up puff of mousy brown hair and her slightly puckered mouth, she had the inquisitive look of a large rat. Her tight blue and tan shirt showed off her small, slightly sagging breasts. "What can we do you for, son?"

Bo hated it when anyone called him son. Even his own mother had just called him "kid." She waited, and her attention made him sweat, as if she were waiting for him to name some wild and illegal form of perversion, or perhaps waiting for him to run away.

"She's got long, wavy black hair and blue eyes. Slender. She looks Black Irish, if you know what I mean." Bolander looked around, as if invoking the description might cause the package containing her to stand up of its own volition, call to him, plead to be taken home. "I saw her here once before, but I don't remember her name."

"I know what you're talking about. There's only three on tri-disk, and the other two are blondes." Janet slipped into the back room before Bo knew she was leaving. There was nothing mousy about the way she moved. She was quick and lithe, and when she returned, she seemed to glide to a stop in front of him, the package in her hand waving under his nose like the bough of a tree in a breeze. "This her?"

Bo tried to speak, but only managed to mouth the word, "Yes."

"Cash, or can we debit it discreetly from your personal account?" Abbe finally asked. Bo handed over the tightly rolled wad of large bills he'd picked up at the bank. Abbe unrolled the money and handed it to Janet. "Cash customer. The mark of a real gentleman. Always deals in bills."

"There's only eight thousand here," Janet said after counting the stack twice. "Perpetual license is fifteen."

The words made Bo go cold, the way looking into the rearview mirror and seeing police lights turns the flesh to gel. He couldn't wait long enough to save up another seven. Not after coming here and seeing her up close. If he left without her, he'd lose his nerve, probably spend most of the cash on booze, trying to forget about the whole thing.

"What can I get for that?" he asked, his voice dry and cracked. She thought about it several seconds.

"One year unlimited usage license, renewable or upgradable at added cost."

"Whatever. I'll take it." Bo didn't even have to consider the options. He could come up with the other seven in a year's time, maybe. What mattered was having her, now. Janet filled in the license agreement and coded the init disk while Abbe bagged the purchase. Somehow, Bo had imagined her coming gift wrapped, not tucked into a brown paper bag. Seeing her face there, shadowed by the coarse, unbleached paper, a touch of reality tickled at the back of Bo's mind. After all, she was just a program . . .

"Good call, kid. You'll like her. She learns how to be the lay of your lifetime. Anything you want, she does it. Here you go." Abbe handed him the bag, and the clean smell of him broke the morbid spiral of Bo's thoughts. He took the bag and left, glancing back once to wave, awkwardly, at Janet and Abbe, deep down, perhaps, wondering what they thought of him.

Outside, in the fading heat, he turned down the block to avoid the gauntlet of pimps and pushers. A bus was just pulling to a stop at the corner, and he dashed to make it, slipping through the doors as the old diesel groaned away from the curb. He ran his pass through the reader and slipped to the back of the bus. He was alone there except for a small, slightly heavy blonde woman in a business suit and white sneakers, who was reading a self-help guide to AIC interfacing. She didn't even look up when Bo collapsed to the seat across from her.

It was full dark outside, or as dark as Boston ever gets at night, the humidity like a curtain dimming the streetlights. All the lights were out on the bus, but Bo could still see to read. He pulled her package from the bag and started going over every detail, the specs on the back, the advertisers' pitch on either side. He'd seen it all in the magazine ads. Then, on the front, he stared several long, breathless seconds into her eyes.

I'm just going to read the documentation, he swore to himself. Just the docs. He slipped the tip of his pocket knife into a crease in the cellophane wrapper, slit it all the way around the bottom, and slid the top slowly off the box. A breath of flowers, gardenias and lilacs, rich but too sweet, drifted up to him from the perfumed papers inside. Bo would have thought it tacky, had he not been so thoroughly enthralled. Wrapped in another cellophane bag, tucked under the curled and creased paperwork, she was there. Not much to look at, just a shiny gold and green ROM disk and a plastic-coated magnetic RAM, sandwiching a thick black MASIC wafer. The plastic mounting piece was the same color as the ROM. Without a second thought, he broke his oath, reached into his canvas bag, and pulled out his 'Face.

The slim black case was no thicker than an old cassette player, with one slender wire that snaked back to a power cell in Bo's bag and another thicker wire with a gold, brush-shaped probe attached to the end. Bo pulled aside his hair and flipped open the cover of his jack with the same quick, casual ease as someone pops out a contact lens. An electric tingle ran across the base of his scalp as he slid the probe in and secured it with a half-twist.

Being wired was like being inside the TV looking out, like being the electron, fired toward the phosphor screen and becoming part of the image. Being wired was visual, aural, olfactory, tactile. So wonderfully tactile. Even the startup routine was a caress that ran the length of his body, the light, tender touch of a friend that would have tickled if it hadn't felt so good. It was the breath of a lover on bare skin, a mother touching the cheek of her sleeping child. All by itself, it was worth the risks of wiring, worth the loneliness of nights lost on the net, the madness, the days when the headaches made his vision turn red.

Bo ran his imprinted thumb over a hidden sensor, and a panel slid away with a barely audible sigh. He fit the media into the slot, and the gold plastic mounting clip came away in his hand. He fed the thumbnail-sized init disk into another slot and waited. Words in red floated in his lower peripheral vision, seen as if through the lens of tears.

Configuring to Aminoff-4 interface . . . stand by . . .

Then she was beside him, quiet and prim, reading a book of poetry. His eyes wandered over her, soaking in the details of her smooth, pale wrists, the thick tweed of her skirt, the blue-black sheen of her hair. She glanced at him out of the corner of her eye, and she smiled.

Hello? Her voice was much lower than he'd imagined, and soft as a down comforter in winter. There was more, though, a depth of understanding and a predisposition to laughter.

"What are you reading?" He became self-conscious about trying to look over her shoulder and scooted away, putting most of a seat between them. His eyes fixed on a blemish in the blue plastic of the bench where he'd just been sitting.

It's Rimbaud.

"Oh." One of the hot bands on the club set was making fistfuls of loot reading Rimbaud's poetry while playing ragged jazz and electric guitar solos. Bo thought they sounded like posers, so he never listened. But he still recognized the name.

I'm Sarah-Belle. I prefer just Sarah. Her voice drew his eyes up from the seat to her own, and something passed between them, some exchange of trust that Bo knew, deep down, was simply excellent programming. It caught him off guard, and he opened up to her without another thought. He smiled, for the first time in longer than he could remember.

"My name's Jack, but I go by Bo."

Voulez-vous être mon beau? His 'Face subtitled it for him in yellow, just below her lips.

"Don't speak French," he said anyway. "I don't like the way it sounds." There was the barest pause, a slight flicker around the edges of her cheeks, a minor realignment of her straight, dark brow. Bo glanced down, and her book was Donne instead.

"Make love to me." He said it almost before he knew he was going to. The look on her face was an intermingling of amusement, interest, indignation and irritation. He felt somehow he'd broken the rules, and even after he consciously realized the rules were his to make, he still felt uncomfortable under the study of her clear blue-gray eyes.

Here? I don't think that's a good idea.

"Yes, here." He'd said it, and though he wanted to back down, he couldn't. He wouldn't be chastised by a circuit board, even if it was a Turing chip and probably smarter than he was.

Here? she asked again, teasing him with the unspoken promise in her voice. She ran one finger down the side of his neck, and with the other hand, she began untying the sleeves of his fatigue shirt. *Right here? Are you sure? I've never done anything like this before.*

In the lower left of his vision, a single pale icon appeared, pulsing every several seconds, DaVinci's Balanced Man, an indication from his 'Face that he'd entered a much deeper level of input, direct to the tactile centers of his brain. Everything that happened, while it was lit, would be confined to the spaces of his mind, every spoken word, every touch, every kiss. Like a dream, but a dream that paralyzed his voluntary nervous system. His awareness of the world faded to peripheral. Only a few telltale twitches betrayed the activity taking place in the small black box and in his mind.

Bo started to speak, but Sarah silenced him with a kiss, and her lips were soft, forgiving. She had the kiss of someone who smiled often, a kiss that gave way under his, that parted for him and drew him in deep, the softest, most passionate kiss he'd ever had. It relaxed him and drove him to the edge of panic all at once. His pulse pounded in his neck, in his temples, but he felt secure, warm, and content. The kiss said she loved him.

Without breaking the kiss, she slipped onto his lap, wrapped her arms around his neck, ran her fingers through his hair, across his cheek, down his chest. She touched his right thigh, tingling where in reality he had only numb scar tissue. Slowly her fingers walked up the front of his jeans to the zipper, touching lightly, teasing, exploring, finding. She pressed her hand against him, squeezed him through the ragged denim. Bo felt release at last, and he let out a small, whimpering moan.

Sarah broke the kiss, pulled back enough she could see his eyes. Her smile was sly, but her eyes were delighted. With her fingertips, she stroked him firmly, and he tried to smile before embarrassment got the better of him.

We're going to have to do something about this, she said, and burst into laughter as he sheepishly rolled his eyes. Her laugh was as light as sunshine after a cloudburst, but at the same time just a bit silly, and still heartfelt. It reassured him, told him she was not laughing at him but because he made her happy. Bo melted into her laughter, closed his eyes and savored the sound as much as the sweet taste of her mouth that lingered on his lips.

She unzipped his jeans with both hands, took care that nothing caught or snagged. She spread her skirt over his lap and settled onto him, unbuttoned her white blouse, revealed small, round breasts, pale as clouds, and peach nipples. Sarah paused when she saw the expectant, frightened, slightly horrified look on Bo's face. Sarah winked and smiled a slow easy smile.

Hey there.

"Hey." He smiled back and knew he was ready. She threw her head back and slid onto him with a pleased moan. A tingle ran down the length of Bo's body, arched his back, tightened every muscle. Microcurrents ran the length of his body, analog touch poured directly into his brain. Her scent drifted up to him, floral and spicy, enticing. She was there, and she was wonderful. Sarah rocked back and forth, smiling, eyes closed. Bo found the pleasure she took from him more erotic, more stimulating, than the feel of her. She made love to his ego, and it drove him over the edge. She collapsed onto him, her head on his shoulder, and kissed his neck. Sarah kept him afterward, squeezing him with quick, tight squeezes that sent a new wave of endorphins flushing through his body.

Finally, she sat back, let Bo look at her, let his eyes and his mind drink in the woman who had just made love to him. Her hair cascaded around her shoulders like dark silk. For the first time Bo touched her face, found it warm and smooth, her hair soft as cashmere. Sarah turned to kiss his palm before she spoke.

Isn't your stop soon?

"I think we passed it."

Oh. Sarah gave him a quick kiss on the lips and winked out suddenly, reappearing beside him prim and immaculate once again. The thin volume of Donne lay beneath her folded hands, and she looked exactly as she had before except for the sated smile and casually flirtatious wink she gave him. The DaVinci icon faded, and Bo was free to move once more.

He started to get up and felt the slick, sticky wetness soaking through his jeans. He pulled his rucksack across his lap, blushing a deep scarlet. He hit the bell and yelled for the rear door.

"You said it was a bad idea, didn't you."

It's okay. Sarah caressed his shoulder through the thin cotton of his T-shirt. She broke into a broad, enthusiastic grin and rolled her eyes. *Okay? It was great!* They both laughed as the bus squealed to a stop several blocks west of Bo's apartment.

As he bounded down the steps and into the damp, oppressive Boston night, Bo heard the blonde woman mutter, "Wire-head freak." Her epithet drove home the reality to him, that Sarah was just a program, that he was a loser stuck in a fantasy. Then Sarah took his hand, and they walked home together, strolling and chatting like long-time lovers. By the time they reached his place, he'd made the unconscious decision that whatever they had together beat the hell out of his reality apart.

"Gotta turn you off," Bo said when they reached the door. "Ron goes batshit if I wire in the house, and we've been fighting all day." Before she could speak, he thumbed the power stud and unjacked, then stuffed the 'Face back in his rucksack.

The apartment was nearly empty when he opened the door. A couple pillows on the floor and milk crates used as a table. All of Ron's AV gear was gone, as was his computer and the beatup brown sofa where Bo sometimes fell asleep. Bare hardwood floors littered with empty fast-food drink cups and microwave burrito wrappers greeted Bo and informed him that something was very wrong. He checked the door again to make sure it had been locked. It was.

"Hey, Ron?" Bo checked his room, found it as he'd left it, then checked Ron's. The futon was still there, but the tangle of silk sheets was gone. The house plants and bookshelves no longer filled the corners. Bo's footsteps echoed off the bare plaster walls. "That bastard."

Bo found a note on the refrigerator. "Bo, gotta jam. Moved in with Elisa. Later." He'd emptied the fridge, too. Bo went to his room and curled up in the pile of blankets on his bed. He didn't feel like changing clothes or showering, just sleeping it off and worrying in the morning. Worry refused to wait, and after staring at the water marks on his ceiling for almost an hour, he reached for his ruck, for the comfort of her company.

Hey, tiger.

Sarah wore a white silk camisole that reached mid-thigh and fell loosely across her breasts. When she dropped to her hands and knees to kiss him, it dropped away from her, and Bo saw all the way down the pale, tight curve of her belly. Her body stirred something inside him, but instead, he said, "Can we just talk?"

What's up? She flickered at the edges again before settling down beside him in a half-lotus. She wore an I-Love-NY nightshirt which she pulled down over her knees.

"Ron moved out. No notice or anything." Bo pulled a pillow into his lap and hugged it tight. "He was a real shit, but at least he was company. And I needed him to pay the rent."

Well, we can find you another roommate, right?

"I hope so." For a while, Bo just stared off across the room, realizing after a while he was gazing at the stacks of AIC and MASIC disks piled in a milk crate in his closet. He could sell off most of it and pay for another month, if he got ten cents on the dollar for his original investment. He'd have to find a real sucker to pay those prices for unlicensed disks. He considered selling his 'Face and paying for a half-year, in advance, or taking Sarah back and using the cash to get out of the city, move some place cheaper. He regretted throwing the suit's business card away, even though he could probably find the guy again if he tried.

I'll help you find something. In the morning. Come to bed with me, Bo? You need rest.

"Sarah, why are you so good to me?"

She didn't answer for a while, long enough that Bo wondered if he'd hit a glitch in the softsoft. *You make me laugh. I like being with you. I don't exist without you.* She took his hand in both of hers, her touch warming and reassuring. She made him feel needed.

"I guess you don't." Somehow, her need for him felt like a responsibility, a reason to work it out. He knew he'd been smudging the line all evening, and finally physical reality was merging with volitive reality somewhere in the wire. He knew better than to lose touch, but in the end, it didn't matter to him all that much. "I'm really screwed."

We'll come up with something. I'll help you. You have unlimited usage, remember? I'm not just some AIC-format slut. I think. And I'm clever. She kissed his neck, insistent. *Come to bed?*

Suddenly, physical and emotional exhaustion pulled at his limbs, insistent. "You're right. I need to sleep."

He rolled over and reached for the power stud on the 'Face black box, but Sarah stopped him with a hand on his shoulder. *No. I don't like it when you turn me off,* she said. She curled up tightly beside him, and the DaVinci icon faded into his vision. *Leave the power on. I need to think.*

Joel Dailey

PROGRESSIVE
LIGHTING

AT BIRTH I was fortunate to be blessed with the largest phallus on record at Southern Baptist Hospital, New Orleans. The exact measurement of my much-exclaimed-over member would both astonish and embarrass you, so out of discretion and since this is a serious literary work, I will refrain from naming the actual figure . . .

Moments after my birth a surrounding gaggle of nurses alternately giggled and cooed, tape measures at arms' length, or so I have been informed. To this day I maintain it a falsehood that later that night one adventurous nurse crept through the hospital corridors to my cribside and, through ardent application of professional skills for which there is no appropriate degree conferred, encouraged me to full erection, so amusing herself, not to mention hours-old me, till dawn interrupted our lusty liaison . . .

You may be wholly unaware of this, so allow me to clue you in: being in possession of a humongous penis, sometimes stiff, mostly limp, is not entirely a picnic in cutoffs near dusk . . .

Years later, my wife, did I mention I married the richest woman in the state of Louisiana?, died tragically in a skiing accident. She loved to be seen on the slopes, but as I pointed out to Beverly on several occasions, post-coitus, she simply had no aptitude for shooshing . . .

No, shooshing was not Bev's strong point, lovemaking was. She married me for one single, tumescent reason. Day, night, in front seats, on limo floors, on tricycles, on handlebars, fern bars, wet bars, dry bars, S & M bars, or candy bars, Beverly would give me The Look, snap her wealthy fingers, bark, "Let's do it!"

On such occasions there was no stopping us. We did it over and over. We did it so many times, so often, in so many places . . . There were times, I swear, when we even did it while we were doing it . . .

Beverly demanded first syllable arousal.

Snap!

"Let's do it!" And I'd be See Rock City, stroke the local sky-scraper . . .

All that happened in a swirl. Bev was drawn to those slopes, the mountain ranges . . . I was nowhere near the accident scene, as I have testified under oath repeatedly. All rumors to the contrary, spread by the press and sick individuals who somehow haven't yet received their press credentials, are flagrant lies. These complete knob heads from the start of our idyllic romantic association have attempted to pull my wife and I asunder . . .

Did I mention my irresistible impulse to scarf down stale grocery store bought chocolate cakes, three at a clip?

It's true, and if you could but view them for yourself, you would readily agree; my wife's surviving relatives closely resemble pigs who want immediate butchering. Hogs, sows, arms, a symphony thereof, dagger lightning . . .

My wife's Final Will and Testament, generously and primarily mentioning her beloved, that's me, slalomed out of Probate, and I, suddenly the richest hombre in the state of Louisiana, the "Sportsman's Paradise" as the license plates proclaim, I quickly skedaddled . . .

Would you care to familiarize yourself with my complete dental history? Just say the word; I can fax it out in less than a jiff . . .

After months of travel, of cosmic hemming and hawing, after dark weeks and weekends of bottomless Weltschmerz, I woke to find myself ensconced in a tiny Bulgarian village hotel. Lickety-split, I slapped together creative financing and threw open the freshly painted doors, green, of my own educational venture, THE TONYA HARDING INSTITUTE OF WHITE TRASH OBEDIENCE AND DISINGENUOUS CHARM. You ought to see that translated into Bulgarian!

O many's the inspiring love song I've played upon my love muscle for my throngs of Bulgarian lovers . . .

The Institute took off like an exaltation of larks with the Bulgarian people. Framed on my office wall, black velvet background, gold trim, and right behind me as I'm writing, is the following observation, to which I owe so much, "Never Underestimate a Bulgarian."

Have I revealed that green is my favorite color? If so, please disregard this extraneous point of information. Not to worry; no extra charge . . .

Yes, grateful, rather graceless, Bulgarians in desperate need of obedience training flocked to the Institute with such regularity and in such demanding numbers that we went franchise all over eastern Europe in less than a calendar year.

Those first weeks of instruction are especially fixed in my memory. Even now I can see the tenderfoot Bulgarian pupils forced to run the gauntlet, comprised of our aggressive teaching staff, thereby receiving their appropriate moral spankings multiplied times thirty-six with complete and unabridged sets of the Oxford English Dictionary balanced atop their shaven heads.

Now if that's not coaxing obedience and charm, what is? Only months later did it occur to me that perhaps there was an Oxford Bulgarian Dictionary . . .

Did I inform you that I'm a very spontaneous person, especially in an elevator . . .

Now that I'm even wealthier and I've turned daily operation of THE TONYA HARDING INSTITUTE OF WHITE TRASH OBEDIENCE AND DISINGENUOUS CHARM empire over to competent bureaucrats and managerial types who are under finger-close 24 hour surveillance, I have shifted my attention to writing. It is my belief that a high percentile of my essence, my self, exists in the words presently cradled in your hands . . .

After being born with such an award-winning sexual organ, First Place in the *Guinness Book of World Records*, Length, after having wedded the richest woman in the state of Louisiana and having stood at her gravesite and inherited her vast financial holdings, despite the legal objections of her pathetic, whining relatives, and after having fathered THE TONYA HARDING INSTITUTE OF WHITE TRASH OBEDIENCE AND DISINGENUOUS CHARM, and made it a rousing global success, my next goal is to become immortal, to insert myself, via these words, into your brain, into all brains worldwide, permanently.

Did I tell you I abhor table tennis?

Robert Gluck

From

JACK THE MODERNIST

1. A MAN PASSING grazes my right nipple; he hears my gasp and returns interested. He traces a voluptuous circle around the nipple; a line of feeling shoots into my chest like the smell of gasoline. He looks at my face hard, meaning he means it, then at the nipple. First there's a membrane that wants a caress: the rest is history. Do I describe his face?—two dots and a line. He's giving me an erection—that interests him. I asked my dad about nipples and he said yes, that's why he always wears cotton T-shirts, even cotton irritates them: During puberty I could make myself come by caressing my nipples if toward the end I laid one finger on my cock. The man who is interested tongues my left one; it makes a hot entrance into his mouth and then he sucks the hard tip in and out gently and patiently between his teeth: it causes air to rush through me. I fondle his hair and ears, I love him so much I would do anything he asked me to, my arms are weak.

His thumbnail lightly skirts the tip of the right one again and again; pleasure sets up the roll of a snare drum in my teeth, in the membrane under my cockhead and around my asshole—pleasure so aggressively familiar it registers as an affront and my chest is about to cry or shout out as though deeply refusing again and again increasingly released. The erect tip, faded pink, my nipple's leader, stands out against its rose circle; it has become the farthest point of me; sometimes when I eat chocolate my nipples get hard and the hairs around them stand up. I always admired nipples like Jack's—two dimes casually dropped on a table—my own are such peonies. When this man pinches and kneads and mistreats them—I always knew he was a heartless beast, they *act* like they love you, sure, and you end up bruised and sore—the sensation was confined to my nipples and I negotiated the pain into an even stronger and more telling happiness.

2. YOU'RE not a lover till you blab about it. From earliest memory I've been excited and lonely, like a membrane that needs a caress during lovemaking, one caress and then another. I met Jack at a forum in April 1981; we exchanged eyes during the presentation while his arm draped around the back of the empty chair next to him as though it were a boyfriend. He cocked his head and a two-day growth outlined a high delicate cheek; my life was bereft of that contour. During intermission my face lit up but he bounded past and wrapped a man in a bear hug that rocked them back and forth. Jack was short but he expanded, surrounding this man whose face, pinned against Jack's shoulder, suffused with pleasure and embarrassment. Jack's friend was suddenly famous. His struggle to disappear made him the center of attention; he didn't know what to do with his eyes and he tottered back a little when Jack released him.

I leaned against a door, thumbs hooked in my belt loops and forefingers starting two paths that converged in my crotch. I thought, "Now I'm really alone." The combined effect was supposed to register as passionate narrowed eyes clicking toward Jack on flamenco heels: Jack nodded and I parlayed tension into a few sentences about the forum. He replied, "The Right correctly feels we threaten its unconscious life."

I said, "My flat's a few blocks away."

Jack looked past me, smiling into the crowd. "Let's read the *Divine Comedy* together out loud."

"Jack, we hardly know each other—how about some TV and then sex?" We settled on a walk.

The next day he knocked at three-thirty but it was still spring weather. Yellow sunlight fell on his face; I touched the indentation above his lip, breathless. We took Lily, a big dreamy dog who lived the walk so keenly it became hers. I concentrated on Jack: Prep school and Harvard accounted for my pleasurable fear and his overalls and red chamois shirt; I knew others who used poverty for depth. In New York he worked in a famous theater troupe: "We pissed on stage and took our clothes off." My libido rushed forward to claim that information. I guessed forty by the skin on his hands. I talked brilliantly; he must be a good director, I thought, if he can enlarge people this way.

Lily checked resumes too—inhaled them from hubcaps and the corners of buildings, from strangers who stooped to admire her blond tail and ruff, her apricot ears. She scouted bones and delicious dabs of filth, slyly eyed children's ice cream cones, frankly implored construction workers in orange hats who sat on the sidewalk crosslegged behind their open lunchboxes; she searched their faces, trying to locate an invitation, eyes misting before the giant concept (fragrance) of chicken and ham.

"You'd be a fool to pass me up, Jack."

Jack's features attempted a graceful bow off his face. He was small, slender, barrel chested, descended from French Jews. He looked like a sparrow, glossy black curls the color of raisins, bright black eyes and for a beak the small blade of a pocket knife, the likeness enhanced by a tendency to bounce on his toes. Or his face resembled a maraschino cherry, full of refined pep. I was so attracted I was bursting with news, personal news to launch intimacy—to put my hand where his body caught and softened the denim, for that to be a destination—so I recited my catalogue of ships: "Two blacks, one Puerto Rican, two Irish Catholics (one of them went on to S/M—he'd always said 'You can do whatever you want to me'—wasn't I already doing everything I wanted? Later he appeared with black eyes, etc.—he had great legs), one German Catholic, two WASPS (one was Episcopalian, the other from Los Angeles), one Japanese-German, one Marxist Art Historian, one Chinese, one Italian and three little Jews. Jack, I always had a soft spot for little Jews with big noses, maybe because of my first lover; I loved Andy so intensely I used to wonder if I would be scarred. When he left the apartment I gathered up his cigarette butts and smoked them even though I didn't smoke. During puberty I kept hoping my nose would grow big. Everyone else in my neighborhood had a big nose."

Jack's eyes *twinkled*. "You can't depend on those biological clocks—don't stop trying, Bob—you may still get one."

"Jack, I try. I answered a sex ad from the *Advocate*. The guy wrote 'For Love' and went on to describe himself as a small Jewish dancer. What could be nicer? When we met, he turned out to be a converted Jew. His nose was Portuguese from Salinas but he learned Hebrew and lived in Israel and he choreographed ballets based on Jewish legends like the Dybbuk. He had great turn-out during orgasm. I think we made each other nervous. I would say, 'There's a Jew in this bed!' And we wouldn't know if I meant a fallen Jew (me) or a believing Jew (him) or a real Jew (me) or a fake Jew (him). When he dumped me I wanted to sue for false advertising."

I opened up in Jack a territory named Bob; I anticipated in me a sister city named Jack. He replied, "I want a black lover—that's one reason I attended the forum." He submitted this obstacle to our romance with the cheerful heartlessness of a folk tale. At once

I was tired of my past and where it led me—a boring melancholy that trained me to be good at death. I'd exhausted my possibilities and nothing new started up; I could see why people kill themselves. My jurist's voice countered, It's not a *big* deal, and I had to agree: my writing's okay, friends, teaching. Writing, sex, money, friends—as we walked along I felt a vague guilt—I hadn't done justice to my experience. I wanted to trade on it, shabby currency. The way I told these stories exhausted me and I saw my lovers as a form of stasis. To make it more lifelike, I'd gladly have given a statue the past and the sarcasm.

A jay chided, aggressive. The aroma of wild fennel, a lure. A sportscar drove by, an impulse. Lily chased a cat, fun. We stepped off the curb. Our elbows touched, a hinge. Pieces of fog hung in a tree, perception. We walked across some grass—pastoral—and talked about the past—pastoral-historical. When we passed La Victoria the sky was parquetry of beaten gold. Our walk tired me out with its little steps; I wanted to take one giant step across town and into Jack.

"I'm sorry my list is so short, I was with Ed (Japanese-German) for eight years." Identity seemed remote as the village our grandmothers came from. Ethnicity, storytelling—my lovers sounded like so many flavors, strawberry, lemon, lime . . . "How about you Jack?"

"What about me?"

"Tell me where you've been, who you've seen, how they looked, and what they said."

"I had two lovers, one for six months, the other for a year."

"Two?"

"That's it."

"Two brief loves in a man of forty."

"I'm thirty-four and I never met the right individual."

"You seem to know everyone."

If Jack described the other, I can't remember; something about a playwright or a producer, a nice guy. I only remember Joe-Toe.

"Joe-Toe is an actor who left a few months ago for New York, which to an actor equals breathing. What an actor means to New York is more like another sneeze for which someone may or may not bless you. I gave him the name Joe-Toe when I was teaching him to pronounce Giotto in a play I directed. He takes baths hot enough to make steam." He rubbed (meditatively?) his two-day growth and his eyes relaxed on the distance. I figured they were still involved.

"Is he handsome?"

"Not really, he's funny looking." Spoken with a lover's pride, I thought.

The buildings we passed were mostly nineteenth-century gingerbread and they understood each other in a cozy and irrelevant way that excluded their inhabitants and faltered before the existential glamor of a tract house or highrise. Jack lived in one of those bleak Victorian slag heaps around General Hospital, but the old staircase with redwood wainscoting remained and each landing had a lamp of hammered brass and stained glass. The first two were lit against the twilight but Jack's landing was dark. He hunted for his key, then knocked. Jack's roommate opened. Lily exploded into a blur of huffing and wagging and shot past him into the flat. She made a beeline down the hall and into a room where some finches cried out in alarm and bashed themselves again and again against the bars on the far side of their world, their voices piping a bright feeble terror. They had dark blue tails, red bills, baby blue sides and they gave off an odor of sage.

I caught Lily's neck and Jack held her rump—then he told the birds to sing for me, as though they were canaries! Lily's eyes rolled back in voluptuousness and she licked her chops with a moist pink tongue. We dragged her away, closed a door and outside that door she remained, titillated, absorbed, her downcast eyes conveying an impression of unseeing abstraction. Later, when I passed her on my way to the toilet, she turned away from my caress, unwilling to be distracted. Jack's roommate was a

British law student studying for the Boards. He immediately vanished but his anxious smiles and incomplete gestures permeated the flat. Jack went into the kitchen to pour us wine. The kitchen was yellow—its cheerfulness more an academic point. The color said "Life is Great" but was contradicted by shabby cupboards, weary linoleum, chipped dishes and cookbooks shelved too high for use. I explored his bedroom.

It was on the sunset side. Two windows spilled amber light onto four walls of books, a bed, a beige chenille bedspread, a small hill of brown corduroy pillows, a drafting table with a high stool and a file cabinet. The room smelled like chocolate, a sweet smell of books. I explored further: an analytical spirit asserted itself in the face of Jack's bed and the oblivion I intended to enjoy there. Self-preservation advised me to act fast, but there was nothing in the papers on his drafting table except for his handwriting. It was amazingly sleek and deliberate as set type: the y's descended and the r's ascended, flags and pennants. I could love that. I couldn't understand how he earned a living. From an envelope I learned his name was John. Jack was a nickname. I relished it: *Jack* is so flat, like a flat rock or a landing strip between the flights a sentence can make. I could love that. I was against his boots, they supplied a false amount of height to his small frame and made him bottom heavy. He had only overalls, the good pair and the bad pair. He covered his bulletin board with quotations and the heads of friends. His hair parted at the back. Soft clear voice. His eyes twinkled when he smiled because they scrunched up, gathering their liquid onto a smaller surface. Herbal toothpaste. A file cabinet. Small hands and feet. I figured that would stand me in good stead. I figured he would teach me and encourage me and smooth out my hysteria and distress. His library appealed to me as a source of great potential energy. The books stood two deep, shelved with a free hand—mighty classics and plenty of books I'd never heard of sped up my heart with their flirtatious glances. Then they lost their individual contents and became comprehension and speed. My throat tightened with a pang for the new life. I felt seasick. Many of the books I opened were signed by the authors and inscribed with a friendly note to Jack; in all of them Jack had circled passages. I love intelligence and eagerly fetishized Jack's; I half-reclined like a starlet. He returned with a glass in each hand and sang to the books, "You made me love you, I didn't wanna do it, I didn't wanna do it." He was addressing civilization.

"What do you trust?"

"Not who but what? Jack, I trust gossip."

Jack sat next to me; he looked worried, said, "Gossip is crude." I reasoned that the depth he missed in a single story could be found collectively in a hundred. He cocked his head, attentive, so I became interesting. "The people who know your story are as important as the plot. Gossip registers the difference between a story one person knows and everyone knows, between one person's story and everyone's. Or it's a mythology, gods and goddesses, a community and a future."

Jack took my hand. That was exciting. I finally stopped smiling, let desire bewilder and reorganize us. He asked, "What do you mean by community?"

"Ecstatic sexuality."

"Whew."

Sex was the reply to any question. Jack was problematic but great potential; he saw our relationship as the development of raw material. "Let's do exercises together." "Let's study conversational French." Svengali dives into Trilby's mouth, draws back astonished and cries, *Your palate is like the vault of a cathedral!* I wanted my soul thrilled—Jack was the man for the job. He talked freely and openly on every topic (but himself), displaying technique and an acquaintance not only with the world's knowledge but with its wisdom, which he circled. Jack swirled a purple crescent at the bottom of his glass, a sliver of wine slid down his throat, tannic. I wanted to follow. It would be a light comedy to pair myself again, the witty gravitational weights and balances of the twin star a couple makes. Still, I ached for Jack to engulf me and rewrite my life in bolder script. The tenderness I felt for him would chart out that impulse. There wasn't a single sentence that equaled the tenderness I intended Jack to bear me: only shared gestures over a period of time could express it.

I laid my tongue—my whole body—on his lower lip. We looked better without clothes. It was getting dark. We frenched for a while and then tipped backward onto the bed. I opened his hand and kissed his palm because my life seemed bereft of passion. Jack turned away—rightly I admitted. His hand slipped around my waist, a firmer pressure meant roll over, then it lightly skirted my ass. I didn't dare feel that much pleasure. I changed the subject by taking his cock in my mouth, leaning over him, absorbed as though he were a difficult book. I liked his cock, it had the clear smell of cut grass and it was refined as his other features so I could take it in easily. Each time I drew my tongue along the shaft a discreet spasm crossed his face; suddenly he sat up and broke into pieces, faced all directions at once; I thought Jack was starting to cry. It filled me with wonder. His face dangled midair, features rotating separately like the parts of a mobile, then he literally pulled himself together, nose, ears, two eyes, mouth. He stretched out on top of me and whispered, "Put your hand on my lower back, lower, that's it, now the other on the back of my lungs." I rose to any of Jack's occasions—I started to kid but he turned his head away and didn't speak; he initiated a long silence whose mournfulness I shared but couldn't interpret. I could have said, I love you. Jack's weight was like agreement. Beneath my hands his breath became sharp and fast.

Although I like to pitch and catch, I just wanted Jack *in* me. Accepting my body and the world took that form. His cock kept alternating between stiff and flaccid, a weathervane constantly shifting as we framed and reframed our attraction. We eroticized a finely honed attention which challenged terms as soon as our bodies invented them, which addressed my sudden shifts of context, his mid-gesture costume changes. Instead of an oceanic welling with its always-in-the-future-until-it's-in-the-past crescendo, we remained moment by moment; we aroused Choice, crowned Wit—a woman can curtsy, a man can remove the hat from his head with a grand gesture while bowing elaborately—Wit, Choice, and the Particulars. Our attraction for each other expressed itself as a problem to be solved, a topiary maze, each new distinction a turn in the inquiry until the pleasure grew so intense I had to look away. I would call that first lovemaking *dusky*, we kept slipping through each other's hands—hide and seek by moonlight—it was charming.

It charmed me; we ate, talked, showered, slept, more talk, more sleep, tomorrow, four or five nights a week, and for the first time since puberty my body was at rest. Jack simply converted without resistance or even a mood swing. When he called me up I felt like a contest winner. "It's Jack. Want to go to dinner, a gallery, demo, movie, party, concert, café?"—whose worth we did or didn't agree on but with the same understanding and pitch; or Jack said "great" and I said "stupid" but to Denise and Bruce I found myself saying, "a masterpiece." I could grapple and I could surrender—that meant a lot to me. I pictured me at my full height and I intrigued and even aroused myself; teary and improvisational, I looked for developments that equaled my mood and waited to see what I would do next.

This concludes the first chapter of a love affair told with infinite safety from my house to yours, first person. From that beginning an image of Jack remains that continues to define tenderness for me. Two cups and two plates, blue and white, disappear along with the pine table and the kitchen and the hall and the living room when I turn off lights one by one as though I were dispensing with every part of my life except Jack, lit by the 60-watt next to my bed. Jack, already a legend, lies on his back, sheet up to his waist, hands clasped behind his head, nipples—whole notes—

floating above his rib cage, a vertical line of black curls insisting on symmetry, arms with their perfect flex, arms making delicate wings. He's hot—he's calmly waiting to have sex: I climb up beside him, pull back the sheet and run my hand along his hip. Suddenly everything shifts, his thigh moves with my hand, his buttocks shift down and toward me voluptuously and at the same time he sighs as his hip tips sideways like an Indian god, his balls slip over each other and his cock slides across dark curls. I feel very grateful. His breath is stepped up, lips parted and already a bit swollen, chest expanded, skin smoothed out, nipples whirling like gyroscopes—I want to cup them in my hand—whatever I do they will continue in suspension and motion—lips, skin and nipples taking on their sexual meaning, his dark eyes lively, interested, interpretive.

Shar Rednour

MEOW?

STEL PLAYS GUITAR in a local dyke band—actually, it's a band with two butch women, one baby dyke (yet to claim a description other than "eager" or "kid-in-a-candy-store") and two men—one heterosexual transvestite in pumps and on drums, and a beautiful gay queen on bass. You might have heard of them; they're quite popular. Stel's totally hot on stage and has half the town waiting for her next show. So, Stel plays guitar, mostly at her house or at Siddy's (her girl's).

To play at Siddy's, she sits in Siddy's hanging wicker chair while Siddy does her stuff. Siddy's job? Well, Stel would probably lose the newlyweds; because, when asked, she would say that mostly Siddy tells people what to do and how to do it. She can definitely be bossy at times. Siddy talks on one of her phones as she walks through the house, her silk robe flowing behind her lean dark legs, drinking a martini. Stel likes girls who drink martinis, though she can't say she's dated that many.

But working isn't what Stel likes to watch Siddy do as she ponders new songs; no, Stel likes to watch Siddy—it always seems like Sunday afternoons—do her girly stuff. Siddy sits in the sun on her rose comforter manicuring her toenails and fingernails, polishing them with various layers of paint and rubbing scented creams into her feet and elbows.

Like a cat, Siddy's so prissy, prissy and clean. She would lick herself if she could, and if she could lick herself, she would do it all day long—spreading her legs wide in the sun so that it shone into her pussy.

Much of Siddy's grooming is done behind closed doors; and, although she doesn't yell if unspoken rules are broken, Siddy makes it clear that Stel must knock before entering a bathroom. Stel, of course, would do nothing less than give a femme room to preen; after all, who reaps the rewards? One time, though, she was already in the bathroom and opened the shower door to find Siddy perched on the toilet, her eyes half-closed and a serene smile on her face.

"Oh, honey, you look so pretty when you pee," Stel said, reaching for a towel.

Siddy smiled bigger, but then pouted a little. "You don't need to see me pee."

Stel bent down and kissed her. "Why don't you pee on me?"

Siddy stamped her foot, "Get out, get out, get out! I need to finish peeing! Go away! I'm not going to pee on you!"

"Oh, please, just in my hand." Stel sort of laughed as she left the bathroom.

Siddy slammed the door and Stel heard from the other side "No! I can't even pee if you listen. Now, get away so I can finish!"

QUITE a few of Siddy's personal quirks reminded Stel of a cat, but she didn't really add it all up until one night—the first time she let Siddy tie her up.

Stel was tied up, spread across the bed face up, and Siddy was being especially evil. Not with pain—no, Stel can take pain—but with teases and taunts. After securely hooking the restraints to the headboard of the bed, she disappeared into her closet then came out in a shiny dark purple G-string and her plum suede thigh-high boots. With one quick but quiet leap, she was over Stel. She put her knee between Stel's legs. Supported by her arms, she hovered close above Stel. Purring into her ear, Siddy nibbled on her neck and shoulders softly, then bit hard. Every touch was light, like a breath or the wind. Goose bumps soon covered Stel's flesh in trails following Siddy's mouth, fingertips, nails, or hair.

Siddy leaned back onto her heels, and whipped her head around a few times, ran her tongue across her teeth so that Stel saw her fierceness. But just as Stel thought she was going to touch her hard, Siddy bent down and simply trailed her braids across her stomach. Siddy's mouth paused above Stel's pussy. Then she put her lips just barely against the hair, and with hot, puffy breaths said, "Oh, you want to be touched?" Siddy's mouth curled up on one side. Her eyes lifted slowly to meet Stel's while the rest of her didn't move an inch. Stel could still feel her breath against her pussy. At least five thoughts were colliding in her brain, and Stel opened her mouth; but before anything came out Siddy said, "Don't you want to see me stick out my tongue and . . . *lick?*"

Stel thought, *Oh, yeah, bitch, here, lick!* She realized that she simply had to thrust her hips up one millimeter, and Siddy's mouth would be on her. Siddy must have read Stel's mind because she closed her mouth, lifted her chin a bit, and nodded side to side. "Tsk-tsk, what evil thoughts you have . . . See why I have to tie you up!" She laughed, leaned back, and resumed her tickles and torture.

Stel's forearms tensed as she fought against herself—primally, instinctively her arms raised to rip the leather and chains and the goddamn bed out of the wall, to grab Siddy by those queenie braids and force her head down and her ass up then fuck her 'til she cried. But those same muscles fought to hold back as Stel's head kept cool and said *Let Siddy do her game this one time.*

Siddy stood on the bed and began dancing all around, kneeling over Stel, flaunting her bald pussy. She straddled Stel's face and said, "Smell my pussy." Childlike, she smiled. "Don't you want to taste it?"

Stel took a deep breath and looked up with pleading eyes, "Baby, please, yes, yes, I do." Stel knew Siddy wanted her to behave, that she would be upset if Stel didn't cooperate and let her have her way. Stel knew that sooner or later Siddy would get bored and the tables would turn. At this moment, though, Stel just really wanted to shove her face into Siddy's pussy, rip at her with her teeth and tongue and lips—make Siddy come with the part of her that wasn't tied down.

"Yes, please, baby," Stel repeated.

But like a cat who won't stop torturing the mouse and eat it, Siddy wasn't finished teasing yet. Suddenly she pouted. "Oh you poor thing! I can't believe how mean I'm being! Why, I forgot to do this." She popped her forefinger into her mouth, sucked it, then turned around, bent over, and began fingering her asshole—which, Stel thought, "she never lets *me* fuck enough."

Stel began to moan out loud. This was way too much. She had to touch Siddy. "I have to touch you, I have to touch you," became a mantra in her head as her fists started automatically to open and close.

"Enough of that," Siddy said. "I'm bored. But oh, my"—Siddy put a finger to her chin, as if deep in thought—"I have to pee, I guess—"

"Pee on me," Stel interrupted. "Piss on me, piss all over me," she screamed.

"You *would* like that, wouldn't you? No! I won't piss on you," Siddy frowned, "but I can't leave you." She grabbed a clear crystal bowl filled with potpourri from her nightstand and dumped the contents onto the floor. "Here," she said and brought it to the side of the bed so that if Stel strained her head to the right, she could see the crystal bowl on the floor.

"Baby, *please!*" Stel tried again.

"Shut up!" Siddy snapped. "If you don't shut up and close your eyes, I won't be able to do it!"

"I'm sorry. You can pee in here. Do it," Stel reassured her and closed her eyes.

Siddy collected herself, then squatted over the bowl and pissed a stream of bright yellow urine. Her childlike tone returned. "My, how yellow, from my vitamins, so healthy." The stream continued and, although Siddy didn't know it, Stel became thoroughly wet from a different kind of juice.

"Please, come on, save me some—just a little, piss on my tits," Stel couldn't stop herself from begging. She thought she was going to come spontaneously.

Siddy crawled up onto the bed, straddled Stel's belly and sat down on it.

"Oh, baby!" Stel moaned as a few droplets fell to Stel's stomach and ran into her belly button.

Siddy slid her wet cunt up and down the length of Stel's ribs and belly. She bent down and whispered, "Are you happy, now?" Then she put her lips on Stel's. Their kiss lingered long and wet. Siddy sighed and relaxed, putting her full weight on Stel, almost forgetting her top mission.

After a minute's rest, she took a deep breath and sat up. "Well, I'm turned on now. I guess I'll have to touch myself," Siddy said, setting a chair right up on the bed, its legs straddling Stel's. She grabbed the vibrator, sat on the edge of the chair so her pussy was spread and easy to see, and proceeded to masturbate in the most exhibitionistic fashion. She moaned and rolled her hips around, licking her lips, putting on a performance to equal the finest Mitchell Brothers' stripper. Suddenly she pulled out a dick. "This is your favorite part, isn't it, Stel? Oh, my sexy butch just likes to fuck so much," she purred, "Do you imagine yourself on the other side of this dick? Holding my hips while you plow into me, making my luscious round ass shake from each pound against me? You like that, don't you? Don't you wish you could fuck me right now?" She paused. "What do you want, Stel?" she asked, her tone mocking the one Stel uses when she asks that very same question, from quite a different position.

"I want to fuck you," Stel said with a slow intake of breath.

"You what?"

"I"—Stel's voice was low, restrained, and she paused between each word—"want to . . . fuck . . . you."

"Oh, Stel, yes fuck me!" Siddy closed her eyes and leaned back into the chair, bringing her feet up, resting her heels on the edge and began really fucking herself. The headboard began to pound as Stel starting ripping at the restraints. Siddy's voice became full and low, and she began to moan like she does when Stel fucks her. She moaned as if Stel *were* fucking her, breathing, whining, moaning, "Oh, Stel, that's it, oh, yeah oooooh yeah, oh, fuck me like that, Stel. Oh, Stel, fuck me, please, oh, fuck me . . ." Siddy rammed the dick into herself while grinding her hips around and rubbing her clit.

"Fuck!" Stel screamed, "Siddy, goddamn it, unhook these. Siddy!"

Siddy's eyes flew open. She bit her bottom lip and suddenly looked really scared about what she had done. Her top persona was completely gone. "Oooooh!" she whined, "Stel, I want you to fuck me. If I let you loose, you'll fuck me, right? You won't be mean," she said, almost as if reassuring herself. "You *want* to fuck me, right? You won't be mean." The dildo dropped to the bed. Frantically, she cleared off the chair and her toys.

"Siddy," Stel growled.

"Yes?"

"Just fucking unhook me!"

"But the bed . . . right, okay." With her pussy so swollen that she could hardly crawl across the bed, she hurriedly messed with the chains on the headboard. The instant Stel felt release from one arm, she released the other arm. The leather restraints remained as bracelets on Stel's wrists because the time for removing them had passed long ago.

WITHIN seconds, the chair flew across the room. A glove snapped against skin, and Stel grabbed Siddy's ankle as she tried to scramble away. "Get your ass over here. That's it. This is what I need." Siddy didn't have the time or the inclination to protest. Stel pulled her into arm's reach and did as she had imagined only minutes ago. She shoved Siddy's head down by her hair and pulled her ass up, spit on her latex-covered fingers, and started talking as she shoved her fingers into Siddy's pussy. "Yeah, baby, oh, fuck." Every other word was punctuated with harder, quicker, or deeper thrusts, "You got me so *fuck . . . ing . . . cra . . . zy* I can't even put a fucking dick on, huh? You like it? Huh?"

Siddy's nails dug into the sheets as she tried to hold on, get leverage so that her swollen wet cunt could take all of Stel's knuckles. Her moans flowed out as high-pitched cries, then screams turned low and guttural. Snot began moving through her head to her nose. Tears pushed from under her face to the corners of her eyes. Her words rang out long and shaky over the sounds of their sex. "Yes, please fuck me, I love you," she panted. "I love you, I love you, I love you fucking me."

"Yeah baby, I know you do. Huh? That was funny, huh? Here—is this funny? Is this what you wanted? *Is it?*" Stel pulled out her fingers and slapped Siddy's ass hard. "Keep your ass in the air. We're not finished yet. What, are you bored now? Answer me!" Stel smacked Siddy's ass several times, then commanded again, "Answer me!"

Tears ran down Siddy's face, "No, no, I'm not bored. I'm not bored. I just want to make you happy."

"Yeah, baby, you're gonna be making me happy real soon. Roll over!" Stel tossed a vibrator onto the bed, "Keep your pussy swollen for me." She grabbed the dildo and her harness from the toy box and pulled them on, then squirted some lube into her palm.

Siddy licked her lips at the sight of Stel's muscle flexing as she ran her hand up and down the length of the dildo to lube it up.

Siddy's hips were moving fast with the vibrator, but her eyes weren't moving from Stel's, seeking approval. "It made you so excited . . . right? I just wanted to make you happy. You like it when I tease you. Oooh!" She forgot her rationalizations as her clit throbbed insistently.

Stel stood at the side of the bed. "You're gonna make me happy. Crawl over here."

Siddy whimpered and crawled across the bed. She bent down and licked a long stroke up from Stel's knee to the base of the dick, then bit gently into Stel's flesh.

"Turn over. I want your ass."

SIDDY'S screams, curses, and Stel's oh-fuck-baby's were heard all the way down the block. After the orgasms coursed through Siddy's body and neither of them had any thigh muscle action left to speak of, after Siddy had curled up in Stel's arms and was purring something about making her happy and just give her a moment, waves of orgasms were still going through Siddy's body. She ran a fingernail down one side of Stel's neck while she nibbled on the other side. Then Stel got it. Maybe it was Siddy's purrs, but more likely it was light nail trail. Or maybe it was the deep nail scars still stinging that Siddy had only just moments ago torn into her back . . .

"Siddy, do you want to make me happy?"

"Anything," Siddy whispered against her ear.

"You say that, but do you mean it?" Stel asked.

"If it turns you on, then I want to," Siddy said simply. "I told you I'm an object of desire. I want to be your fantasy come true."

"Do you promise to do *anything* to make me happy?"

Siddy looked up from Stel's chest into her eyes, "Yes. I promise."

Stel pulled herself slowly out of Siddy's arms and went to the toy box. She grappled around behind the headboard until she found what she wanted.

"I want you to be my kitty," Stel's voice was low, thick with desire. "My precious little kitty."

Siddy's eyes were droopy with love and she smiled. "Your kitty?"

"Put on this collar and be my kitty. Get on all fours, here, down on the floor."

Siddy moved very slowly but did indeed crawl off the bed and sat on the floor. Then Stel fastened the leather collar around her neck and put a chain on it like a leash. "Am I a pretty kitty?" Siddy asked.

"Hmm-hmmm," Stel surveyed Siddy's body and felt a rush of blood into her cunt. "Oh, baby, you are very pretty. Now, do you know what kitties do?"

With her feet tucked under her, Siddy leaned on Stel; her belly and breast pressing warmly into Stel's leg. She ran her cheek in upward pulses against Stel's thighs, willing her head to be scratched. "What do kitties do?"

"Kitties . . . like to drink from nice little bowls—"

Siddy's nuzzling stopped and she sat frozen at Stel's feet, her mouth gaping. "No!"

"Don't you want to make me happy?"

"Yes, but—"

"It will make me *so* happy." There was a long pause until Stel reached down and stroked the length of Siddy's back. "Pretty, pretty kitty. Crawl over here." Stel led Siddy to the bowl.

Siddy sat perfectly still and stared at the bowl, then finally spat out, "It won't make you happy. You're just doing it to laugh at me!"

Stel's mouth parted as she realized why Siddy was hesitating,

"No, Siddy, I won't laugh at you. Baby, it will turn me on so much."

Siddy looked up past her long brown lashes. "You promise it will turn you on? Will it really make you happy?"

Stel, knowing she was so close, could hardly stay calm, but managed somehow to say slowly, "Siddy, my divine kitty-cat, it will make me very, very happy." Stel stroked behind her ears, then bent down and kissed her.

Siddy ran her cheek up Stel's calf and nuzzled against her ankles, then stuck her ass up in the air, swayed it back and forth slowly, and bent over the piss-filled bowl. She wrinkled her nose, then stuck out her pink tongue and dipped the tip into the piss—wiggling it a lot so that it made little ripples in the bowl. Stel groaned as Siddy's tongue dipped in and out. After a few moments, Siddy looked up from the dish, licked her lips slowly, while keeping Stel's gaze. Then a grin curled up from the corners of her mouth as she said, "Meow?"

Brandon Judell

HOLLYWOOD
SQUARED

I THINK I HAVE AIDS TODAY, even though I have been tested about thirty-two times and have always come up negative. For the last two or three months my stool has always been soft and long—like long snakes decomposing. Today I stared at one of these boa-like creations for a rather long time, searching for parasites. I also think I might have worms. I found maggots in Pumpkin's food last week. I thought maybe she ate a maggot and transferred it to me.

But anyway, I picked up a man on the crosstown bus at 86th Street the other day, and maybe we'll fall in love. He called me the very next day. He has gray hair and eyes that don't open all the way. He appears to be a failed novelist and playwright, the type of person who once you know him well will be totally neurotic. I can't wait.

I'm reading the letters section of *Harper's* right now. Someone tearing apart Raymond Carver throws in some distaste words for David Leavitt, too. David's probably getting very depressed in Spain right now. He can't handle interviewers who criticize his clothes, so he must be foaming that his psyche is getting a trouncing, too.

I think my breath is terrible all the time. How can I kiss a man with a tongue tasting like moldy chopped liver. I keep mints under the mattress in case I get a guy home. Then I stuff my face while I'm going down on him.

That's how Louis gave his girlfriend her wedding ring. He was performing cunnilingus between her thighs (which is the best place to perform it), when he started choking. He said in a garbled voice, "There's something in there that I swallowed."

Denise said in a panicked tone, "What?"

Louis went, "Mmmwhawhawhammmwhawha!"

"What's wrong?" Denise shouted.

"I'm choking. There's something inside of you!" gurgled Louis. Then he pulled the $6000 designer ring out of his mouth. "Look!" After Denise realized it wasn't a dislodged IUD, she started laughing. That's so romantic, but I'm not supposed to know about it.

ANOTHER idle Sunday. If I had a salaried job with coffee breaks, I wouldn't feel guilty about doing nothing. Just made rice pasta and topped it with French salad dressing. I'm out of butter. Out of sauce. Too lazy to do anything but play this Columns game on the computer. You get three blocks of the same color abutting each other and they disappear.

Called Kenny Lasser, my possible love interest. He's the guy from the bus. We might get together tonight. Cleaned the living room floor. It's the only room you can now walk over and your feet actually touch the linoleum.

Haven't masturbated for days, either. I'm going through my non-sexual phase again. Clint Eastwood is on the living room TV.

My stool still hasn't hardened. I guess nothing puts a damper more on erotic thoughts than shit problems. Haven't really been exercising. Maybe forty minutes this week.

I think my life is getting a bit too passionless. I did let a strange Hispanic suck my cock in the George Washington Bus Terminal bathroom this week. I pulled out before I came, yet he spit into a tissue anyway. I felt great.

Someone had actually wanted to mouth my organ, play my harmonica, wet my whistle . . . I'm a sex object again. Thank you, Lord. Thank you, anonymous Hispanic.

I'm getting exhausted . . .

Kenny just called. We're meeting at Pumpkin Eater's at seven. He's a vegetarian. This story might actually get off the ground. A true gray-haired love interest. He's young, just prematurely gray. I wonder if I have enough time to henna. But then I'll have that henna smell. I guess I should do the mudpack to tighten my pores and exercise a bit so my tits swell.

This kind of fiction is a real headache to write because it's basically fact with names changed—and a few inches added to the cocks. If nothing happens in my real life, we're *both* out of luck.

The positive side of writing about factual orgasms is that if a critic writes, "This is unbelievable crap," I can say, "Fuck you, asshole. Everything here is the whole truth. I *was* gang-banged by twenty albino pygmies and have Polaroids of their footprints on my ass to prove it."

The problem is that Kenny looks like the kind of guy who doesn't leave behind any marks.

TWO years later, maybe.

I've just discovered this piece and I hardly remember this Kenny. Anyway, I recall I walked him home. I think he lived in the Ansonia or someplace near. I started grabbing his crotch, and he warned me that he might not be able to get it up because he takes Prozac. I accepted the challenge. So after he lit the incense and rearranged the Indian print bedspreads around the room, plus put on the mood music, I got to business. He might have come. I don't remember. I don't care. I probably jerked off.

Maybe I should reread *The 120 Days of Sodom*.

I just remembered about a guy I blew in San Francisco in the seventies. He was coked out and couldn't get hard. Blond with looks good enough to make him appear average in dark light. He said, "Don't worry. It feels good even if I'm not hard." So there I was on my elbows for hours giving this guy I didn't want to be with a great blow-job. Well, at least an immensely long one. I recall my jaws locking, my cheek hollows aching, and my back stiffening. I think I finally said I had to go and pick up my schnauzer or something. Otherwise, I'd probably still be there like one of those Walt Disney automatons at the 1964 World's Fair going through some very precise but limited movements.

New York Times just did an article on penises and impotency. It said in so many words that if you don't have sex regularly, not enough air gets into your cock, and some type of skin cell grows and the veins get clogged, and you have trouble getting an erection. Now I'm going to have to masturbate twice a day.

Nowadays, I just masturbate before I sleep. I jerk off to an old issue of *Drummer* or *Stroke*, then I answer a few clues in *New York* magazine or the *New York Times* crossword puzzle. Immediately, I conk out. That's why I'm afraid to jerk off during the day, since I've trained my body to snooze about six minutes after ejaculation.

Anyway, before I get to my hot experience in Turkey, Carl, one of my tattooed nephews (I have four), pointed out a beautiful black girl to me that he had sex with in the past.

"My friend and I met her in a bar. Then we danced with her. Then she blew us. I wound up going home and to bed with her. Almost, at least. Because when I put my hand in her pants, I found out she had dick. I was freaked out. A dick, man. I yelled at her, 'You should have told me!' She said, 'Then you wouldn't be here right now.' I said, 'Right you are!'"

He was freaked it seemed because when he was eleven or so, his evil stepmother used to go around to his friends' parents and say that he was gay. So even though he's as straight as a Buckingham Palace guard's spine, that accusation had always made him slightly uptight about homosexuality.

I'll be right back. I have two of those new sandwich-sized Thomas' English muffins in the toaster. Also I should masturbate to get some air in my cock.

SO, anyway, I was lying on one of those filthy cots in the old Everard bathhouse when who should come swishing in but Paul Lynde. He said in as butch a voice as he could muster, "Baby, you're beautiful, and I'm going to make you feel good." He was wearing a towel and a gold chain with some oversized medallion hanging from it, and there was a pack of cigarettes stuffed between the towel and his waist.

I thought to myself, Well, he is a celebrity and maybe I could use this sometime in the future. Then I thought, Well, I'll probably be too embarrassed to tell anyone I *schtupped* with Mr. Lynde. But it was too late. He had closed the door and had thrown his towel to the ground. His locker key was around his right ankle.

Mr. Lynde's stomach was more than a little fleshy and his legs were calveless, but he surprisingly had some tits. Also his cock looked to be close to eight inches and was thickish. He also had big balls that hung low.

(I usually don't remember these details, unless they're about a celebrity or the sex is exquisite.)

Anyway, I'm lying there and he starts licking me from my balls to my chin. Then he sticks his thick tongue down my throat. I remember wishing he hadn't worn so much cologne. Anyway, I close my eyes and I imagine myself lying on the desk of the center square of *Hollywood Squares* as Paul Lynde rims me in front of an appreciatively applauding audience. The other squares are filled with the likes of Joan Rivers, Oscar Wilde, Marcel Proust, Fabian, the Gabor sisters, Eddie Cantor, Ann Sothern, and I can't remember who else. They're screaming, "Do it, Paul! Do it, Paul!" Suddenly, I open my eyes to Paul and reality, and I see the *Bye Bye Birdie* star lifting my legs over his shoulders, spitting on my asshole and on his cock. "Oh no! Now I can't tell anyone this story. It would be all right to fuck Mr. Lynde, but to be fucked by the queen of queens. Shit!"

So I close my eyes again, but he slaps my face and says, "When you get fucked by Lynde, baby, you keep your eyes open." And, truthfully, it was a great fuck. Lasting for over twenty minutes or so. I was moaning and screaming. It felt like he was hitting my prostate with every stroke. Sadly, the medallion kept hitting my nose, but I didn't care.

"Chew my nipples," he ordered. I did.

Then he screamed, "I'm coming, baby. I'm coming." But instead of coming inside of me, he shot all over my face ... drop after drop after drop. Then he licked the cum splatter all up. "I love how I taste, baby. Now turn over."

I did. Suddenly I felt him writing on my ass. He must have had a pen or tiny marker or something in that cigarette case. He then turned me over and kissed me good-bye.

Ten minutes later, I ran to the bathroom and checked out what he wrote.

It said on my firm left ass cheek: FUCKED BY PAUL LYNDE.

ANYWAY, what I really want to write about is Turkey, which was where my first sexual bout of this year with another human being took place. Except I just want to quickly mention last night. I had called up (212) 550-1000 and listened to sex messages left by others with the hornies. Well, someone was having an orgy on the Upper West Side and they needed a fifth. I passed phone inspection and headed over there.

I was the second-best-looking person there with possibly the first- or second-best body, which tells you this was not some chic group with membership at the World Gym.

Everyone there sucked, and a few fucked with condomed penises and dildos, and we had to blow the host who was overweight with a small penis, but friendly.

Anyway, the next morning I'm looking into the mirror. I have my glasses on, and my vision is blurry . . . *schmutzy*. For some reason I can't figure out what is wrong. Are my glasses smeared, is the bathroom mirror dirty, or is something floating on my pupils? Instead of solving the problem, I just keep staring at the messy visage, unable to function. But I'm often like this after lots of sexual activity. My brain cells which are no doubt connected to my penis get burnt out.

IT'S been about four months since I last looked at this piece. I wonder if I'll ever finish it. I just got an invite in the mail to a water-sports party in two weeks. Maybe I'll go. That'll make a good ending.

Lucy Taylor

CHOKE HOLD

THE ROPE snugged tight around Angelo's neck. Almost at once, he felt lightheaded. Red embers, like bloody fireflies, swirled behind his eyes.

His dick, already engorged to veiny stiffness, felt like it had added an inch in circumference and two inches in length. He pumped it with a savage finesse no lover's hand could ever have accomplished, while the constricting rope pinched shut his carotid arteries and shut down the blood flow to his brain.

The rope around Angelo's neck was looped up over the top of the bunk bed over his head (the bed where his older brother Mark used to sleep before he shoved a Colt .45 into the face of the wrong Vietnamese grocer one night and got his brains blown out his asshole for his trouble). The other end of the rope was connected to a triangle formed by a bicycle chain and two feet of broom handle that hung down over the bottom bunk. Angelo had drilled holes at either end of the length of handle and secured the chain through them, creating a pushbar for his feet.

By pressing his feet against the jerry-rigged bar, he could control the amount of pressure on his throat, could bring himself to the verge of unconsciousness and beyond. The Device was foolproof, too, Angelo figured, because the minute he passed out, his feet ceased applying pressure to the bar and the rope around his neck went slack immediately.

Now came the dance of control, restraint. To stay conscious as long as possible but not lose his hard-on, then pass out while the tremors of orgasm were still rocketing outward, concentric circles encompassing his dick, his groin, his belly, while the rope brought ever-expanding ripples of darkness flooding into his brain. Where the two waves of concentric circles met and overlapped: there lay ecstasy.

It had to be just right, synchronized just so. He thought about the sex books he'd read that counseled men on how to hold off on their orgasm until their partner climaxed. A simultaneous orgasm—that was supposed to be big shit. Well, fuck that. Angelo had his partner right here, his good hard dick in his good right hand. The goal was to make it happen simultaneously—the coming and the passing out into Nirvana, then the delicious throbbing afterglow of coming back to consciousness. So good was the experience that sometimes he did it several times a day.

Now he was almost there, teetering on the verge, hand stroking ever faster while his legs caused the rope to snug tighter, his brain all pyrotechnic dazzle and incandescent sheen.

Except that . . . right *there* . . . was . . .

Just as he came, Angelo glimpsed a figure undulating sinuously, snakelike, along the darkening labyrinth of his blood-starved brain.

It had wide-set, dark, bruise-colored eyes.

Billows of black hair curtaining a face of almost skeletal angles.

No mouth that he could see.

A woman, yet incompletely formed, her lush anatomy eroding even as he watched, pearlescent neck flowing into translucent, blue-veined breasts that dissolved into the tatters of a pelvis.

Like some kind of pallid water snake, the woman swam up from the seabed of his fading consciousness, a wraith thing that grew more insubstantial by the instant until what passed as flesh was no more than a transparent veil.

Just before she disappeared, the creature stared up at Angelo.

The blurred and wispy tendrils of a hand came up, silently imploring.

"I'm yours," he thought he heard her say. *"Help . . . me . . ."*

Then Angelo lost consciousness.

"I wish this country'd go to war," huffed Danny Marston.

He and Angelo and their buddy Erik Jehle were cruising up Colfax Avenue in Erik's banged-up Datsun to a 7-Eleven where the fatty dweeb behind the counter would sell them beer, no ID required, in exchange for the joints that Danny slipped him from time to time.

Angelo was riding in the back seat with Erik driving and Danny in the passenger seat next to him.

"You know why I wish this country'd go to war?" continued Danny, even though neither Angelo nor Erik had indicated interest: "'cause you know what soldiers get to do, a soldier in the field gets to fuck the piss out of any woman he finds, no questions asked. She makes a fuss, he can just go ahead and waste her. Who's gonna know?"

"I think rape's what they call a war crime," Angelo said absently.

"War crime," mocked Danny in a derisive falsetto. "It's a fucking *tactic's* what it is. They done it in Bosnia, they're doin' it in Haiti—you want to de-morale your enemy, you know what you do, you rape his women. His wife, his daughters, sisters, his old momma, too, plus you get all that pussy. That's why I wish this

country'd go to war—so I could go over and get me some enemy
ass."

They pulled into the parking lot of the convenience store. The
Twins, two sophomore girls that Angelo and the others knew from
school, were bouncing out of the store chewing candy bars. They
weren't really twins at all, but had gotten the name because they
hung around so much together. The name was also meant as an
ironic joke, for while the "Twins" both had bleached-blond hair,
here all resemblance ended. One of them, Denise, topped the
scale at upward of two hundred pounds, balloon breasts big
enough to nurse a calf, the other, MyraAnn, all knobs and bony
angles, looked like a guy trying to fuck her could cut himself on
her pelvic bones if he wasn't careful.

Both had spotty skins and peroxide had left their hair looking
like something you'd cut with a scythe, but they were female,
they were notoriously loose, and that was all that mattered.

They sashayed past, looking away and giggling when they
passed the swaggering boys. "Fuckin' snooty pieces of tail,"
sneered Erik, while Danny stared at them the way Angelo'd seen
tigers look at raw meat just before the zookeeper slung the bleed-
ing chunks down into their enclosure.

Inside the convenience store, they got three six-packs, which
they paid for, and a collection of Slim Jims and Baby Ruths that
Erik stuffed into his jacket while Danny and Angelo were trans-
acting for the beer. They took the booty outside and sat in the car
and ate and got buzzed and talked about what they always talked
about, which was snatch—how to get it, where to find it, the many
ways to do it, fuck it, suck it, jerk off on it.

The talk and the booze made Angelo horny.

Not for the Twins. Not for any woman at all, but for the Device
and for his fantasies.

For the ball-popping, mind-fucking pleasure of blasting into
unconsciousness propelled by an orgasm so strong it felt like his
brains were being shot out the end of his dick.

He could hardly wait until Erik dropped him off at home and he could go to his room and get it on.

This time, though, there was more than just the orgasm he wanted. He wanted another glimpse of the eerie, undulating swimmer, to see if he could stay conscious long enough to see her clearer.

IT was Danny who'd taught Angelo about the awesome un-fucking-believable orgasms that were possible if you could figure out a way to choke yourself at the same time that you jerked off. Of course, faggots did it to each other all the time—according to Danny every fag apartment had a few ties and sashes next to the bed for just such use—but real men couldn't do it to each other, and you certainly couldn't let a woman do it to you (even if any of them had known a woman willing to participate in such a thing)—no, giving a woman the upper hand during sex was worse than being queerfucked.

So Angelo had dreamed up the Device all on his own.

One thing Danny had warned him about was that, frankly stated, guys sometimes accidentally offed themselves this way and wouldn't that make a pretty picture for your mom to walk in on, you stone dead on the bed, with a hard-on the size of a gourd in your fist lying in your own stink and your eyes staring up and your mouth open with your tongue stuck straight out like some kind of flesh dildo?

Seven seconds, Danny said he'd read someplace. Seven seconds from the time the noose tightened until you went out so if anything went wrong, that's how long you had to save yourself or that's it, buddy, you're tomorrow's dirty joke in homicide division.

"You fuck up and let yourself pass out with the noose still tight, you dead meat, man." And Danny had chuckled around a mouthful of chili dog, a sound like gravel being ground under one of his Doc Marten boots. "Man, you be dead with your dick in your hand."

Careful now, thought Angelo, *not too fast. Make it last as long as possible, go easy.*

Angelo's knees were quivering as he gave the bar a push. The noose around his neck dug in. Blood beat behind his eyes and surged into his cock. Angelo shut his eyes and watched the blackness in his head turn dazzling, starry, a liquid, crimson phosphorescence like lava flowing into purple waves. And from this strange, internal ocean the woman from his vision pieced herself together like a pattern made by moonlight on an obsidian sea.

She was better formed this time, but still incomplete, whole areas of pelvis and ribcage left either shockingly absent or pitifully concave, her breasts nippleless, translucent globes behind which a single-ventricled heart could be seen beating feebly.

Angelo's legs felt numb. He couldn't feel the bar beneath his feet, couldn't tell how hard he might be pushing it.

The woman had no ears. No mouth except a lipless, toothless orifice no bigger than a bottlecap.

But her yearning, hungry eyes fixed on Angelo, beseeched him.

Her hands reached for him, long fingers weaving patterns like underwater fans, nails the color of arterial blood.

The pitiful mouth pursed and strained, passed words.

"Help . . . me . . ."

Angelo felt her pain, her sadness. He took his hand off his cock for just an instant, tried to reach for her, flailed empty air.

"Who . . . ?"

His vision was the color of her nails now, a sea of floating crimson dots, edged in an ever-expanding black frame.

"Help me, Angelo, I'm . . ."

He wanted to touch those reaching hands—she was so real now, so close—but he had to stroke himself again—quickly—or lose the chance to climax.

"I'm yours," she murmured, her insubstantial form aquaver like

a fibrillating heart, pulsing fainter and fainter as the blackness swallowed her up.

Help me, help me, help mehelpmehelpmehelpmeeeeeeee . . .

Angelo came and then came to seconds later, unconsciousness having rendered his legs limp and the rope slack. His hand and dick were glued together by a sticky paste of cum. The blood drummed in his temples like tiny fists, tapping him awake.

For long moments afterward, he lay there, staring up at the bottom of the bunk bed over his head, remembering every detail of the woman in his dream who claimed that she belonged to him.

Some bizarre variation on a wet dream, he figured, although he'd have wished the woman's face and body could be more like a centerfold and less like some kind of seductive leper, with parts of her unformed or fallen off.

What most disturbed him, though, was that the vision inspired more than just a hard-on. It was as though the woman from this drowned world was inducing new emotions in him or resurrecting old ones, those frightening feelings that he thought he'd put aside in little boyhood: tenderness and gentleness, the desire to protect, defend, and love.

The way, a long time ago, he'd felt about his brother.

Before Mark toughened up and muscled up and got to be a tattooed, colors-sporting, queer-bashing badass who called Angelo a fuckface punk and once handed him a glass of rum and Coke with a fat, bloated worm at the bottom and told him, *Be a man now, drink it, gulp it down*, and Angelo still gagged when he remembered that slimy, awful slickness on his tongue, like swallowing a baby turd, but he'd done it, he'd done it so he'd be a man in Mark's eyes, and even so, Mark had only laughed at him. *(You dumb fuck, do you always do what people tell you?)*

Now Angelo felt the pricklings of tears behind his eyes and an unspeakable sorrow and longing, something old and vast, eternal as the ocean, *female*, threatened to seep up out of some hidden crevice in his soul and overwhelm him.

Tears that threatened his manhood, his maleness, everything tough and hard and pussy-fucking-tough-assed-mean mother-fucker son-of-a-bitch that he was trying to be.

So Danny would like him. So Erik would like him. So Mark, if he were still alive, would respect him.

So he would be a *man*. (But he wanted to be held, he wanted to be cared for, he wanted . . . something different . . . what?)

Fucking shit, why was he crying? What was *happening* to him?

Twisting on the bed, Angelo brought his cum-encrusted fist up and rammed it into the ridge of bone above his eye.

Searing red, rainbow-spangled pain. Blood running warm along his cheek instead of tears.

The image of his brother, of the woman, faded with the pain.

"HEY, man, I'm at Erik's house. You gotta get over here. Now."

It was Saturday afternoon, the middle of a Lakers game.

"What for?" said Angelo.

"Look, just get your ass over here. Erik's parents are gone for the weekend and we got us a surprise."

"So what is it?"

"Fuck you, man, I don't have time to jive with you. You comin' or not?"

But Angelo had already punched the remote and switched off the TV.

"Comin'."

THE basement rec room of Erik's house reeked of a testosterone cocktail—booze and semen and sweat.

Over all of it hung a thick, nauseating layer of fear, like the ripe scent wafting up from the carcass of a roadkilled animal.

The shades were all drawn, and Angelo couldn't see well at first. Then as his eyes adjusted, he saw the mattress thrown down on the floor and the two bodies on it.

Three bodies actually, because Erik was part of whatever the scene was down on the floor.

The Twins lay naked on the stained and grungy mattress. Erik's white ass moved up and down as he fucked the thin one.

Angelo's first, horrified impression was that they were dead. But then the fat twin moaned and flopped around. Erik came over and slammed a bottle of vodka up against her mouth.

"Drink," he said. "Drink this or I swear to God I'll break the bottle over your fucking head and shove it up your cunt."

Whether or not she even heard him Angelo didn't know, but she sucked weakly, coughing every now and then like a baby suckling a poisoned teat.

The other one, the skinny one, didn't move at all.

Erik shuddered into the thin Twin's body and hauled himself off her. "My man, you got here just in time. We invited these two young ladies over here to party, but they both seem to have, uh, overindulged and are sleeping it off." He bowed and made a flourish with his hand. "So, which of these beautiful buttered buns would you care to start with? You got your big tits, you got your small tits, you got your fat ass, you got your tight ass, you got all afternoon, my man, the day is young."

Angelo stood there, staring at the room, the women passed out on the mattress, feeling sick to his stomach. He felt like a little boy again and Mark was giving him the drink with its disgusting garnish and he wanted to flee, oh God, he wanted to run from all of them, his grinning, gleeful buddies and the women with the awful furry, grinning mouths between their legs, and they were expecting him not just to thrust himself between those cum-caked lips but to do this terrible thing while they watched, and he wished to God he'd never answered the fucking telephone, wished he'd stayed at home with the Device and the visions that it brought him.

"Whatsa matter, our leavin's ain't good enough for you?"

"Maybe he just can't make up his mind," said Danny. "Maybe he's like the mule that starved to death between two bales of hay cause he couldn't make up his mind which one to eat."

Oh God, I never expected it to be . . . not like this . . .

"Hey, man, get going. You makin' me nervous."

Erik had hand-jerked himself erect again and began to fuck the fat one, her breasts jiggling every time he thrust into her, a dribble of saliva burbling at the corner of her lip.

"Hey, what kinda man are you anyway, don't want good pussy? Maybe you not a man at all. Maybe you a faggot oughta lie down here and get fucked with the girls."

"Shut up," Angelo said.

He closed his eyes and thought about the woman in his vision, the yearning and the sorrow that he'd felt for her, but he couldn't see her clearly now, the memory had departed like the image of his brother as a young boy—before his brother turned into a brute he didn't recognize—getting dimmer, vaguer.

Something inside him, something good and valuable, that might have changed his life, had been choked into unconsciousness, and he hadn't even felt it.

Then his penis overrode all hesitation and sprang to life like some battery-powered sex toy as he began to remove his pants and underwear.

He crawled atop the thin Twin, forced his cock into her pussy, and began to work his hips. At first he was distracted by the newness of the sensation, the repellent fleshiness of the girl's interior. After a while, he had only one thought: God, he hoped they didn't guess this was his first time. God, he hoped he was doing it right, hoped he fucked her like she'd never been fucked in all her sorry life, fucked her so she'd never walk straight again, because he was a man, a man, because he was a man . . .

HOW was it possible he was still horny? He'd fucked three times—twice with the fat girl, once with her skinny friend. He'd fucked their dry, sandpapery snatches until he thought the skin would peel right off his dick, but he was hornier than ever.

Because I want to do it the way it feels best.

Not with a girl.

Not a squishy-soft, dickless girl who had that awful hole between her legs, that terrible God-awful hole like some kind of smelly burrow surrounded by those lopsided lips that looked like the fatty trimmings off a piece of pork, and he had to think of the Twins that way—not as people but as vile, disgusting sex organs—or else he knew that he'd start crying and that he'd never stop.

No, he was just horny, that was why he was hurrying home. To be alone with the Device and his good six inches.

To be alone with his fantasy.

He lay on his bunk now, the rope tight around his throat while the inside of his skull turned into a planetarium full of wheeling, dipping stars and at the same time, as his sight dimmed and his mind blurred, he began to see the woman gliding up from underneath the water, resplendently, shimmeringly nude.

Complete now. Perfectly formed.

Created by him.

For him.

She was different now, no longer pale and maimed and incomplete but plush and buttery, breasts so full and peachy you could pillow down forever in the cleavage, and if she had a hole between her legs at all, Angelo knew intuitively it would be neat and clean and small and never emit foul odors or menstrual blood or babies and she was beckoning to him now and smiling a lover's smile with her scarlet, vulval mouth.

Angelo, come here, take my hand, take it . . . Angelo, I belong to you . . .

But he'd already guessed as much. She was some part of him he feared and kept in exile, a shadow creature who emerged only when unconsciousness was creeping in, when the synapses in his brain were ceasing to transmit.

She frightened him, and yet he longed for her, and the more intense his longing grew, the greater was his terror.

He put his feet down on the bed, temporarily relieving the pressure on his throat, pumping his meat with desperate vigor, aroused as he'd never before been in his life by this female ghost, this lost soul in a limbo he couldn't understand but which he sensed held all that was forbidden, terrifying to the world of men, all softness, seduction, *womanliness*.

This was the place it wasn't safe to go, the place of female longings. And yet . . .

Help me, Angelo. I need you. I'm yours.

His dick was as hard as a crowbar, as pumped as a biceps after fifty curls.

He put his feet back on the bar. Pushed hard.

. . . need you, want you, please . . .

She reached for him, not just with her hand but arching toward him with her entire body. It was more real than any Virtual Reality game he'd ever witnessed, more real than the mattress underneath his bucking body, more real than his hard-on in his hand.

He strained for her with his free hand. She seemed to pull back a little, withdrawing tantalizingly . . . a little deeper underneath the watery twilight but still smiling, smiling . . .

. . . and he wriggled sideways, still reaching out because he could almost touch her face now, her sweet, sad face . . . her long fingers were so close and he could . . . just . . . almost . . .

He lost his balance.

His angled body slid sideways off the bed, the bar twisting so that the bicycle chain looped twice around his upraised ankle, all his weight holding the rope taut, grinding it into his neck.

The noose tightened brutally.

Oh, Jesus, no.

Seven seconds.

He tried to scramble off the floor and back onto the bed.

Six . . .

Vision gone to test pattern, scarlet at the edges, trying to catch the side of the bed, pull himself up, free his trapped foot, his agonized throat . . .

Five . . .

Again, come on, COME ON, but his fingers were like plugs of Silly Putty, they had no strength, no grip, like they were sculpted from mud.

Four . . .

The woman-ghost was swimming up out of the dark water behind his eyes. He could see her now with terrifying clarity. She wasn't lovely now, but malformed and hideous, her eyes pinched, demonic slits, her mouth a foul, red-rimmed pit miming the obscenity between her legs.

Three . . .

His eyes felt like eggs dropped into boiling water. Copper burned at the back of his tongue.

Two . . .

Come here.

No, please, I didn't want to hurt those girls, I didn't want to do it, I only wanted to be a man, to be a man, to be . . .

One.

Angelo, you're . . . MINE.

Camille Roy

From
THE ROSY MEDALLIONS

THE DAY I first saw her was a day the fog didn't clear. Whiteness smothered everything, a kind of extinction. I'd been spending my days off wandering aimlessly, and that day I'd gone to the park, stopping on a footbridge to watch the ducks. A dank little lake filled the bottom of a ravine and there were very few ducks. It seemed hard to move or think; maybe I was hungry. I was staring at the oily water when someone appeared, walking towards me through the tangled groves of eucalyptus. She drew near and then stopped, leaning over the railing next to me. I shifted my gaze to her feet—men's shoes, narrow, with the thin creases of expensive leather. Cuffed pants. Her dark grey gabardine coat was cut generously, well below the knee, and belted like a trench coat. I turned towards her but the stranger was oblivious, her dark blue eyes looking down at the water. Everyone has her own private thoughts, but her disdain was striking. It was as obvious as the creases in her skin and the steely grey of her closely cropped hair. This was a pervert, remote as a vampire who has aged. Shock settled into my shoes; I had never seen anyone like her before. A pervert with money. The thought made my teeth hurt, but filled me with modesty. I wanted to dance about in a white embroidered gown, to show how dreamy I was; it was the only quality of mine I could think of which might be attractive to her. The inadequacy of this idea rattled me, and I was staring at the water with a twisted expression when she spoke.

"The poor dog has arthritis. This damp weather doesn't agree with him."

There was a small white poodle at her feet.

"What happened to him?" I asked. He had three legs and a grim expression.

"Claude had an accident with a bear trap."

Nothing about her encouraged questions, and as I looked at the maimed poodle I felt caution slow my breathing. It was oddly pleasurable, to stand next to her and notice my own apprehension.

"How far do you think the dollar will fall?" she said eventually, in a soft voice.

"Has it fallen?"

"It's lost 25% of its value against the yen. And about 13% against the deutsche mark."

"Oh," I said, jumping on a feeling of rich disdain, "capitalism goes on binge and purge cycles. You can't stop it."

"Yes. Things have gotten out of hand," she said with interest.

"The profit motive!" I said dismissively. When she didn't respond I added, "What can you expect but slime and corruption!" I felt so sure of myself I spoke ridiculously, and laughed out loud. She was quiet for so long I was afraid our conversation had ended. I felt ashamed for using the word "slime." Finally, she turned to me with a quizzical expression.

"Currency speculation is a dangerous game. I myself recently averted disaster—in ways I should be ashamed of. But I find it impossible to remember why, exactly, I did all of this. Any of it."

I knew you would never be wholehearted. I recognized your sly face as soon as it appeared, making light of my disappointments. Your witty evasiveness likewise, and then your boredom. With anyone else this would have meant no sex, I sense these things from the start. But with you I was impelled, awkward, even grabby, and I feel at fault, though all that happened also seems somehow entirely your fault.

"I followed you. I think you're interesting." At her doorway I suddenly acquired my father's clear enunciation, each syllable a protruding embarrassment. She took my shoulder, gently steered me into the house, and shut the door.

"I noticed you."

I followed her through a dark hall, though the rooms on either side seemed full of light. It led to a library, comfortably outfitted with built-in bookcases and a velvet couch with deep cushions. All the colors were rich and dark, while outside the windows a willow stirred in a breeze, making a panel of rippling green. She seemed clear and unworried, picking up a few things, laying her coat over a chair. Her disdainful expression had shifted to amusement. That's what I am, the amusement, I thought, and felt tired. I hoped I wouldn't have to do most of the talking, and sat down cautiously on the couch.

"You caught us by surprise." This in a wry, but friendly, tone.

Writing this, there's a sharp sense of visibility decreasing. The literalness of my desire feels disjointed, slides off from the target. All this breath between myself and what I remember—a body and its pleasures. You invited me in. The shock of that disconnects me.

She stopped and looked at me with misgiving, as if registering my presence for the first time. "Why are you here?"

"I don't know, you asked me." It's too late, I thought, you can't kick me out. The weary sliding away of her eyes made me pushy—I lit a cigarette and put my feet on her coffee table.

She shook her head irritably. "Sorry. I get annoyed when I don't know what I'm doing."

I could stay. Relieved, I sank back into the cushions and surveyed the room. There was a black table with swollen claw feet, and something shiny above me, a brass chandelier. My neck is a lure, I thought, laid out on her brown velvet cushions. I felt its muscles contract as I slowly said, "I like it here." Then I took a long drag on my cigarette.

She smiled sideways, a sharp smile not directed at me. "You're ridiculously young." She swung around to the chair next to the couch, sat down, leaned forward, and nudged my leg with her finger.

"So what's your name?" she asked.

"Patty Hearst."

She laughed with a gratifying hard burst. "Would Patty like a drink?"

"A whiskey sour please," I mumbled, feeling drunk already. But she didn't have sour mix, just whiskey straight up, which was soon swirling in the bottom of my glass. Whiskey reminds me of my mom. For some reason this struck me as really funny and I smiled foolishly at her.

One thing I like is she makes me feel I don't need to know much. It's a relief not to have to understand your own experiences. The room was warm, the books seemed packed and secure in their built-in bookcases. Suddenly I wanted to talk for a long time, or else be very quiet on that soft brown couch, leaning back and studying the layer of whiskey in my glass.

Lifting my hair off my neck as if it were very heavy, she gently touched my neck with her lips, then her teeth. Then she leaned against the back of the couch, swirling the ice in her glass with her finger. Her eyes had that hot look adults get when their routines are busted and anything could happen.

"How you doing? You ever done anything like this before?"

Have I ever—that's funny, I thought. I bared my teeth and a weak smile turned into "Yes." I sounded like a liar.

She shrugged and traced the outline of my lips with her finger, ran her hand down my throat. "Nice skin," she said.

Leaning back, she draped her hand across her lap. That shift on her face I thought must be a smile, perhaps an ironic one. A sexual flare had followed her hand across my face. I wanted to cover myself. I thought of striking her, the interesting sparks off that hard, long life.

"Anything special I should know about?" she asked me.

"No, of course not."

It was a good time to get up and walk around the couch, to get myself between her legs. But I seemed to move slowly, I couldn't get used to the speed.

"No of course not," she said gently, mocking me. Hand on my shoulder, the slow approach was beginning to make me suffer. "We'll see."

HER mountainous perversity is like buckets of hair. Buckets of finally hair, at a time of night when I get my pronouns confused. It's the kind of image or scene you want to describe to your friends but it's so weird that no openings come up in regular conversation.

HER hand on my shoulder, that first gesture of invitation, was characteristic of her. Circular as a huge conscience, something to follow indefinitely. Her fingered good-byes marked my body. Even this story, its thin crust, marks her evasions.

So the room was either dark or light, or was two rooms. There were implements beyond my consciousness. Sharp cravings make narratives, also subjects. So it was easy to let her carve it, warble wobble. Only by turning on her with all my teeth bared could I regain ground already lost. Of course I did it. Of course yearning made it impossible. Pleasures of the rupture, rack and screw.

All over her, squall. Green wet rose, puff of smoke.

She had a collection of crops framed under glass. Each one had a name under it: Lady Fastbuck, Mary Mountbatten. She said these were mementos of the days when she rode in steeplechases. "It is hard to do this," she said, kneading my breast in the rhythm of her breath.

My moment in the hallway: I want to sit on the French inlaid bureau under the crops and get fisted. Marks rise to the surface of my neck. When did she put on that leather jacket; it's causing long prickly emotions down my back. Pulling at her shirt I attack the decency of white cotton, attaching myself via red lines I draw in her flesh. She's rubbing her crotch. "Let me see your tits," she says.

I drop my shirt for her, push my breasts together hard enough to feel their resistance. Then I slide out of my jeans, my shoes. Dropping item by item on the rug, I'm oddly comfortable with my body. There's a curious sense of touching the thick carpet only with my heels, perfect rounds of skin.

She pushes me towards the next room. Her bedroom—a place for my shiny and submissive death—I'm reluctant. If I'm going to abandon the real world, the one made up solely of dressed people, I want her to, also.

I want to say *shut up* though she is silent. Instead I twist out of her grasp & lean against the window. The glass is cool against my cheek and hardening nipples, then below there's a grassy sloping garden and the willow. Her hands are on my hipbones, they slide down slow & firm as if following a groove. "Slow down," I say. "No," she says, her voice calm and flat. "I'll slow down later." Then she laughs, and her teeth graze my neck. My breath fogs the glass. "Please baby," I say. "What?" I twist around to look at her face. There's a slight smile but her eyes are wide with desire. I slip my arm beneath her shirt and run my lips along her jaw line. "Fist me," I whisper and what slides up my cunt and unfolds is a smooth genital pain.

Then her hand disappears in my fur and I tighten my thighs around her leg to grasp it. Sliding down, riding her knuckles, the juices of my cunt, her expensive pants. Hand on my shoulder, she looks down at the wet mark and laughs. I suddenly like her; this new affection streaks through my body like aggression. I undo her pants and push them down; her clit is warm and wet under my tongue. She slides down the wall into a heap, leans her head to one side. "What do you think you're doing?" she asks quizzically.

"Making advances," I say. She leaps forward and we're rolling on the floor like dogs. What orders the flow is aggression—hers. Maybe she's not really a sadist. Possession is the deepest, thickest point. I could work that, and draw out desire even when she's not interested. I twist over, guilty. But she's grasping my buttocks with both hands. Bent over the edge, a lattice of hands, her rosy palms smacking my tin flesh.

I'm getting rosier and rosier. There's no telling where we are. These large sensations come and go. I want to be a star. I want to be adorable. Instead there are the larger sensations, so open there is a sense of leveling. What is inside slips out and vanishes. So when I am finally on my back again and she fists me with her total possessiveness, I am wholly (not) there having left (come), fucked to heaven.

Thomas S. Roche

TEMPORARY
INSANITY

I LIVED IN HEALTH CLUBS among glittering mirrors
and dropped by mansions when I wanted to relax. I posed
for a trillion nude photos, a skin-flick slut seduced by the
photographer—and generally his or her assistant(s)—at
every shoot.

I lost my virginity a thousand times, spread like succu-
lent marmalade on canopied king-size beds, tangled in
satin sheets and caressed by baby oil and vibro-fingers
massage. I did red-hot virgins whose need consumed
them. I took on cruising bimbos three at a time. I seduced the neighbors (all of them) while my husband was
at work, sunbathed nude twenty-four hours a day, owned
two thousand black garter belts and a million pairs of fish-
net stockings, eighty leather jockstraps, a hundred split-
crotch panties and forty thousand pushup bras. I had a
fifty-foot cock and a pair of hundred-pound tits. I invari-
ably deep-throated on the first try, and juices were con-

stantly running down my thigh. I went to a tanning salon at eight, noon, six, and midnight, serviced each time by the helpful massage therapists in their skintight tank tops and nylon gym shorts.

I haunted bars replete with domestic cigarettes and hard alcohol, a cocktail waitress who didn't own underwear. I was, perpetually, a freshman in college with enormous breasts and/or blond pubic hair. I spent most of my time in Southern California, occasionally dropping by Hawaii for the weekend. I was going for my Ph.D. in Sexology and used this as an excuse to seduce every hot young stud and flirtatious virgin in my class. I used my position as CEO of an enormous corporation to get me pussy. I drove around pedal-to-the-metal in Daddy's Porsche 911 convertible, cruising for hot young flesh.

I was badder than Satan. I turned out porn novels faster than a printing press turns out wedding invitations. I ate latex double-headed dildos at sundown and shit tiger-striped nylon jockstraps just before dawn. I pissed French Roast and slept with my boots on.

I was the god(dess) of Sleaze, the Damned Thing, the Pornographer, a vision of Sex with its tits on backward.

I had a stack of published porn novels twice the size of my roommate, all with my name on them (or someone else's, I forget whose). Half again that many books were in transit awaiting publication. I was paying the rent. Nothing could touch me.

THE publisher I had been writing for had gone out of business, taking several of my porn novels with it before I knew what was happening. I was left with a credit card balance approaching infinity and a stack of unpublished pornography that was now almost worthless. I was in the death-grip of capitalism, and the end of the month was approaching.

I got wind of a shady outfit in Brooklyn that published original novels, hardcore S/M she-male and bestiality books for an ab-

surdly low fee provided you sent it on disk so they didn't have to
retype it. I could not work for such shitty wages, and resolved to
starve rather than prostitute myself thus.

It was thus that I submitted, with a sick, curious pleasure, to
the ultimate degradation beneath the booted feet of the System.

I submitted myself, wrists crossed, to temporary insanity.

SO it was that I came to stand before the dark tower, dildo in one
hand, begging bowl in the other, tie loosely knotted, to the foot of
the forty-story building to answer phones for $12.50 an hour. I was
greeted by a middle-aged woman with a frilly white shirt and a
wool blazer with an "I LOVE SF" button on it. Her name was
Deirdre. She led me through miles of winding cubicles, under fluorescent lights through the valley of the damned. I was not afraid.
She spoke to me about the duties I would be fulfilling, but she
seemed to be speaking ancient Greek.

Finally, we reached my cubicle, deep in the belly of the beast.
There was a Garfield doll hanging from the light fixture, and a
computer in one corner of the tiny cubicle.

"Susanne is on vacation," Deirdre told me. "She normally an-
swers this phone. People will be calling in if they have problems
on the network. They'll get put on hold in a queue at the service
desk. If they want to speak to someone immediately, they hit the
pound key, and they'll be transferred to you."

"And what do I do with them?"

With a straight face, she told me: "Ask them to wait a moment,
and transfer them to the service desk."

THE hum of the fluorescent lighting grew in volume until it filled
my entire being. The phone had not rung at all. The boredom was
like a fine espresso or a cigarette I savored but did not enjoy. The
minutes grew exponentially longer; 11:23 lasted for eight years.

My tie seemed to be choking me. The polyester pants, all I

could afford on such short notice, were a field of ants crawling over my balls.

I stared at the black computer screen.

I couldn't. I wouldn't. It was crazy.

Tentatively, I switched the Damned Thing on.

AROUND four, Deirdre dropped by to make sure I was doing OK. I quickly switched screens and sat there grinning nervously.

She regarded me as if I were a maniac. Her gaze gradually softened, and her lips parted slightly. I noticed that her tits had gotten larger, her eyes bigger and more seductive. Her gray-streaked hair was now bleached, teased in an inviting mane of an unearthly color. She breathed deeply, her breasts heaving, as she sat on the arm of my chair.

Deirdre's palm grazed my cheek as she gazed into my eyes. Her own baby-blues were shaded by mascara-black palm fronds.

She spoke in a low, harsh whisper.

"How is the day going?"

"Fine," I mumbled.

"Do you have any . . . questions?"

"Sure," I mumbled. "Do . . . uh . . . do you need me back tomorrow?"

"Oh," she sighed, "we couldn't do without you. We need you back for the rest of the week. Susanne doesn't come back until next Monday. You're doing great. Everybody here likes you."

I was a bit confused, since I couldn't recall having met anyone, but I let it slide. "You can go ahead and pack up to go home," said Deirdre. "We don't get many support calls in the last hour of the day, so just go ahead and leave at five . . ."

I didn't have the heart to tell her that I hadn't gotten a single call all day, except for a wrong number around noon.

After she left, dancing in perfume and hallucination her way out of the cubicle, I turned my attention back to my computer, and the novel in progress that lay within.

I was the she-male, an androgyne with a flawless pair of silicons and a foot-long schlong undamaged by hormones. I was a creature of desire.

I cursed. I hadn't brought any floppy disks, and there were none to be found in the office. Chapters One and Two, where the she-male in question visits a weight room and thereafter an ice-skating rink, were on the hard drive.

There was nothing that could be done, so I secured the files, turned off the computer, and left.

ALL night long, I was tormented by visions of some perverted hacker working his way into the office in the middle of the night and feeding random combinations to the word processor until he found the password to those files.

But when I arrived the next day, the two chapters were still there, intact, and the hair I'd placed on the keyboard was on the same place. Some people tell me I read too many spy novels.

I went back to work. There were a lot of calls that day, particularly during the especially steamy scene involving the she-male and a kitchen full of pastry chefs wearing nothing but aprons that said "KISS THE COOK."

The phone rang like an avalanche of Tibetan wind chimes.

"Hello," I mumbled incoherently, sweat pouring down my back and soaking my undershirt. "I mean . . . Technical Support, can I help you?"

"I can't get my machine running," the young woman on the other end of the line said breathlessly. "It seems to be giving me error messages. Do you think it might be going down?"

I had to think about that one. "If you'll hold for a moment, Ma'am, I'll transfer you to the service desk."

"I don't want to be transferred to the service desk. I want *you* to help me." It was said with husky, breathless desperation.

"Can you hold?"

"Oh . . . I guess so."

I transferred her away into nothingness and went back to Chapter Four, introducing a phone call on the kitchen phone from a woman desperate with need. The she-male invited her over and the bread was effectively kneaded while the chefs kept doubly busy on biscotti with unusual shapes.

The she-male finished off with the pastry chefs, leaving them caked with flour, spread out across the kneading table.

The phone rang again.

It was a panting, desperate being of questionable gender, but the voice was rough and whispered. "My terminal tells me *access denied*, but I know the password's right. I need to get in. I need in, right now—open up? Please open up and let me in? I want to enter . . . at the highest possible baud rate . . . open up! Open up for me, She-male!"

I frowned. I seemed to be suffering from intermittent hallucinations, something numerous colleagues of mine had experienced. I shrugged.

"If you'll hold a moment, Ma'am?"

"That's 'Sir' to you, punk! On your knees and give me access! *On your knees, She-male, and take my data stream right into that steaming hole!*"

Things had gotten serious.

"Hold, please," I said. "I have a hallucination on my other extension." I transferred him away. "Technical Support," I said to the next caller.

He responded with a desperate plea. "Need it! Want it! Gotta have it! Help me get it running! I need my access! Lines closed up! Need them opened! Please! Please! Open me up—wide!"

"Oh shit," I said. "Let me get you the service desk."

"No, oh God, please," he wailed, his voice crumbling into a dancing desperate moan. "Not the service desk—they're limp-dicked pansies! I need you! I need the she-male! Bring me back on-line!"

"Holy fuck," I muttered. "Hold on a minute."

I transferred him.

Again and again, three lines at once.

"She-male! Fuck my tits and help me reestablish my carrier!"

"Jesus Christ. Uh . . . wait a minute . . . hold please . . ."

"Oh God! Fucking oh my fucking God, She-male, put those luscious lips together and give me the 800-number for 9600 baud access, now! I need it now . . . oh please give me the number . . ."

"Um, excuse me, but you'll have to wait . . . holy fuck . . ."

"Swallow it! Swallow it, baby, and cough up the terminal type, cough it right into my ear, baby, I need it!"

"Shit!"

"I'm sitting here naked at my terminal, She-male, and I've got my cat in my lap. I want you to put that collar on and meow like you've never meowed before . . ."

"Oh, son of a bitch . . . hold, please . . ." There was nothing to be done. The calls would keep coming until she-male gave in to the desire of the callers and became their eager-dreaming pleasure pumpkin.

"Let me swallow your hardware . . . let me tongue your software . . ."

The she-male laid her bed of satin sheets and switches to speaker phone.

AT the end of the week Deirdre signed my time sheet with a puckered red kiss of her blackberry-slathered lips across the words "Supervisor Signature," and with a friendly wave bid me farewell.

I carried home the better part of "She-male Software Slut" secreted away deep in my valise among ancient *Guardians* and dog-eared Paul Bowles novels.

I finished the novel sitting at my computer at home playing Lydia Lunch's "In Limbo" at top volume. Her erotic moans evoked the desperate hallucinatory dreams of people trying to reestablish their carrier.

She-male ended up in a villa in Switzerland, sharing it with three dozen nuns, two Russian construction workers, and a German shepherd.

I sold the novel, all rights, to the aforementioned shady outfit in Brooklyn for the colossal sum of $200. That roughly approximates the $1 a page that Henry Miller made some half-century ago. I started work on something a little slower paced.

William Borden

DESSERT FOR
THE GOURMET

ALYSSA WANTS TO DO IT in public. I tell her we'll get arrested. She says I don't really love her.

The phone booth is a tight fit. So is Alyssa.

When I close the door, the light comes on. I leave the door open a crack.

Even still, it's really hot and stuffy.

I sit on the little seat, and Alyssa straddles me, but the phone cuts into her breast, so she turns around—she has to open the door to give herself more room—and hikes her skirt up, and I unzip and pull myself out, and I pull her panties down, and her butt is cool on my palm, and she sits on my lap, but with all the fuss I've gone limp, so she sits on my lap anyway and pulls on me, but it's all just too confusing and when a guy comes with a quarter in his fingers and stares through the glass door we give up. She stands and smiles at him while I stand behind her and stow myself away and zip up.

Alyssa says to meet her in the park at noon, so I do, even though there are hundreds of people sitting around eating their lunches out of paper bags and hundreds strolling around and some dropping crumbs to the goldfish in the pond, and Alyssa walks up wearing a raincoat, even though it's sunny and no chance of showers, and she backs me up against a tree—people stroll past on the path a few feet away—and pulls her raincoat open but only so I can see, she makes a kind of tent, with her raincoat stretching from her to me, so I can look down and see that she's completely naked under her raincoat, so by the time I'm unzipped I'm sturdy as the tree I'm backed up against.

But I have to lower myself a few inches and brace myself against the tree, because I'm a little taller than Alyssa, if you know what I mean, and she straddles my thighs and grabs the tree trunk—still holding the edges of the raincoat, of course—and I feel her settle onto me with a terrific ease of slipperiness, and my arms are inside her raincoat holding onto her naked body.

We don't have to move much, what with her slipperiness and the little movements I make to keep my balance, my back hard against the tree trunk and my legs bent at a not very secure angle, and she has to move a little to keep her balance, and we're both breathing fast and I'm forgetting the park and the people eating lunch and the people strolling past looking at us but trying to look like they're not looking at us—when the soles of my shoes begin to slip on the grass, and my knees are giving way, and I'm slipping down the trunk of the tree—"Not yet! Not yet!" Alyssa whispers, frantic, nearly there, but gravity is a force we can't fool with, and the laws of physics, as Isaac Newton told us, are all about leverage and friction—or the lack thereof—so then I'm on my back on the grass and Alyssa is kneeling over me, covering me with her raincoat while I try to zip up, while the mounted policeman looks down at us and his horse's hooves stomp dangerously close to my head, and the mounted policeman gives me a look that says he'd better not see me again in that park for a long time.

It's a trendy restaurant and the white linen tablecloths hang low. I don't think low enough, but Alyssa's gotten us a table in a corner where there's not too much traffic and while her chicken cordon bleu gets cold she just slides out of sight, the table rocks a little, and then I feel her fingers on my zipper and then her fingers on me and then her lips circling me, and her lips are rising and falling and I'm having no trouble rising to the occasion when the waiter appears out of nowhere to worry if Madame is feeling all right, is she in the ladies' room?, and I say she feels fine to me, and he inquires if the entree is all right and I assure him it is as the table rocks a little, the ice clinking in the water glasses and the silverware rattling.

He gets a funny look on his face and I think for a minute he's going to actually raise the tablecloth and look under it, but he walks away, slow, looking back once—just as Alyssa gives an extra little pulse to her suction and I grab the edges of the table and close my eyes, and I feel as if all the troubles in the world have been sucked down into the top of my head and then shot out, squeezed away, transformed into bliss, while a charge of electricity surges through my body in waves, from my head to my toes and back again, several times.

When I open my eyes, Alyssa is seated at her place, primly dabbing her napkin to her lips.

The waiter, a middle-aged man with a perfectly trimmed mustache, clearly a career waiter with a disdain for all but a select few regular customers, takes a long time to come back and ask us if we'd like dessert, which we would.

I'm ready to dig into my Baked Alaska, but Alyssa stretches her arm across the table, stopping the descent of my spoon.

"It's your turn," she says sweetly. "Or mine, depending on how you look at it."

I look down at my Baked Alaska, melting around the edges.

Her hands slide out of sight, beneath the tablecloth. I hear her skirt rustle as she tugs it higher.

It's not as dark under the table as I would have expected. I see other people's feet under other tables. I see a waiter's feet walking. I see Alyssa's legs widen before me.

She eases herself forward on her chair. Her garters stretch across her thighs, from her black garter belt to her stockings. Her thighs are moist against my cheeks. I inhale a sweet aroma, sweeter than any on the menu. I squeeze my face between her thighs.

My head knocks the table. I hear a glass fall, silverware jump, plates clatter.

My tongue licks the soft folds of her moist labia. I flick my tongue across the hardening button of her clitoris. I forget where I am. I forget my Baked Alaska.

Alyssa tastes like Baked Alaska. Like hot cream. Her clitoris is a nut I nibble.

There's a pounding on the table. Is it Alyssa in the paroxysms of climax? Or the maitre d' in the throes of attack?

Alyssa stifles a scream. Is she coming? Or being attacked?

I don't care anymore. I don't care if I go to jail, if I'm on the front page of the paper. I feel her nut between my lips. I nibble it. I suck on it. I nibble it.

Someone pounds the table, as if they were knocking to get in, as if there were a fire. Utensils, dishes dance wildly.

Alyssa screams.

After a moment, her legs ease outward, suddenly relaxed. Her hands appear, her fingers fluttering over her bunched-up skirt. I back away, my knees scuffing the carpet, wondering how I'm going to recover my seat inconspicuously.

My hand falls on the waiter's shoe.

Below the table, a spoon appears in Alyssa's hand. I grab it. I back out. I get to my feet.

The waiter is holding my chair for me.

I hand him the spoon.

I look down at my Baked Alaska, a pool of liquid swirled into a melted desire. The waiter follows my gaze, a certain concern in his expression.

"Another dessert, sir?" the waiter asks, suddenly attentive.

I look at Alyssa. A small smile, like the Mona Lisa's, forms on her full lips. A strand of hair falls loosely across her forehead.

"One's all I need," I say quietly. "Thanks."

Linda Smukler

MORNING
LOVE

MORNING LOVE but I could have gone on all day
where I had you pinned and held in all places I had you
yet the day had to be gone to work to be caught in the
possibilities of discovery by your girlfriend or mine the
day had to take my bag and hide it in your office and the
day had me walk the streets of New York buy books drink
coffee write in public places I saw a friend for lunch and
my nose bled badly I walked into a stationery store where
the clerk (miraculously) let me use the bathroom I got
into my car and drove out to Long Island to a party for my
first ever love 20 years past and found some regret some
carrots some dip and Diet Coke some nostalgia her husband and some truth the day had me come back at midnight to find you exhausted you wore new lingerie for me
which I could barely enjoy because you would not let me
see your breasts I did see your ass in a black lace thong
and I loved you through that then decided I did not want

you to have it so easy even if it took 3 weeks I wanted you to remember how I turned you over and looked at your ass but you
were somehow far away and it didn't seem to matter and because
my neck was breaking I turned you over again and sucked you off
and felt like I was in the sea off the coast of Labrador the next
morning you found me and I saw my chest thin and barely boy-
formed and you thought I might be too skinny and you took me
as a boy and I came hard on my back but there was scarcely time
to let you explore me when I had to go back into the living room
to get my cock like a person running full force over a cliff-trap
finding himself in mid-air still running still shooting light and
semen but now not into your open mouth I retrieved my cock
and strapped it on pulled my sweatpants over and I could see my
hard-on as I ran back with the lube and got to the bedroom to find
the new tube was sealed and needed a pin or a sharp instrument
to open the plug and that did it I got angry with the time going
by and we had already canceled breakfast and I threw up my
hands and could do nothing but stomp back to the living room
click flapping to find the other already-opened lube which I did
find and came back and in my anger made you suck my cock and
told you not to get me frustrated I fucked your throat and wanted
to choke you into having me into being mine into revealing
everything inside out then I fucked you hard in your cunt and my
cock could have been fatter and shorter like you prefer and for a
moment you did forget everything I sweated and worked and
rode you and my cock came out twice and each time it was a little
more difficult to get back in then I turned you over and took you
in the ass while I touched your clit and you came and then we
were done and suddenly it was very late and the dogs hadn't even
been out and we were both afraid of your lover coming home and
we had to leave so I ran into the bathroom and showered a short
time much shorter than I would have liked and rushed out and
took the dogs and one would not poop but that was too bad and I
tried to call some friends but no one was home and it was all too

much and I had heavy bags and make sure everything is out and there you go and we walk to the car did we miss anything? a pair of dirty underwear? my toothbrush? you looked at me in the car and said I don't know what's going to happen already I heard the distance in your voice I'm late for work you said and I dropped you off to pick up orange juice and we all stop drinking and feeling bad about ourselves eventually is what I thought and what I thought is that a letter would be coming from you which would say stop don't talk don't make love to me on the phone that's enough forget I ever said I loved you forget all of it I cried when you got out and shut the door I tried not to show my face but you knew and goodbye it's too much and goodbye and I stopped to get coffee which was very bitter and left to drive upstate and that was it I cried again when I finally walked into my house at the snow and the sweetness of my dogs and the great emptiness and the tightness in my chest and that was two days ago and that was the sound of two-and-a-half months pinging between my head and heart like a pinball or a tiny missile of lead which finally shot out of my lungs as I panicked and screamed into the cold air for my German shepherd who I thought might be lost and goodnight my dog did come back and now for two more nights I say goodnight and thankyou you said and thankyou

Amelia Copeland

HIS LITTLE
PLAN BACKFIRED

"WELL, his little plan backfired," Suzanne chortled to herself gleefully, but without any real rancor.

She couldn't really blame Frank for trying. She had a record as long as, well, nearly as long as The Thing for misbehaving herself in the past, and he had always taken it with remarkable good humor. He did get a little pissy sometimes, but under the circumstances that was generous. And the way in which he attempted to assure her fidelity this time was certainly innovative.

"Come on, honey," he'd said, "just try it. It's only for five days. I had it customized especially for you."

"It's a goddamned *chastity* belt, Frank. I will not wear a fucking chastity belt."

He'd smiled at her choice of adjective. "Well, no, honey, it's *like* a chastity belt, but you'll have fun with it. It's made out of that flexible silicone you like, you can run it at three speeds with three different kinds of action, and, get this, sweetie, it has this great water attachment which you can use either for hygienic purposes or to stimulate yourself!"

"And it just happens to *chain on!* How convenient!" She'd been trying to sound angrier and angrier, but had begun to crack. It was a totally ridiculous idea; on the other hand, Suzanne was dying to try the thing out. It did look like fun. And she couldn't imagine a more good-natured way for Frank to assure her loyalty.

"Just try it, Suz," he was saying, "if you don't like it, I'll never ask you to wear it again."

SO they'd made a little ritual of installing it, testing all the speeds and action types: three speeds, three actions: nine different configurations! Adding the water attachment and another attachment for clitoral stimulation, well, the possibilities were just endless. Frank had always been a master with a vibrator, and The Thing (as she took to calling it) was just the tool for the job. After he'd showed her how all the switches worked, they'd strapped it on and had the hottest wrestling match that Suzanne could remember as they'd grappled between her legs for the controls. Just when she'd been ready to let out a yell the size of all outdoors, Frank had yanked The Thing out and plunged The Real Thing in, pinning her arms down to the bed.

"Well, The Thing is great, Frank," Suzanne said when her power of speech returned, "but it's the giver I truly revere." She bit him hard on the neck.

"Yeh, don't you forget it."

SHE wasn't quite so accommodating when he strapped The Thing onto her the next morning before she left for Chicago. She felt like a naughty child, and discipline was to her like throwing down the gauntlet. But she succumbed as she had agreed, and stumbled out the door strapped into her luggage and her personal cage.

Because Suzanne was in a self-righteous, independent mood—and she wasn't going with Frank—she denied herself the luxury of a taxi and elected to take the Train-to-the-Plane, or what she referred to as the Train-to-the-Stairs-to-the-Bus-to-the-Escalator-to-the-Plane. Bad idea. Not only was it packed, but it was late, and she had to run to her gate, encumbered.

However, her travail did give her the opportunity to note how comfortable The Thing was; she really didn't notice it at all. It wasn't until she finally plopped herself down in her seat—next to a weary-looking business type—that she felt it . . . and let out an involuntary "Oooh." Her neighbor glanced at her over the top of his glasses, and with a pleasant little plastic smile, Suzanne said, "Nice to sit down." Then she jumped back up to grab a blanket out of the overhead bin.

"Chilly in here," she muttered, flashing him the smile again.

"Mmm," he muttered back, noncommittally.

Spreading the blanket over her lap, she did some experimental wiggling around and discovered a nice comfortable position which drew firm but indirect pressure from the clitoral stimulation contraption—akin to how it felt when Frank stood behind her and pulled her toward him with his hand between her legs. Rocking her butt under and back, she found she could get some nice friction going.

She made herself a promise that she wouldn't come (the first time) until after the movie started. During long trips she liked to set some milestones . . . But she worked herself into quite a frenzy during the in-seat exercise video! Press, relax, press, relax, she kept their tempo dutifully, and actually performed the appropriate arm movements too, taking special care to brush up against her hardening nipples whenever possible. When her seatmate looked over, probably incredulous that Suzanne was actually doing these ridiculous exercises, she wanted to grasp his head to her breast and yell, "Shut up and chew!" but instead she deflected him again with her best toothpaste-commercial grin.

At the end of the video the plane hit some turbulence and Suzanne was hard pressed not to blow it. She tried to slither back in her seat, out of range, but kept slamming down onto The Thing, and each time, little pangs of pleasure would shoot through her. The inevitable tension from flight anxiety wasn't helping a bit (although knowing her neighbor felt it too made her less self-conscious). Soon all Suzanne could think about was her cunt, how slippery The Thing had started to feel inside her. She was just dying to enlist any passing body from the aisle on her left and her bespectacled neighbor on her right to suckle and chew on her now engorged tits. She yearned for the exercise video so she would have an excuse to stimulate her breasts, but really she just wanted to whip one out of her blouse and suck hard on it herself. Eventually she took out a book which she pretended to read for just a moment, then leaned it, open, against herself to rub and press it into her sensitive nipples with the top of the binding.

Thank God the movie was about to begin. But, alas, her neighbor was not going for a headset. Suzanne was getting sort of irritated with him and was dying to lean over to him, rip open her blouse, and say, "How 'bout these for a headset, fella?" She stole a look at his ear and wondered how he'd feel if she just jammed a nipple into it, and the other in his mouth. She imagined grabbing his glasses, setting them on one of her breasts and making him try to get them back on his face without using his hands. She considered reaching over, grabbing his crotch and saying, "Pleasure or pain, the choice is yours," but fortunately, the movie was starting. Neighbor be damned, she plunged a hand under her blanket, ready for action.

"When the opening credits are over," Suzanne said to herself. Director, producer, starring . . . music by . . . lift off; she set herself to vibrating. Oooh, she liked this toy. Her legs had that don't-try-to-stand-up feeling. She could feel the sensations building up through her torso and traveling into her arms. Already quite aroused, her orgasm was beginning to take shape, expanding throughout her entire pelvic region. She pressed her cunt forward and took the full pulse against her clit. At last the feeling focused into a bright hot spot at her clit and a flash of intense pleasure shuddered through her body. She couldn't stifle a loud sigh and noticed her little businessman glance at her, then up at the screen, and quizzically back at her. She turned her head to hide a smirk.

It was a lovely flight. Suzanne checked into her hotel with a smile on her face, looking forward to a quiet evening of personal hygiene. She tried to call Frank, but got his machine, so she left the message, "I've been unfaithful to you already. But the man of my dreams won't take me away—he says he can only marry a silicone girl."

IN the morning, she had to catch a shuttle bus to the convention center, and because she was late as usual, all the seats were taken. This, Suzanne thought, was probably for the better. She needed to keep her professional edge to meet her competitors; she couldn't be arriving all soft and floppy. She had consigned herself to a perfectly agreeable pole when she noticed a pleasant warm feeling inside her vagina. No, no, it was more like a pulsing. She realized that The Thing had somehow turned itself on, and just when she realized it, it speeded up and began to really shake her! Her clothes felt constricting as her vulva began to swell, and she became extremely aware of the friction from her lacy bra. She had a moment of panic, but it was quickly superseded by the pleasurable feeling emanating from her cunt. The clit stimulator was pressing into her at insistent intervals, and she was immediately, incredibly, overwhelmingly aroused. She looked around nervously, but everyone seemed to be chatting amiably. A familiar face at the front of the bus caught her eye, and a distant colleague waved. She waved back feebly and hung onto the pole. That rubbery feeling was beginning in her legs. She wanted to shut The Thing off, but couldn't just plunge her hand under her skirt, and besides, she was dying to come, and dying to get it over with, soon. Suzanne tensed her legs as best she could and grasped The

Thing hard with her vaginal muscles, pushing her clit forward. Oh god, the man who'd waved was making his way toward her. She grasped the pole with both hands and bore down, concentrating on climaxing. Then she squeezed her eyes shut and prayed. The shudder went through her and she gasped, regaining her presence of mind just in time to hear a voice say, "Suzanne, are you all right?" She looked at him absently and said, "Yeh, yeh, just a little dizzy," and then, after a pause, "How *are* you, Jeffrey? It's good to see you!" And it was. She'd always liked him. She wanted to drop to her knees, rip his zipper down with her teeth and suck his cock into the back of her throat.

AT the 10:30 break between lectures, she called Frank's office.

"Frank? Something strange is going on with this thing. It went haywire on me!"

"Do ya like it, sweetie? It's just my little way of saying, 'I'm thinking of you.'"

"You're *thinking* of . . . ? You mean, *you* . . . ? What are you talking about, Frank?"

"Pager technology. Kind of obvious, really. They just combined a vibrator with a paging device, and, WOLLAH! As they say in the ad, 'For a good time—*for her!*—call . . .'"

"Frank, you crazy fuck! I don't believe this. You're so sweet! You're such a maniac! You're a sick fuck! I almost lost it in a shuttle bus! You *know* how my legs get all weak!" He was just giggling uncontrollably.

"All right," Suzanne continued, "so you can reduce me to jelly at your whim. Okay, fine. It has its benefits, I admit. I gotta go, I'll be late for the next lecture."

"Okay. Call me later."

"Okay, bye. NO WAIT! Frank, I'm giving a paper at 3:30 this afternoon. If you even *think* of trying anything then . . . !"

"No, no, don't worry, I won't."

• • •

HE didn't. But he did get her once on the way back from lunch (she ducked into a phone booth), twice at a reception that evening (he always knew just how long to wait after her first orgasm subsided), and once in the cab on the way home from dinner with coworkers. They'd had an early dinner so she must have thwarted his attempt to test her composure. And, of course, he couldn't resist waking her up on high speed at 4 A.M.

The next day after lunch, something dawned on her.

She phoned him. "Frank, you give me that phone number."

"Oh, you think so, huh?"

"Yes, Frank, you give me that damned phone number. I have a long, boring meeting this afternoon and I want to have some fun. AT MY OWN PACE."

He gave it to her. She was armed.

SHE was negotiating a joint venture with a California firm. Although she had complete authority, about two hours into the meeting, Suzanne balked at a decision and insisted upon calling her boss. She ran to the phone and dialed the mystery number.

A sanitized voice said, "Wellll-come. You may make your selections at any time, following each with the 'pound' sign, or hold for a menu."

There was a pause. "Select a speed. Press 1 for low, 2 for medium, 3 for high." Suzanne pressed 2.

"Select action type. Press 1 for vibrate, 2 for standard pulse, 3 for random pulse." This is chaotic enough, she thought, better not choose 3. She chose 2.

"Enter value for duration." She poked in 8.

"Thank you. You may . . ." she hung up.

Ooooh.

She sauntered back to her seat with a smile.

"What'd they say?" someone asked.

"What'd they—? Oh, yeh, they said, everything is fine, fine."

"So we can do it?"

"Yeh, yeh, let's do it." She settled comfortably into her chair, and gave Jeffrey, seated to her left, a friendly squeeze on the arm. He smiled back at her fondly.

THE meetings were to continue all week, and the next day, Suzanne used the same ploy. Jeffrey and she had had a very cozy dinner the night before, and today she was feeling brave. This time when she returned from "calling the office," Suzanne scooted her chair up close to his and rubbed her leg against his. When her orgasm hit her she let him feel the shudder through her leg, after-shocks and all, and she let him hear the little sounds of the breath catching in her throat and releasing. Frank always said that really turned him on. Later, when they were leaving the conference room, Jeffrey grabbed her arm and whispered in her ear. "How did you do that?! You had both hands on the table!"

"I have a little secret," she said and, slipping out of his grasp, ran off to join her coworkers.

ON the fourth day of the conference, at the meeting, she passed Jeffrey a note. It said, "Call this number . . . Do it now."

He gave her a little half smile, and excused himself. The phone was just on the other side of the room, and Suzanne watched his expression change from perplexed to amused as he listened to the recorded voice. He looked over at her and she nod-ded in affirmation. As he started punching in numbers she saw his jaw drop; then he broke into a huge grin and turned to face her more directly. He made some more selections. As the negotiations continued around them, he stood by the phone, watching her in-tently. She felt a slow pulse and allowed a slight smile to play on her face. His eyes were locked into hers; he was still holding the phone. Jeffrey punched in some more numbers. The Thing speeded up and started to pulse randomly. She saw his eyes nar-row on her and a dreamy look came over him as he watched her. Now fast vibrations were coming. When the wave hit her she let her head drop back for a moment, then brought it forward again to meet his gaze. She smiled and he hung up the receiver.

"I'm gonna get me a cellular phone," he whispered, as he sat back down. He slid a hand between her legs to feel the wetness at the crotch of her pantyhose, then affectionately squeezed her thigh.

SUZANNE had to excuse herself early from her dinner with an old friend that evening. It appeared a competition was taking place in her cunt. She got a continual but erratic series of short pulses, fast vibrations, and stillness, which kept her in a state of anxious arousal, but never let her come. She became so frustrated and distracted that she had to return to the hotel. She used her fingers on herself in the taxi to find release, but still felt horny and irritable. When she got to her room, Jeffrey was at the door.

"Did you—?" she began, but realized she couldn't finish the sentence.

"I've just got to see you do that one more time before we leave tomorrow," he said.

He came into the room with Suzanne and took her coat. As he undid her blouse he put his mouth to her ear, saying "I've just got to see how you look when you come just for me. I want to hear you moan aloud and I want to be holding your tits while your body shudders," he breathed. "I want to come inside you and—"

"You can't," she said, abruptly. He had cupped her breasts in his hands and was holding them as if he'd never held anything more precious, more awesome.

"Take off my skirt," she commanded.

He stepped behind her to undo her zipper, and after he did she heard him undo his own. He slid his hands into her silk panties and down her ass, running his thumb along the chain that disappeared between her buttocks. He kneeled to slide her panties down, and as he got back up, he licked a long straight trail from the back of her knee, up the inside of her thigh, deep between her legs and then slowly up along the chain between her cheeks. As he stood upright again, a hand slid around her waist, and he grasped her breast with his other hand, twisting the nipple back and forth. She felt him press his fully erect penis against her butt, working it up and down along the delicate chain. He was breathing hard in her ear and Suzanne tried to imagine how the chain felt as it stimulated the sensitive underside of his cock. His hand slid down her stomach to explore between her legs, and he found the base of the vibrator. With a surprised murmur, he started flicking switches. Jeffrey held Suzanne to him with his hand between her legs, feeling The Thing's vibrations through her crotch, through his hand, through her ass, through his dick. He held her tight to him, squeezing her breast and tweaking the nipple as her arousal built steadily. As her legs started to give out she let the full weight of her body rest on his hand so he was entirely supporting her there. And he felt every shudder and quake as it wracked her body. She cried out, loud, as her body shook uncontrollably, bucking against his penis, and Jeffrey let out a gasp. Suzanne hung onto his thighs and collapsed against his arm. As the continued reverberations shook her, she felt his warm come streaming down between her buttocks.

SUZANNE was relieved to be going home, and sincerely hoped her two lovely men would leave her at peace for the duration of her trip. She was tired. She was spent. She started to nap on the plane, but was groggily awakened by that familiar humming inside her.

"Here we go again," she thought, but she was in no mood.

She started back toward the bathroom because she didn't feel like pretending, but faltered midway because she felt a strange pinch in her vaginal wall. When she got to the bathroom, the feeling became distinctly prickly. Then, just as she was locking the door, she got a sharp jolt and a zap in her clitoris. She cried out in pain, but the aftereffect, red hot and brilliant, was luscious. A long series of random jolts followed, and the skin all over her body came alive with sensation. Suzanne groped at her tits, and tentacles of pleasure shot out from her nipples, activating receptors she didn't know she had. Her clitoris and vaginal walls pulsated threateningly, and then a total explosion of feeling ripped through her body. She twitched and writhed as a screaming orgasm stole a howl from her throat. Draped over the small sink counter, she panted and shook uncontrollably until the spasms subsided.

"FRANK!" Suzanne yelled, as she came in the front door, "Frank, come and get this thing off me!" She dropped her bags and immediately started taking off her clothes.

"Oh, honey, didn't you like it?" He came running from the other room, fumbling with his keys.

"I *loved* it, Frank, but you should have told me about the *electrical* impulses."

He had gotten the chain off and she bent her legs slightly so he could take The Thing out of her. He examined it curiously.

"Electrical?—Huh?"

"You know, that *zapping* thing!"

"Zapping—? OUCH!! What the—?"

"Yeh, that's what I want to know!"

"Why, honey (ouch)," he said slowly, turning The Thing over in his hands, "I do believe your little toy has got a short circuit."

Robert Olen Butler

JEALOUS HUSBAND RETURNS IN FORM OF PARROT

I NEVER CAN QUITE SAY as much as I know. I look at other parrots and I wonder if it's the same for them, if somebody is trapped in each of them, paying some kind of price for living their life in a certain way. For instance, "Hello," I say, and I'm sitting on a perch in a pet store in Houston and what I'm really thinking is Holy shit. It's you. And what's happened is I'm looking at my wife.

"Hello," she says, and she comes over to me, and I can't believe how beautiful she is. Those great brown eyes, almost as dark as the center of mine. And her nose—I don't remember her for her nose, but its beauty is clear to me now. Her nose is a little too long, but it's redeemed by the faint hook to it.

She scratches the back of my neck.

Her touch makes my tail flare. I feel the stretch and rustle of me back there. I bend my head to her and she whispers, "Pretty bird."

For a moment, I think she knows it's me. But she doesn't, of course. I say "Hello" again and I will eventually pick up "pretty bird." I can tell that as soon as she says it, but for now I can only give her another "Hello." Her fingertips move through my feathers, and she seems to know about birds. She knows that to pet a bird you don't smooth his feathers down, you ruffle them.

But, of course, she did that in my human life, as well. It's all the same for her. Not that I was complaining, even to myself, at that moment in the pet shop when she found me like I presume she was supposed to. She said it again—"Pretty bird"—and this brain that works the way it does now could feel that tiny little voice of mine ready to shape itself around these sounds. But before I could get them out of my beak, there was this guy at my wife's shoulder, and all my feathers went slick-flat to make me small enough not to be seen, and I backed away. The pupils of my eyes pinned and dilated, and pinned again.

He circled around her. A guy that looked like a meat packer, big in the chest and thick with hair, the kind of guy that I always sensed her eyes moving to when I was alive. I had a bare chest, and I'd look for little black hairs on the sheets when I'd come home on a day with the whiff of somebody else in the air. She was still in the same goddamn rut.

A "hello" wouldn't do, and I'd recently learned "good night," but it was the wrong suggestion altogether, so I said nothing and the guy circled her, and he was looking at me with a smug little smile, and I fluffed up all my feathers, made myself about twice as big, so big he'd see he couldn't mess with me. I waited for him to draw close enough for me to take off the tip of his finger.

But she intervened. Those nut-brown eyes were before me, and she said, "I want him."

And that's how I ended up in my own house once again. She bought me a large black wrought-iron cage, very large, convinced by some young guy who clerked in the bird department and who took her aside and made his voice go much too soft when he was doing the selling job. The meat packer didn't like it. I didn't, either. I'd missed a lot of chances to take a bite out of this clerk in my stay at the shop, and I regretted that suddenly.

But I got my giant cage, and I guess I'm happy enough about that. I can pace as much as I want. I can hang upside down. It's full of bird toys. That dangling thing over there with knots and strips of rawhide and a bell at the bottom needs a good thrashing a couple of times a day, and I'm the bird to do it. I look at the very dangle of it, and the thing is rough, the rawhide and the knotted rope, and I get this restlessness back in my tail, a burning, thrashing feeling, and it's like all the times when I was sure there was a man naked with my wife. Then I go to this thing that feels so familiar and I bite and bite, and it's very good.

I could have used the thing the last day I went out of this house as a man. I'd found the address of the new guy at my wife's office. He'd been there a month, in the shipping department, and three times she'd mentioned him. She didn't even have to work with him, and three times I heard about him, just dropped into the conversation. "Oh," she'd say when a car commercial came on the television, "that car there is like the one the new man in shipping owns. Just like it." Hey, I'm not stupid. She said another thing about him and then another, and right after the third one I locked myself in the bathroom, because I couldn't rage about this anymore. I felt like a damn fool whenever I actually said anything about this kind of feeling and she looked at me as though she could start hating me real easy, and so I was working on saying nothing, even if it meant locking myself up. My goal was to hold my tongue about half the time. That would be a good start.

But this guy from shipping. I found out his name and his address, and it was one of her typical Saturday afternoons of vague shopping. So I went to his house, and his car that was just like the commercial was outside. Nobody was around in the neighborhood, and there was this big tree in back of the house going up to a second-floor window that was making funny little sounds. I went up. The shade was drawn but not quite all the way. I was holding on to a limb with my arms and legs wrapped around it like it was her in those times when I could forget the others for a little while. But the crack in the shade was just out of view, and I crawled on till there was no limb left, and I fell on my head. When I think about that now, my wings flap and I feel myself lift up, and it all seems so avoidable. Though I know I'm different now. I'm a bird.

Except I'm not. That's what's confusing. It's like those times when she would tell me she loved me and I actually believed her and maybe it was true and we clung to each other in bed and at times like that I was different. I was the man in her life. I was whole with her. Except even at that moment, as I held her sweetly, there was this other creature inside me who knew a lot more about it and couldn't quite put all the evidence together to speak.

My cage sits in the den. My pool table is gone, and the cage is sitting in that space, and if I come all the way down to one end of my perch I can see through the door and down the back hallway to the master bedroom. When she keeps the bedroom door open, I can see the space at the foot of the bed but not the bed itself. I can sense it to the left, just out of sight. I watch the men go in and I hear the sounds, but I can't quite see. And they drive me crazy.

I flap my wings and I squawk and I fluff up and I slick down and I throw seed and I attack that dangly toy as if it was the guy's balls, but it does no good. It never did any good in the other life, either, the thrashing around I did by myself. In that other life I'd have given anything to be standing in this den with her doing this thing with some other guy just down the hall, and all I had to do was walk down there and turn the corner and she couldn't deny it anymore.

But now all I can do is try to let it go. I sidestep down to the opposite end of the cage and I look out the big sliding glass doors to the back yard. It's a pretty yard. There are great, placid live oaks with good places to roost. There's a blue sky that plucks at the feathers on my chest. There are clouds. Other birds. Fly away. I could just fly away.

I tried once, and I learned a lesson. She forgot and left the door to my cage open, and I climbed beak and foot, beak and foot, along the bars and curled around to stretch sideways out the door, and the vast scene of peace was there, at the other end of the room. I flew.

And a pain flared through my head, and I fell straight down, and the room whirled around, and the only good thing was that she held me. She put her hands under my wings and lifted me and clutched me to her breast, and I wish there hadn't been bees in my head at the time, so I could have enjoyed that, but she put me back in the cage and wept a while. That touched me, her tears. And I looked back to the wall of sky and trees. There was something invisible there between me and that dream of peace. I remembered, eventually, about glass, and I knew I'd been lucky; I knew that for the little, fragile-boned skull I was doing all this thinking in, it meant death.

She wept that day, but by the night she had another man. A guy with a thick Georgia-truck-stop accent and pale white skin and an Adam's apple big as my seed ball. This guy has been around for a few weeks, and he makes a whooping sound down the hallway, just out of my sight. At times like that, I want to fly against the bars of the cage, but I don't. I have to remember how the world has changed.

SHE'S single now, of course. Her husband, the man that I was, is dead to her. She does not understand all that is behind my "hello." I know many words, for a parrot. I am a yellow-nape Amazon, a handsome bird, I think, green with a splash of yellow at the back of my neck. I talk pretty well, but none of my words are adequate. I can't make her understand.

And what would I say if I could? I was jealous in life. I admit it.

I would admit it to her. But it was because of my connection to her. I would explain that. When we held each other, I had no past at all, no present but her body, no future but to lie there and not let her go. I was an egg hatched beneath her crouching body, I entered as a chick into her wet sky of a body, and all that I wished was to sit on her shoulder and fluff my feathers and lay my head against her cheek, with my neck exposed to her hand. And so the glances that I could see in her troubled me deeply: the movement of her eyes in public to other men, the laughs sent across a room, the tracking of her mind behind her blank eyes, pursuing images of others, her distraction even in our bed, the ghosts that were there of men who'd touched her, perhaps even that very day. I was not part of all those other men who were part of her. I didn't want to connect to all that. It was only her that I would fluff for, but these others were there also, and I couldn't put them aside. I sensed them inside her, and so they were inside me. If I had the words, these are the things I would say.

But half an hour ago, there was a moment that thrilled me. A word, a word we all knew in the pet shop, was just the right word after all. This guy with his cowboy belt buckle and rattlesnake boots and his pasty face and his twanging words of love trailed after my wife through the den, past my cage, and I said, "Cracker." He even flipped his head back a little at this in surprise. He'd been called that before to his face, I realized. I said it again, "Cracker." But to him I was a bird, and he let it pass. "Cracker," I said. "Hello, cracker." That was even better. They were out of sight through the hall doorway, and I hustled along the perch and I caught a glimpse of them before they made the turn to the bed and I said, "Hello, cracker," and he shot me one last glance.

It made me hopeful. I eased away from that end of the cage, moved toward the scene of peace beyond the far wall. The sky is chalky-blue today, blue like the brow of the blue-front Amazon who was on the perch next to me for about a week at the store.

She was very sweet, but I watched her carefully for a day or two when she first came in. And it wasn't long before she nuzzled up to a cockatoo named Willy, and I knew she'd break my heart. But her color now, in the sky, is sweet, really. I left all those feelings behind me when my wife showed up. I am a faithful man, for all my suspicions. Too faithful, maybe. I am ready to give too much, and maybe that's the problem.

The whooping began down the hall, and I focused on a tree out there. A crow flapped down, his mouth open, his throat throbbing, though I could not hear his sound. I was feeling very odd. At least I'd made my point to the guy in the other room. "Pretty bird," I said, referring to myself. She called me "pretty bird," and I believed her and I told myself again, "Pretty bird."

But then something new happened, something very difficult for me. She appeared in the den naked. I have not seen her naked since I fell from the tree and had no wings to fly. She always had a certain tidiness in things. She was naked in the bedroom, clothed in the den. But now she appears from the hallway, and I look at her, and she is still slim and she is beautiful, I think—at least I clearly remember that as her husband I found her beautiful in this state. Now, though, she seems too naked. Plucked. I find that a sad thing. I am sorry for her, and she goes by me and she disappears into the kitchen. I want to pluck some of my own feathers, the feathers from my chest, and give them to her. I love her more in that moment, seeing her terrible nakedness, than I ever have before.

AND since I've had success in the last few minutes with words, when she comes back I am moved to speak. "Hello," I say, meaning, You are still connected to me, I still want only you. "Hello," I say again. Please listen to this tiny heart that beats fast at all times for you.

And she does indeed stop, and she comes to me and bends to me. "Pretty bird," I say, and I am saying, You are beautiful, my wife, and your beauty cries out for protection. "Pretty." I want to cover you with my own nakedness. "Bad bird," I say. If there are others in your life, even in your mind, then there is nothing I can do. "Bad." Your nakedness is touched from inside by the others. "Open," I say. How can we be whole together if you are not empty in the place that I am to fill?

She smiles at this, and she opens the door to my cage. "Up," I say, meaning, Is there no place for me in this world where I can be free of this terrible sense of others?

She reaches in now and offers her hand, and I climb onto it and I tremble and she says, "Poor baby."

"Poor baby," I say. You have yearned for wholeness, too, and somehow I failed you. I was not enough. "Bad bird," I say. I'm sorry.

And then the cracker comes around the corner. He wears only his rattlesnake boots. I take one look at his miserable, featherless body and shake my head. We keep our sexual parts hidden, we parrots, and this man is a pitiful sight. "Peanut," I say. I presume that my wife simply has not noticed. But that's foolish, of course. This is, in fact, what she wants. Not me. And she scrapes me off her hand onto the open cage door and she turns her naked back to me and embraces this man, and they laugh and stagger in their embrace around the corner.

For a moment, I still think I've been eloquent. What I've said only needs repeating for it to have its transforming effect. "Hello," I say. "Hello. Pretty bird. Pretty. Bad bird. Bad. Open. Up. Poor baby. Bad bird." And I am beginning to hear myself as I really sound to her. "Peanut." I can never say what is in my heart to her. Never.

I stand on my cage door now, and my wings stir. I look at the corner to the hallway, and down at the end the whooping has begun again. I can fly there and think of things to do about all this.

But I do not. I turn instead, and I look at the trees moving just beyond the other end of the room. I look at the sky the color of the brow of a blue-front Amazon. A shadow of birds spanks across the lawn. And I spread my wings. I will fly now. Even though I know there is something between me and that place where I can be free of all these feelings, I will fly. I will throw myself there again and again. Pretty bird. Bad bird. Good night.

CONTRIBUTORS

ERIC ALBERT is one of the few people who earns his living solely from making puzzles. Will Shortz, crossword editor at *The New York Times*, recently called Albert one of "the best five or six constructors in the country." Albert's work has appeared in most major newspapers, including *The New York Times*, *The Boston Globe*, and *The Washington Post*. He has also contributed to all of the top-quality puzzle magazines, completed five books of crosswords for a major publisher, and had his crosswords displayed on boxes of a well-known brand of cereal. He is the only puzzle maker to have received a Wynner (the crossword industry's highest award) three years in a row. Two of his favorite books are *Cress Delahanty* and *I Capture the Castle*, and he will soon be a world authority on anal sex.

KATYA ANDREEVNA's erotic fiction has appeared in *Heatwave: Women in Love and Lust*, *Once Upon a Time:*

Erotic Fairy Tales for Women, and *Power Tools.* Her work has also been published in Norway. The story in this volume was inspired by her never-ending search for the perfect pair of pumps.

WILLIAM BORDEN's novel, *Superstoe,* was reissued by Orloff Press in 1996; it was first published by Harper and Row in 1968. His short stories and poems have appeared in magazines and anthologies throughout the world, most recently in *American Fiction* (New Rivers) and *Winged Spirits* (Bayeux Arts). The film adaptation of his play *The Last Prostitute* was shown on Lifetime television and in Europe. His plays have had more than one hundred productions and have won numerous playwriting competitions.

ROBERT OLEN BUTLER has published eight critically acclaimed books since 1981—seven novels and a volume of short fiction, *A Good Scent from a Strange Mountain,* which won the 1993 Pulitzer Prize for Fiction. His stories have appeared widely in such publications as *The New Yorker, Harper's, GQ, The Hudson Review,* and *The Sewanee Review,* and have been chosen for inclusion in three annual editions of *The Best American Short Stories.* This is his second appearance in *The Best American Erotica.* He lives in Lake Charles, Louisiana, with his wife, the novelist and playwright Elizabeth Dewberry.

AMELIA COPELAND is the publisher, editor, and receptionist of *Paramour,* a quarterly magazine of literary and artistic erotica. She lives in Cambridge, Massachusetts, which is really not as prudish of an area as everyone seems to think.

JOEL DAILEY lives in New Orleans and teaches writing at Delgado College. His recent books include *Audience, Ambiance, Ambulance* and *Public Storage.* A selection of his poems appears in the anthology *American Poetry Since 1970/Up Late.* He has edited and published *Fell Swoop* since 1984.

LARS EICHNER is the author of *Travels with Lizbeth, Pawn to Queen Four, Gay Cosmos,* and numerous works of erotica. His first book was the erotic *Bayou Boy and Other Stories,* which was first published in 1985 when he was thirty-seven. He was elected to the Texas Institute of Letters in 1994. He lives in Austin, Texas.

ESTABROOK is a businessman who writes literature as an avocation. He has three children and two master's degrees in Comparative Literature—one in Latin, one in French. If he had to do it all over again, he'd be a paleontologist.

BONNY FINBERG writes, publishes, and reads in New York City, but prefers India, Morocco, and Southern Europe. She is always at odds with things like gravity and equilibrium, more comfortable in strange places, and moves furniture around every six months. She is currently working on a book of short stories about women on the edge in New York City.

ROBERT GLUCK's books include two novels, *Margery Kempe* and *Jack the Modernist* (High Risk/Serpent's Tail), a book of stories, *Elements of a Coffee Service,* and a number of books of poetry. In 1994, Gluck was named one of the best postmodern writers in America by the *Dictionary of Literary Biography.* His work has appeared in such publications as *The Faber Book of Gay Short Fiction, City Lights Review, Holy Titclamps,* and *Best New Gay Fiction/1995.*

BRANDON JUDELL has been anthologized in *A Member of the Family, Contemporary Literary Criticism, My First Time,* and *Flesh and the Word 3.* He's also the lead film critic for Critics' Choice on America Online, a contributing editor to *Detour,* and on the editorial board of *Lisp.* Currently, he can be viewed ranting in Rosa von Praunheim's autobiographical film *Neurosia.*

SUSANNA MOORE lives in New York City.

SHAR REDNOUR is a writer, producer, designer, and über-femme dyke living in San Francisco with her studly rock-star girl-friend, Jackie Strano. *Virgin Territory* was her first scratch at editing an anthology, and it proved so successful that she is now editing *Virgin Territory II* and *Starf*cker*. She has short stories in various forthcoming books but is currently obsessed with her version of "Rapunzel," from which an excerpt appears in *Once Upon a Time: Erotic Fairy Tales for Women* by Masquerade Books.

THOMAS ROCHE knows he's bad, but he just can't help him-self. His favorite things to write about are cobwebbed attics, four-poster beds, red roses, black wedding dresses, flesh-eating bats, and domineering she-males. He edited the anthology *Noirotica* and co-edited (with Michael Rowe) *Sons of Darkness*. His fiction and articles have appeared in numerous horror, fantasy, and erotic magazines and anthologies, including *Best Gay Erotica 1996* and *The Mammoth Book of Erotica Volume 2*.

CAMILLE ROY is a writer and performer of plays, poetry, and fiction. Her most recent book is a collection of fiction and poetry, *The Rosy Medallions*, published by Kelsey St. Press. She lives on a hill in San Francisco with Angel, Baby R, and a cat.

DAVID SHIELDS's most recent book, *Remote*, was published by Knopf in February 1996. He is also the author of two novels, *Dead Languages* and *Heroes*, and a collection of linked stories, *A Handbook for Drowning*. His stories and essays have appeared in *Harper's*, *Vogue*, *Details*, *The Village Voice*, and *Utne Reader*.

LINDA SMUKLER is the author of *Normal Sex*, which was a fi-nalist for a 1995 Lambda Literary Award in poetry. Her work has appeared in numerous journals and anthologies. She has received fellowships in poetry from the New York Foundation for the Arts and the Astraea Foundation. Her new book of poems, *Home in*

Three Days, Don't Wash, with accompanying CD-ROM, debuted this year from Hard Press.

CECILIA TAN writes erotica of all flavors. Her work has appeared in magazines and books large and small, including *Penthouse, Paramour, Dark Angels, By Her Subdued, The Servant's Quarters*, and *Taste of Latex*. She is also the editor of Circlet Press, for whom she has edited over a dozen erotic science fiction anthologies, with more on the way.

LUCY TAYLOR is a full-time writer whose fiction has appeared in *Little Deaths, Hotter Blood, Hot Blood 4, Hot Blood 6, The Immortal Unicorn, Flesh Fantastic, Desire Burn, Forbidden Acts, Dark Love, The Mammoth Book of Erotic Horror, High Fantastic*, and *David Copperfield's Tales of the Imagination*. Her work has also appeared in publications such as *Pulphouse, Palace Corbie, Cemetery Dance, Bizarre Bazaar 1992* and *1993, Bizarre Obsessions*, and *Bizarre Sex and Other Crimes of Passion*. Her collections include *Close to the Bone, The Flesh Artist*, and *Unnatural Acts and Other Stories*. Her novel, *The Safety of Unknown Cities*, has recently been published by Darkside Press; she is currently at work on another novel. A former resident of Florida, she lives in the hills outside Boulder, Colorado, with her five cats.

DOUG TIERNEY is originally from Virginia, went to MIT, then took root in Boston. He weathers the New England winters with his girlfriend, Rachel, and their enormous orange tabby, Ludicrous. Coming from a long line of police officers, Doug is currently working on a volume of ghost stories told by cops. "The Portable Girlfriend" is his first published work of fiction. In his other life, he writes technical manuals for nuclear reactors. He lives in a co-op with twenty-eight other men and women, cooks Indian and Thai, edits for a small press magazine, rides (and occasionally wrecks) a motorcycle, and plays bass guitar.

AARON TRAVIS is the nom de porn of Steven Saylor, who nowadays devotes most of his energy to writing a series of novels collectively called *Roma Sub Rosa*, stories of mystery and intrigue set in ancient Rome (the first was *Roman Blood* in 1991). Saylor claims that his erotic muse has gone into retirement, leaving his seven volumes of sexual stories already published by Badboy Books as the complete works of Aaron Travis. He divides his time between homes in Berkeley, California, and Amethyst, Texas.

BOB ZORDANI holds an MFA in Creative Writing from the University of Arkansas. He's the author of two chapbooks, *My Funny Barbeque* and *Last Resort*, and his poems have appeared in many literary journals, including *New England Review, Shenandoah*, and *Yellow Silk. The Dazzled Boy*, his first book-length poetry collection, is in circulation.

READER'S DIRECTORY

Alyson Publications

Quality lesbian and gay fiction and nonfiction (adult, young adult, children, and erotic). For catalog or more information, write Alyson Publications, Inc., Dept. CZ600A, P.O. Box 4371, Los Angeles, CA 90078-4371.

Beet 'zine

Just like literary quarterlies, but interesting. Joe Maynard, Publisher. P.O. Box 879, New York, NY 10021. Three issues are $7, sample issues are $2.

Black Sheets

Intelligent, irreverent, sex-positive magazine. Bill Brent, Editor. P.O. Box 31155-A95, San Francisco, CA 94131-0155; (800) 818-8823 for credit card orders. Subscriptions are $20/4 issues, payable to The Black Book, with a statement of legal age required; a sample issue is $7 postpaid.

A free publications catalog is also available with signed age statement.

Circlet Press
A small, independent book publisher founded in 1992, Circlet specializes in erotic science fiction and fantasy with anthologies and collections of short stories on topics from vampires to futuristic erotic technology. 1770 Massachusetts Avenue, Suite 278, Cambridge, MA 02140. Send SASE for catalog or e-mail circlet-info@circlet.com. http://www.circlet.com/circlet/home.html.

Kelsey St. Press
Founded in 1974 to publish writing by women. Publishes books of contemporary writing that challenge traditional notions about form, content, and expression. Specializes in poetry, short fiction, and collaborations between visual artists and poets. They publish 2 to 3 books a year. Rena Rosenwasser, Director. Patricia Dienstfrey, Editor. 2718 Ninth Street, Berkeley, CA 94710. Subscription information and catalog information upon request. Fax: (510) 548-9185. kelseyst@sirius.com.

LIBIDO
The journal of sex and sensibility. Published quarterly by Marianna Beck and Jack Hafferkamp. 5318 N. Paulina Avenue, Chicago, IL 60640. Subscriptions: $30/year, single issues, $8.

Masquerade Books
World's leading publisher of straight, gay, lesbian, and S/M erotic literature. Richard Kasak, Publisher. 801 Second Avenue, New York, NY 10017. Bimonthly *Masquerade Erotic Newsletter* subscriptions are $30/year; book catalogs are free.

Paramour magazine
Luscious, cream-filled pansexual magazine featuring short fiction,

poetry, photography, illustration, and reviews by emerging writers and artists. Amelia Copeland, Publisher/Editor. P.O. Box 949, Cambridge, MA 02140-0008. Published quarterly; subscriptions are $18/year, samples are $4.95.

Pink Pages
The sexy, sleazy sex ghetto of *Beet* magazine. Joe Maynard, Publisher. P.O. Box 879, New York, NY 10021. Subscriptions: three issues for $7, sample issue for $2.

Serpent's Tail
London-based literary press specializing in culturally adventurous material by international authors. High Risk Books, its American imprint, is dedicated to publishing challenging, innovative, and progressive fiction and poetry. Catalogs are available from Serpent's Tail, 180 Varick Street, 10th Floor, New York, NY 10014.

CREDITS

READER SURVEY

What are your favorite stories in this year's collection?

Have you read previous years' editions of *The Best American Erotica*? *(1993, 1994, or 1995)*

If yes, do you have any favorite stories from those previous collections?

Do you have any recommendations for next year's *The Best American Erotica*? (Any nomination must be a story that was published in the United States, in any form, during the 1996 calendar year.)

How did you purchase this book?
__ independent bookstore   __ chain bookstore
__ mail order company   __ other type of store
__ sex/erotica shop   __ borrowed it from a
                               friend

How old are you?

Where do you live?

__ West Coast   __ South
__ Midwest   __ Other
__ East Coast

What made you interested in *BAE 1996*?

__ enjoyed other *BAE* collections   __ editor's reputation
__ authors' reputations   __ enjoy "Best Of" type
__ word-of-mouth   anthologies in general
   recommendation   __ read book review

Any other suggestions? Feedback?

Please return this survey or any other *BAE*-related correspondence to: Susie Bright, *BAE* Feedback, 309 Cedar Street, #3D, Santa Cruz, CA 95060, or you can e-mail me at: BAEfeedbk@ aol.com.

Thanks so much.